PUBLIC ENEMY ZERO

ANDREW MAYNE

PUBLIC ENEMY ZERO

Special thanks to Justin Robert Young.

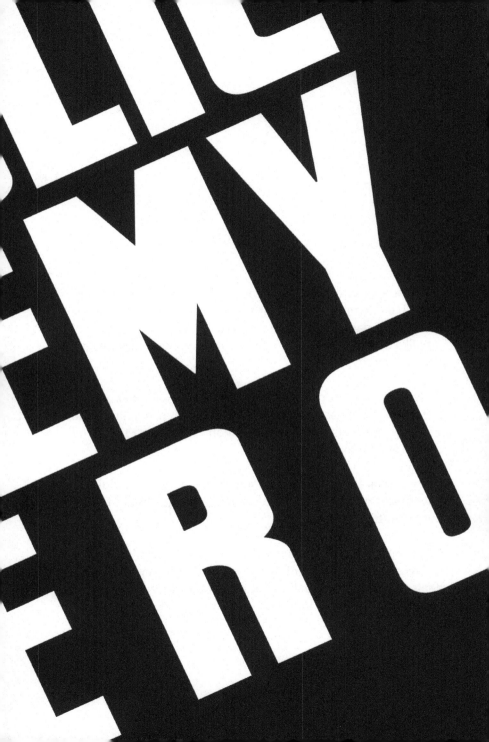

Introduction

This is the first novel I ever wrote – typing away feverishly after I discovered that writing could take you to faraway places and dangerous situations just as easily as reading. It was like discovering I had the ability to send my consciousness out of my body.

It was also when I realized I could make a movie happen on the page and smash tractor-trailer trucks into buildings and derail trains as easily as having someone walk into a room and drink a glass of water.

As an exhilarating of an experience it was to write, reading it now makes me wince, and I'm tempted change a lot of things. But I won't.

Changing it would feel disingenuous. The book you're holding is the same one that got me my first literary agent, movie deals and the opportunity to sit across the table from people I'd only read about in Variety.

Despite the lack of writing polish (that still eludes me to this day) the momentum of the story, my enthusiasm and the scope of the idea, carry it past those humps for some people. I'm releasing it pretty close to the original ebook version because that seemed to work well enough.

Oddly, this was a book I almost didn't release. I was too unsure and nervous about it. Were I to write it again, I'd do so many things differently. But there's the lesson; despite all my reservations, the book found an audience and it launched my career.

That's not to say that every half-baked, poorly edited manuscript should be unleashed on the public; but it should serve as a reminder that in the end, what matters most is your story and your passion for telling it.

Best,

Andrew Mayne

@AndrewMayne
Burbank, CA
2015

PUBLIC ENEMY ZERO

Prologue

The Naked Man in the Forest sat on a rotting ash tree trunk and stared at a tangle of vines on a nearby oak. Sunlight filtered through the leaves casting thousands of pinpoints of light on the ground like tiny golden stars. He could feel insects crawling over him. The moss under his scrotum was making him itch. But he remained still. Even as mosquitoes landed on his bare flesh and drank from him, he did nothing. He was waiting for Her to appear. Sometimes she made him wait hours. It was her way.

He was tiny and insignificant in her presence. He thought he had sinned in her eyes. He'd gotten lost in his Otherself and forgotten who he truly was. Birds chirped and forest things went about their work in the brush around him. He sat quietly, thankful that She had let him sit in her garden.

He watched as the vines on the oak began to undulate. Green leaves formed into supple lips. White flowers formed her eyes. Moss and twigs formed the bridge of her nose and her beautiful face formed before him.

Hello my child.

Tears welled up in his eyes. He was always happiest in her presence. Without her he was nothing. He was worse than nothing, he was a pestilence. Something wicked and dark.

Why are you crying my child?

The naked man cleared his throat. Guilt stifled his words. Her face, so perfect, so wise, encouraged him on. "Earth mother, I have sinned." he said, his face filled with shame. "I have forgotten who I am. I let...I let the Otherself lead me astray."

He wanted to look away but couldn't bare not experiencing her presence. He looked down at his pale skin. "I feel like I've lost my way."

Oh child, your path is a difficult one. But you're here now. You haven't lost your way. The Otherself can be confusing, but where are you happiest?

"Here Earth mother."

And who do you love?

"You Earth mother!"

And you have earned my love. I'm so proud of you. You've gone so far. We've come so close. So very close.

"How much longer must I be the Otherself?"

When my eggs are ready for the world. When the time of the cleansing is upon us. Until then you must be the Otherself. You must continue to build trust. You must protect my eggs.

"Yes, Earth mother." He wiped tears away from his eyes. "I know your suffering is so much greater than my own. Being apart from you is just...I feel so vile."

I know my child. Soon your suffering will be over. The darkness will be gone and you will live in my garden for all of eternity.

The Naked Man in the Forest watched the vines slide away and her face fade. She wasn't truly gone, she was still all around him in the trees, the birds, the dirt beneath his feet. Her mother face was just a way for him to look upon her and know she was looking back.

When he was the Otherself he forgot what her presence really meant. Although the Otherself was doing her bidding, he loathed that being to the core.

The Otherself was everything that was wrong with the world. The Otherself was why Earth mother suffered. Otherself and all its kin were the darkness casting their shadow on Earth mother. Soon she promised, soon that would change. He could cast aside the Otherself once and for all and be the child of Earth mother forever.

The Naked Man in the Forest walked back to the clothes the Otherself wore. He brushed the itchy moss off his backside and pulled on his underwear. When he picked up his pants a small Ziploc bag fell from his pocket. He picked it up and tossed it aside.

It had been over a year since he'd had to take the blotters of LSD to clearly see the Earth mother. Now she came just as vividly as ever without it. Of course in the forest was the only place he could see her. But he could *hear* her all the time telling him what to do.

The Naked Man in the Forest put on the rest of his clothes and the Otherself walked back to his car.

The light turned red and Mitchell pressed the brake pedal. Although the street was deserted, he looked around self-consciously as the worn down brake pads let out a squeal when they brought the car to a stop. Up ahead, a row of street lights seemed to stretch on to infinity into the horizon. Each one casting a small protective circle of amber light on the wet ground. On the side of the intersection he noticed the blinking hazard lights of a car that had pulled over to the shoulder.

A heavy-set woman in a waitress uniform struggled with a spare tire at the rear of her car. Mitchell instinctively looked at his broken clock then to his iPhone. He was going to be late. He wondered why she didn't call someone to help her fix the tire. Then he noticed the condition of the car. It wasn't much better off than his. Maybe she didn't have anyone to call or a phone to call them he wondered, feeling sorry for her.

The light changed to green. He decided to go slowly through the intersection.

When his front wheels touched the crosswalk on the other side he watched the woman fall over where the grass met the side of the road. The tire went rolling before falling on its side, in a parody of her fall.

Mitchell let out a sigh. He turned on his blinkers and pulled his car up ahead of her so he didn't pull in behind her and scare her. She was having a bad enough night, he didn't want to make her think she was about to get raped.

He left his car door open as he stepped out. At his back bumper he called out to the woman.

"Need any help?"

She looked up from the ground where she was assessing her situation and her life in general. Rivulets of mascara ran down the sides of her eyes. She wiped the tears and snot from her nose. "Yeah," she paused for a moment trying to make out the figure in the dark. He looked young and clean cut. "My boyfriend is on the way, but I could use a hand."

Mitchell questioned the existence of the boyfriend in his mind but said nothing.

"Let's take a look."

He walked over to where she was sitting and offered her a hand up. He looked to see where the tire had rolled to. Suddenly his left eye saw a flash of red as his temple felt something hit. Mitchell let go of her hand and stumbled backward.

"Fuck!" Confused, he looked to see where the rock had been thrown from.

The woman balled up the fist of the hand he had just let go and let loose another punch. This one landed on the side of his jaw.

Mitchell jerked back trying to understand.

That's when he saw the expression in her eyes and her teeth bared at him.

She screamed and came at him with her hands outstretched. Her fingernails swung at him like claws. He jumped back as they grazed his chest. He opened his own arms wide in an instinctive gesture. She came at him again. Her thick legs pushing against the ground as she tried to catapult at his neck.

Mitchell jumped back again and she fell flat on the ground making a thud. Mitchell thought he heard something crack. She shouted incomprehensible swear words at him in a voice that sounded more animal than human.

He stepped forward to see if she was alright. Bloodshot eyes looked up at him. Red was pouring from her nose and her cheek had road rash. The woman screamed at him again then came to her feet much more spryly than he would have thought possible.

Mitchell backed up again. He was trying to understand what he had done. What had he said?

She ran towards him again. He backed away and turned into a jog.

He could hear her feet clopping on the ground as she chased after him. She was getting closer. Mitchell wanted to shout back and ask her what was going on but he was too panicked to say anything. He didn't even know what to say.

Behind him her pace slowed down as her body began to give out. She screamed out in a horse voice.

Mitchell turned around. She was half way between him and his car. He could keep running or make a break for his car and count on his greater speed to get him there fast enough to lock the door.

She got a second wind and burst towards him. Blood and snot dripped from her face as she pumped her arms and screeched out in a hoarse voice.

On impulse, Mitchell ran towards her. She raised her arms out to claw him. He jumped to the side and felt the wind as she overstepped and went past. He ran to his car without looking behind.

Footsteps grew louder as he jumped into the open door. He pulled it shut as her fists came pounding against the window. Furious, she smashed her head against the window trying to break the glass. Blood and snot splattered the window as her face made a sickening thud each time it struck.

His heart beating out of his chest, Mitchell fumbled through his pockets to find his keys. He threw his tangled iPhone ear buds on the ground before he felt his key ring. He turned the ignition, put it into drive and stepped on the gas as the woman started beating the glass with bloody knuckles.

The car's bald tires spun out for a moment on the wet grass.

Mitchell screamed out, "Fuck! Fuck! Fuck!"

The car finally got traction and lurched forward.

Off balanced, the woman fell into the muddy grass.

In the rear view mirror Mitchell watched as she pulled herself up and ran after him. Her uniform was a mess of dirt and blood. She let out another scream then came to a stop and stood there blankly watching as he drove off.

Mitchell sped through a light as it turned yellow to gain as much distance as he could. His mind raced for an explanation for what just happened. He reached down to touch his fly in a moment of self-conscious panic, afraid that he'd approached her with his penis hanging out. His fly was in place. Mitchell felt stupid.

When it was obvious she wasn't going to chase him down in her car with a flat tire he began to relax. He pulled out his iPhone and contemplated calling 911.

And tell them what? All she had to say was that his fly was open or that he'd attacked her and it would be his word against hers. Her bloody face looked a lot worse than his. He put his phone back.

After he ran out of reasons to blame himself, he finally realized that she was probably just bipolar or something. For all he knew, she was racing home to get her medication before she flipped out. He just caught her at the wrong time. *Crazy.* That's all.

He began to pity her like someone with uncontrollable Tourette's. It's not a condition anybody wants. After she got medicated she'd probably feel horrible about it.

Of course, he'd never got an apology from a girlfriend who started silly arguments during a period, so maybe she wouldn't feel bad about it either. He knew it was an asshole thing to think.

With the threat diminished and the decision that she was just psycho, Mitchell began to calm down. He realized his seat belt alarm had been beeping since he drove off. He clicked it into place and headed towards the radio station.

By the time he reached the parking lot, he was already debating whether or not to tell the story on the air.

He grabbed his backpack, got out of his car and looked at the bloody mess on his window and the kicked-in driver's side door.

Seeing that, he felt a little less sorry for the woman. Then felt guilty about that.

Mitchell swiped his card at the entrance and walked into the building. He decided to keep the story to himself for now.

2

At that hour of the night the lobby and the rest of the building were empty except for Rookman in broadcast booth two. He ran the 10 PM to 1 AM shift. His show was a call-in conspiracy program with special guests who used nicknames like Truthseeker, Indian Joe, The Ghost Stalker and Dr Annihilation.

Mitchell walked by the window and waved. Inside, a man in his late forties wearing a trucker's hat pointed at his watch and gave Mitchell the finger.

Mitchell gave an apologetic shrug. Rookman grinned and waved him off.

All the station's broadcast booths were about as big as a bathroom with the exception of the conference room where the morning crew did their show. It was usually filled with silly props and those magazines they give out at strip clubs. One of the hosts was in the middle of trying to avoid time for cocaine possession. The reason that it hadn't made it into the papers was based in part because he used a fake radio name and the fact that their station was so under-listened to, nobody cared.

Mitch once heard that the advertising manager was talking about leaking the story to help their Arbitron numbers. It was that kind of station and that kind of business.

Mitch reached his booth and opened up the door. The smell of bad coffee permeated it.

Oddly he thought, he kind of missed it. He'd been gone for a week and as much as he hated his job, it'd been the only connection he'd had with the outside world since Rachel broke up with him.

Granted, getting cursed at by drunks and having teenagers call in to scream obscenities wasn't an ideal connection, but it was something.

He flipped on the monitor to listen to Rookman's show while he did his own show prep--which basically consisted of pulling up some of his iTunes genius lists and thinking of inane questions to ask people to hopefully generate some interesting calls.

Rookman was way better at that. At that moment he was talking to a man who claimed that a recent meteor spotted over the skies of Los Angeles that crashed into the ocean was actually a manned Chinese spacecraft on a secret mission.

The caller had a disarmingly calm voice that didn't sound like a crackpot. He sounded like Kiefer Sutherland to Mitchell.

"You've said it over and over again Rookman. People have to wake up. There's a new Cold War going on. This fireball that came down wasn't a meteor. It was a spacecraft. Talk to any scientist and they'll tell you the re-entry doesn't make sense for anything else."

"So what was it?" asked Rookman.

"It goes back three years ago. Remember when the Space Shuttle made that secret mission to fix a military satellite? They found something. Something that scared the hell out of them. Now we all know that World War III isn't going to be fought with nukes. It's going to be with computers and biological warfare and in space. "It's not going to be over in years or even months or days. It's going to be over in minutes. Whoever has the tactical advantage wins. One day, those of us that survived the night are going to flip on the television or go to Google's home page and see that someone else is in charge."

"So what does this have to do with the meteor?"

"Spacecraft, Rookman. We're talking about a spacecraft. So NASA sends their payload specialists up there. Guys who get their orders from underground in Langley and they see something on the satellite that's not supposed to be there."

"Describe for us what they saw," asked Rookman.

"Maybe the size of a cigar. It's got an antenna, a large battery and piece of plastic explosive the size of your fingernail. When a call comes down and the powers that be decide it's time to strike, you don't have time to launch missiles or scramble jets or change satellite orbits. It's going to happen in seconds. One minute everything is fine, the next minute all those Chinese-made computers that are routing our email and handling our phone calls and store photos of our pet dog are going to run a piece of code written in some University back in Beijing. Guess who's in charge then?"

"I'm guessing not us," replied Rookman.

"Well the only thing stopping them is our military advantage. The problem with that is it's all controlled by satellites. So the solution there is to take them out. But it's got to happen quickly. Instantly. So what do you do? You don't try to shoot them with a laser that may or may not work. You don't shoot missiles at them. You need something simple. You booby trap them."

"So that's what the Space Shuttle found? A booby trap on one of our satellites?"

"Exactly. Now you're about to ask me what does that have to do with those Chinese astronauts that burned up over Santa Monica Pier. That was payback. The Chinese launch was a secret mission. They sent a small Soyuz capsule covered in radar absorbing material into one of the same orbits as one of our birds.

"Only this time we're ready. We hit them with a blast of microwaves from one of our communications satellites; it's all it takes. We fry them in their capsule and everything goes haywire. Remember when half the country lost satellite TV four days ago? Guess the real reason why? So the astronauts are dead and the equipment is malfunctioning. The spaceship eventually loses orbit and come crashing down to earth and lights up the sky over LA."

"That's an incredible story."

"Of course the Chinese can't say what happened and we can't say anything either. Neither one us wants to let on to what we can do or what we know."

"And that's why it's a cold war. Thank you again for calling in. I know I can say for everyone listening that we all appreciate the risk you take in bringing this to us."

Next came the touch Mitchell loved the most about Rookman's show when he had callers with government conspiracy stories.

"Now just to make it clear that we're not asking anyone to violate state secrets and commit what some would call treason in doing their patriotic duty, I have to ask if you're working for the government."

At that point the caller hung up. Or at least to the audience it sounded like he hung up. Mitchell suspected that Rookman simply hung up on them to create a dramatic effect.

"Doctor Lovestrange? Doctor Lovestrange? Huh, it appears he hung up on us. Well, we can look forward to his next call."

When Mitchell first heard Rookman he thought he was the kind of crank that felt Fox News was too liberal. After listening to the show he actually looked forward to it. The mix of crazy conspiracies and ghost stories was compelling. After a while they began to sound plausible, until some guy would call in talking about the orgy he had on a flying saucer at Woodstock.

Mitchell couldn't figure out where Rookman really stood on all of it. He had to believe some of it. Sitting in the booth in his trucker's hat and camouflage vest talking about buying up gold coins, he looked the part of the conspiracy nut. To talk to him face to face he didn't really seem like the kind of guy that believed a race of lizard people ran the world. But he was the type that would sweep his home for bugs if he heard a click on the line.

The show was actually just a hobby for Rookman. When Mitchell found out that his day job was as a community college guidance counselor, he was strangely not surprised.

Working the late shift for barely above minimum wage on a station nobody listened to, Mitchell wished he could have gone to a guy that kept copies of Guns and Ammo, The Economist and Penthouse on his desk.

The phone in the booth rang. Mitchell picked it up.

"WQXD, this is Mad Mitch speaking."

"Go fuck yourself Mitch," said an adolescent voice followed by giggling in the background.

Mitchell took it as a compliment that the call came in before his show started. That meant they were waiting for him.

Callers like that were never deterred by the fact that all calls were time delayed and ones like that never made it to the air. For some reason they thought that they would be the first one to call in and tell him to eat a dick live on the air.

When he first took the job the station manager told him to expect some abuse and showed him a list of numbers to look for on the caller ID. They were known nut jobs that obsessively called the station.

The morning crew guys would make jokes about them and refer to them by their last four digits of their phone number.

4788 once called the station 320 times in one day. Anytime someone answered, it didn't matter if it was a male or female, a loud shrill voice would scream "Faggot", then hang up. The guy who made parody songs for the station made an auto-tuned version that got 400,000 views on YouTube.

Mitchell thought it ironic that probably more people heard that guy than ever listened to the station.

The phone rang again. Mitchell picked it up.

"Try not to eat too many dicks tonight Mitchy boy." Mitch recognized the voice.

"I'm sure you already ate them all Rookman."

"I'm a survivor man. Have a good show."

"Thanks man. So that Chinese satellite thing. You believe that?" Mitch didn't want to sound like the gullible fan boy, but he couldn't help it.

"Nah. It's horse crap. It was Russians." Rookman hung up.

Leave it to the Rookman to wrap a mystery in an insult.

Mitchell flipped on his intro music then gave out the number for requests. Three calls came in. He took line one.

"WQXD, this is Mad Mitch speaking."

"Fuck you Mitch." Click.

Line two.

"WQXD, this is Mad Mitch speaking."

"Faggot!" Click.

Line three.

"WQXD, this is Mad Mitch speaking."

"Hi Mitch. This is Amy," came a sad voice. "Long time listener. First time caller."

Her words came out hesitantly. Like someone holding back tears.

"How you doing tonight Amy? What can I do for you?"

"It's been a rough day for me Mitch. Can you play some Taylor Swift?"

"Sure thing sweetheart. Want to tell us what happened?" A juicy breakup story always made a good intro to a love song.

"I got into an argument with my boyfriend."

Please make it about sex, thought Mitchell.

"Then on my way home from work my car got a flat tire and..." She paused. "...some guy attacked me." The last part came out in halted breaths.

Mitchell's body went numb.

3

Mitchell stared at the microphone for what felt like an eternity. His back began to tense up. He looked over his shoulder then through the window into the darkened hallway.

It was empty. Rookman had left and he was all alone in the station.

He looked over at the security panel that would flash when someone came through a door. It was dark.

"Mitch?" came the sad voice.

He tried to find enough saliva to speak. "I'm still here Amy. That sounds...that sounds horrible." He took a breath. "Attacked?"

"I was trying to change my tire and then this psycho comes out of nowhere." She sniffed her nose.

Mitchell remembered to breath. "Did he hit you?"

"My nose is bloody. I think so. It happened real fast." Sob. "I called my mom to come get me."

Knowing that there were others listening, Mitchell had to ask, "Amy, are you sure you don't need medical attention?" He tried to hide the tremble in his voice. "Or the police?"

"I think I scared him off. I just want to go home. Could you play my song please." It was the voice of a scared little girl and not the portly demon that tried to kill him hours before.

"Alright sweetheart." Mitchell typed in her request.
'You belong with me' began to play.
"I love you Mitch." Click.
Mitchell sat back and exhaled. His knee was shaking. His stomach was ready to bail out its contents.
The girl sounded like she was still in shock. What was going to happen when her mother came to pick her up and saw what a bloody mess she was? He began drumming his finger on the table then realized he still had an open microphone.
He raced through the hypotheticals. What if they called the police?
Could she remember his license plate? What he looked like?
She sounded disoriented on the phone. She seemed confused. He was pretty sure she couldn't remember enough to directly finger him. Pretty sure.
He thought for a moment, if she called the police, the first thing they'd want to do is run a rape kit on her. That'd of course come back negative. At least for him.
So then they'd be dealing with possible assault.
There was a fax machine in the radio station that was dedicated just to police reports. Mitchell would sometimes read them. He tried to think of anything relevant.
If he went to the police right now it'd scream to them like he was guilty and feeling remorseful about it.
He knew there was no way he could convince them of the hysteria, the blood lust in her eyes or the panic he felt. They'd just see the scared girl who asks for a Taylor Swift song when she cried.

He had wanted to pry her for more information, but knew that would have been a bad idea over the air.

On the caller ID he could still see her number. Should he call her back off air and talk to her?

Mitchell loaded up the track list. He turned off his microphone and reached for his iPhone. He was about to type the number into the keypad when he realized that would put his contact information right on her phone.

He put his phone away. What about the station phone?

He didn't know how much attention he could pay towards her without looking guilty or callus.

Fuck it. He picked it up and dialed. It went to voicemail.

Mitchell didn't know what to do next. He heard the beep.

He hung up.

He rationalized that by at least calling back he could justify that he tried to make an effort to follow up. If the station manager asked, he did his due diligence.

This girl was confused, probably bipolar and a fan. If he just let it go, it'd probably go away.

Mitchell began to relax. He leaned back in the chair and looked at the ceiling.

If she couldn't remember anything specific about him then it'd never trace back to him. There was nothing connecting him to what happened.

He ran his fingers through his hair and tried to think of something to say when the song ended.

"Hey everyone, it's your pal Mad Mitch here in the late night hour." He thought about saying a white lie about being dropped off by a friend or having showed up at the studio an hour earlier. Then he realized the stupidity of that.

He tried to think of a question to throw out to callers. Everything he could think of sounded like it would point directly back at him.

Favorite song to do it to. *Attempted rapist.*

Weirdest thing that happened. *Attacked a girl.*

Biggest fear. *Getting caught.*

Biggest wish. *Getting away with it.*

"Fuck! The blood on my car!"

Mitchell looked at the display. The microphone was live. He felt all the blood drain out of his body. He was light headed. His cheeks burned with fire.

He looked down at his right finger. He didn't remember doing it. But it was there. It was pure instinct that made him click the drop button when he heard the word "fuck".

He counted off the syllables of "The blood on my car." He was well under the seven second delay.

Mitch threw to commercial and queued up his play list. No more audience interaction tonight. At least for now.

He set the timer on his iPhone and ran out of the studio. Mitchell grabbed a bunch of paper towels from the break room and ran out the backdoor to the parking lot. He'd parked it under a bright light so it wouldn't have made as big of a target. Now it just looked like a bright neon sign pointing to his guilt.

His guilt.

Why did he feel guilty about this? Was it because she was a woman?

Mitchell looked at the driver's side window. Her forehead, cheek and part of her nose were imprinted with her blood. He could even see the ridges where her knuckles struck the window.

For a fleeting moment he thought about taking a photo to prove his case later on. To whom and what would he prove?

A bloody, angry girl tried to smash and claw her way into his car? Or did it look like he ran her face first into the window? He was sure a clever forensics person could tell the difference. If they wanted to.

Screw it. He began wiping down the window. The blood just smeared around covering it in a red film.

"For fuck sake, can't I get a break?", he screamed under his breath.

He damped a paper towel in a puddle and used that to wipe the window.

He looked around the parking lot. His was the only car.

The blood finally began to come off. He used the entire handful of towels to get the rest of it.

His alarm rang. He almost pissed himself.

Mitchell gave the car another look over. The window looked okay. He was sure the police could find it if they looked. But at that point he'd tell them everything anyway.

His door was still kicked in, but oddly, that made him look like the victim. A kicked in door showed, at least in Mitchell's mind, that he was the target of aggression. He knew other people may not see it that way. But for him it was physical proof that what happened, happened the way he remembered it. The door was physical proof of her violent rage. Oddly, that made him feel better.

He ran back to the station.

He flushed the paper towels down the toilet. He waited to make sure they went down then jumped back into the booth as the play list ended. He flipped on the microphone.

"Alright gang, here's your question. I want to know what super hero you wanted to be when you were a kid? Besides the holy trinity of Spider-Man, Batman or Superman."

The Invisible Woman came immediately to his mind.

4

The rest of the night was mostly panic free until he remembered Rookman. He used the same parking lot as he did. He had to have seen his car and the blood. What did he think?

Crazy for sure, but Rookman was a perceptive man. Mitchell once wore the same shirt two days in a row and got a call from Rookman congratulating him for getting laid.

When Rachel broke up with him and he wore a shirt two days in a row again out of depression, Rookman called him up and said let it go and move on.

It was the same shirt.

Rookman knew something happened. Mitchell tried to think if there was any kind of clue in his phone call. That's how he would have told him he knew.

Maybe he didn't notice. Or if he did he was keeping his mouth shut.

Mitchell had to resist the urge to run outside and look under his windshield wiper for a note. Rookman's style would have been to leave the business card for a lawyer or bail bondsman.

Guys who talk tough have a habit of being the first to fold. He thought Rookman was pretty genuine. It wasn't all an act, was it?

No. Rookman was a sincere guy. He was a ball-buster for sure. But he had character. If Rookman noticed the car, he probably decided it wasn't any of his business.

Mitchell thought about the crazy stuff he probably heard from students every day. This was minor in comparison he was sure.

If Rookman mentioned it, Mitchell would tell him everything. He was pretty sure Rookman of all people would believe him.

He opened up the phone lines again for requests. He kept his finger on the drop button fearful that he was going to get another call from the girl. Only this time she was going to call him out and publicly accuse him of trying to rape and murder her.

Every time he heard a female voice he clinched up a little bit.

When a man called in and said he wanted to be Daredevil, all Mitchell could think about was the fact that his day job was being an attorney. *Guilty!*

He also got the usual amount of insults. People invited him to do all sort of lewd acts to himself or family members. The interesting thing was always that the later it got the more they sounded like some kind of Freudian expression.

"Whore."

"Junky."

"Faggot," of course.

The most disturbing calls were the rambling ones from drunk people. They always had something important to say. They just never could get around to saying it. If you cut them short they'd call you any or all of the previous insults.

The last hour felt pretty normal. He screwed around on his iPad during the play lists and just did what he did on a normal night.

A calendar reminder popped up and he felt sick to his stomach for a much more mundane reason than being accused of attempted rape.

That was the day he'd promised to drop off his ex-girlfriend's keys. He'd wanted to just send them, but he didn't want to look like a coward. He was pretty sure there was a new guy living with Rachel. He hadn't known that when he agreed to drop them off.

A three week turn-around from Mitchell to that guy. It was probably faster than that. It just made his gut hurt even more. The last thing he wanted to do was to see her or him, worst of all her and him together.

Thinking about it was like having every negative emotion in the world explode inside of him like a grenade. Jealousy, sadness, anger, inadequacy, impotency and a million others he could describe if he took the time.

By agreeing to drop them off, he told himself he was outwardly doing what a person who feels none of those things feels. Another part of him felt that he was only justifying her actions by going along with her nonchalant attitude about the situation.

Whatever, he thought. He'd drop the keys and the whole thing would be done with. He didn't want to spend any more time dwelling on it than he needed. He had other things to worry about.

Christ, the other thing. He couldn't decide which was worse to worry about.

He watched the minutes tick down on the station clock. He'd go drop the keys off then go home and sleep through the rest of the nightmare while everyone else went to work.

Damn. He realized that she wouldn't be up for another two hours. That meant he couldn't go home and crash. Mitchell would have to sleep in his car while he waited for her to get up.

Fine, he thought. Whatever it takes.

The last hour passed uneventfully. He saw the alarm pad light up by the door as the early morning shift host was coming in.

Bonnie walked by the window and gave him a wave. Mitchell felt it wasn't an unfriendly wave, but it had the feeling like she was kind of just waving at him and the station furniture alike. Waving to him was just one part of the ritual she had for realizing that life hadn't turned out like she wanted. *Hello Mitch. Hello fern.*

She was in her late forties and was probably very pretty once. She had that deep voice too many late nights and too much alcohol gave women. Mitchell and his friends used to call that a 'boozer' voice.

Someone had told him she'd been an MTV veejay for a little while back when kids knew that term as someone who announced music videos and not as slang for vagina.

Mitchell could believe it. She was good at what she did and acted like a pro. You always got a sense that she felt she was too good for the place and she probably was.

Mitchell wondered what it was like to go from MTV celebrity to obscure early morning host. Was it a gradual slide? Or an overnight thing you never recovered from? He looked around the tiny booth he was in and wondered if he'd be grateful in twenty years to even have the job he had there. That scared him.

He'd struggled to find a job in broadcasting without any luck. The current job came about because a friend from college was leaving the station and pushed really hard for him.

The station really never let you know if you were doing good or bad, so there was never any security. He didn't have a gimmick like Rookman, so he really didn't have a following. People knew him, but he wasn't known for anything other than being on the radio.

He'd gotten a date with Rachel because she was fascinated by the idea of a radio personality. When she realized that was the only interesting thing about him, her interest began to wane.

He couldn't blame her. He had an audience and nothing to say to them.

Mitchell played his out music, flipped a switch and turned the station over to Bonnie.

It was still dark outside. As he walked towards his car he contemplated sleeping in the parking lot, but then the kicked in door made him decide to put some distance between himself and the station.

He'd decided to park a few blocks from Rachel's house and nap there. He'd then give her the key and his life could go back to its pathetic trajectory to nowhere.

5

Mitchell found a parking spot two blocks away from Rachel's apartment and pulled in. He'd become somewhat adept at sleeping in his car. When Rachel had asked him to leave he'd told her with foolish pride that he had some other place to stay. The other place being his old Toyota.

A friend of his had helped him eventually find a small place in a former retirement community. It was a virtual ghost town where most of the residents were shut-ins or absentee owners holding out for property prices to go back up. The rest of the units were in foreclosure.

In the three weeks he had been living there he could recall seeing another neighbor maybe three times and always at a distance. Afraid of anybody under the age of 60, they'd scurry back into their apartments and lock the doors.

For Mitchell, the lack of neighborly contact wasn't a bad thing. He kept such odd hours it really didn't make a difference. Another upside for him was that the complex was next to a grocery store accustomed to dealing with the elderly and home bound people. He could order anything he wanted online and have it waiting on his doorstep when he got home. That alone kept him from starving while he'd been sick the past few weeks.

He unfolded the sunshade and placed it into the windshield to keep the morning sun out of his eyes. It was cool enough now that with the windows cracked he could turn off the engine and not worry about suffocating from the Florida sun.

His after-work meal consisted of a bottle of iced tea, a stick of beef jerky and a power bar he'd bought at a gas station by the radio station. The meal had become such a routine that the old Haitian man who worked at the gas station would place the items into the tray as soon as he saw Mitchell's car pull up. Mitchell would drop his money in the slot and get his change, never having any kind of an exchange other than a friendly nod.

Still feeling a little bit anxious about what happened the night before, he pulled out his iPhone. He opened up a browser window to pull up the local newspaper. He spent several minutes reading the crime bulletins looking for anything that might refer to the incident the night before.

Nothing came up that sounded like what happened. There was the usual shop lifting, DUI and domestic disputes, but other than that it looked like it hadn't been reported. Although that didn't mean she hadn't filed a police report, Mitchell felt better knowing that it wasn't front page news and there was no active manhunt out to get him.

With that little bit of peace, Mitchell pulled the lever on his seat and leaned back to go to sleep.

Mitchell was awoken by the angry bee buzz of his iPhone as a text message popped up on the screen.

It was from Rachel: **what the fuck? r u dropping them off or not?**

He'd forgot to set the alarm and now he had to deal with the pissed off wrath of Rachel. There was a time when she could make him feel good about himself and like a complete asshole. Now it was all asshole all the time.

His chance to drop the keys off and act like it was all no big thing was shot because he knew she was going to read his hesitancy like he was still holding out for things to go back to the way they were.

He yawned then typed in a reply: **Sorry. Overslept. Almost there.**

A moment later she texted back: **how long? bout to take a shower after rick.**

For fuck sake. Why did she have to add that? He felt the knife go into his side.

Intellectually he knew it was her way of saying not to make the thing into something stupid and awkward. It still hurt.

For a fleeting moment he had the childish idea of texting back, "got to drive girlfriend to work. can't stay to talk." But he knew she'd just say something positive about him having a new girlfriend and have the upper hand back.

He thought one way to make her doubt herself would be to tell her he was seeing some other guy. She'd write back that she always knew he was gay, but secretly feel inadequate. Or at least he imagined she would.

That was a horrible idea, he realized.

Since the passenger side door didn't reliably lock, he took his backpack with him and headed towards her apartment. He could smell the ocean air as a breeze swept by. He had missed living that close to the ocean. Not that he ever went there all that much, it was just nice knowing that it was near.

He'd slept through the morning rush hour. The streets were empty of life except a woman across the way struggling with two dogs and a delivery truck that flew by.

When Rachel's apartment building came into view he felt a little butterfly in his stomach. He panicked for a moment thinking he forgot her keys. That would have been great, showing up at her doorstep without them. He could only imagine how big of an asshole she'd make him feel like if that happened.

On the first floor he looked over at the apartment where the two little boys lived with their mother. Mitchell used to sit out there and play Transformers with them after school while they waited for their mom to get home. He'd been meaning to stop by and say hello, but never got around to it.

He reached the foot of the stairs leading up to her apartment and paused. Could he time it so her new boyfriend was in the shower? The last thing he wanted to see was another guy standing in the apartment filling the role he used to fill. Worse was the idea of meeting this guy and finding out that he was better looking and younger than him.

Rachel was five years younger than Mitchell, which wasn't a big gap, but the idea that she broke up with him partly because of his age was a nagging feeling he had. He did a slow walk up the stairs and pulled open the screen door to knock. In his mind he rehearsed what he was going to say. She'd ask him how he'd been. He'd leave out the part about being sick because he knew it would only make him sound even more pathetic. Instead he'd tell he'd been busy with radio station stuff and tell a white lie about getting an offer to go to a bigger station in a bigger market.

He knew she'd say he should take the job to either call his bluff on the lie if she saw through it or to get him as far away from her as possible. He'd already thought of a follow through for that though when he was home sick on his couch. He would reply that he loved South Florida and the station was thinking about putting him on earlier in the day. Like early enough that she would be driving home from work and turn on her radio and accidentally flip to his station and hear his voice. He grinned at the idea of her being afraid to turn on the radio at the risk of feeling remorseful about the break up. Or better yet, have his face up on billboards around town.

His grin faded when the sad reality that it was a fantasy brought him crashing down to Earth. He'd be lucky to still have his job in three months. An earlier time slot when people who weren't insomniacs or alcoholics was more far fetched than any one of Rookman's conspiracies.

Rachel's dog began barking from behind the door. He could hear footsteps and then Rachel's voice yell at the dog. From behind the door she called out, "Hold on Mitch."

He could hear her undo the chain and then unlock the deadbolt. She opened the door and a wave of longing swept over Mitchell as he saw her how he'd seen her a hundred other mornings in her shorts and tank top. A little sleepy, but radiant and beautiful.

She gave him a half smile. The smile turned into a snarl. He'd seen that expression before, but never on Rachel. That was the look the mad girl last night had given him before she tried to rip out his throat.

Rachel's eyes opened wide as her mouth seemed to unhinge. She lunged forward at Mitchell and let out a scream so shrill he felt his knees go weak.

6

Mitchell took a step back as Rachel leaped forward. Her fingers came at his chest clawing like an animal.

His right foot overstepped on to the stairs and he stumbled backwards. He felt the railing with his right hand and clung to it so he didn't fall down the steps.

One of Rachel's hands grabbed his shirt and yanked at it. He could feel the elastic neckband burn against his neck as she pulled. His trip had actually helped him stay out of her reach. Rachel overshot where he stood and fell down on the edge of the stairs with the upper half of her body hanging over them. The aluminum railing made a gong-like sound as her spine hit it.

Frustrated and furious, she let out a scream and started kicking at his shins. Mitchell jumped up spreading his legs to avoid the blows.

"Rache..." he started to ask.

He was trying to understand what was happening. Had she fell? Was it like the night before?

All he could do was react.

She looked up at him and reached a hand towards his belt and tried to pull him towards her.

The hand slid and latched onto his ankle. Mitchell yanked his foot away and reflexively stomped on it pinning it to the ground.

Rachel's left foot hit him in the knee and he let her hand go.

She was beginning to pull herself up.

Mitchell looked at the open door. Should he try to make it inside and lock her out?

Just then a male voice called out from inside. "What the fuck is going on?"

Mitchell ran down the stairs in two bounds.

Rachel got up and chased after him.

He rounded the edge of the complex and headed down the sidewalk. He could hear her running behind him.

They used to jog together. He was the faster sprinter while she had better stamina.

Behind him he heard her pace quickening. She was gaining. He made a quick left and ran down a shortcut he used to take. Rachel overshot it before turning around.

He could hear her snarling behind him.

Mitchell ran down the gap between the buildings and took another turn. He'd made some distance from her, but she was still gaining on the straight aways.

Across the street he could see an apartment complex with a white metal gate between an alley. The gate was open. If he could reach the gate he could close it and separate Rachel from him, at least temporarily.

Mitchell ran up the steps and jumped through the entrance. He shut the gate as Rachel's body slammed into it.

The latch had no lock on it so he held it shut with his hands.

Rachel pulled at the bars and screamed. Her eyes widened as they saw where his knuckles were vulnerable on the outside of the bars. Her mouth snapped at his fingers trying to bite them off. Mitch pulled his hand free and her head slammed into the metal bars. She furiously banged her head against the gate then she tried to bite his other hand. *What the hell?*

Mitchell moved his hand to another part of the gate and tried to hold it shut. How long could he do that before she bit one of his fingers off? He hoped somebody would call for help soon. The entire neighborhood had to hear her screaming and the sound of her body thrashing against the gate.

He could hear the sound of someone running down the alley he had just came from.

Her boyfriend, Rick, ran into the street. Still in his boxers, he was Mitchell's height but much more athletic.

He looked over at them and came charging.

Rick let out a guttural cry, leaped up the small set of stairs and slammed into the gate with his shoulder. The concrete fitting where the gate was bolted into began to crack. Bits of painted plaster fell away in chips.

Rachel stretched her hands through the gate and tried to claw at Mitchell's throat. He let go of the gate entirely and stepped back. Rick charged at the gate again. Mitchell could hear the sound of metal bending.

Mitchell looked at them confused. Their eyes were blood shot and their teeth bared all the way to their gums.

Something was going to give. He could either stay there and wait for help to come or use what time he had before they bothered to just undo the latch and come for him.

Screw it. Mitchell ran down the alley and hopped over the low wooden fence that separated it from the service road in back of the complex. He spotted a large trash can and pushed it in front of the fence. It might trip one of them up if they didn't see it.

He headed up the service alley and came to the cross street. A car drove by. He tried to flag it down. It kept on going. From behind he heard the sound of aluminum hitting the ground. The crashing gate echoed down the canyon of buildings that lined the service road.

Mitchell turned around to see Rick leap over the fence and pass right over the trash can. *Fuck.*

Rick looked to his right, then to his left and stared right at Mitchell. He pumped his arms and came at him like a sprinter out of the starting blocks. Mitchell ran into the street, not caring about traffic, and ran straight down the middle.

His best hope was to spot a cop or someone who could help.

Already in pain, his body was crying out to stop. He could feel bile build up in the back of his throat. He couldn't keep this up much longer.

The only thing that kept him going was the thought of what would happen if Rick caught up with him.

The sound of bare feet hitting the pavement was getting louder. Rick was letting out the loud puffs of air sprinters sometimes do when they are trying to use their lungs as a muscle to pull themselves forward.

A smaller set of footprints was further back. Rachel was following them.

Mitchell heard a scream right behind his ear. Something reached out and touched his backpack. The adrenaline gave him a burst of energy. For a brief moment he felt something of a high.

He reached another intersection. A car was driving across it. Fuck, it was going to be close.

Mitchell jumped. His could feel the wind of the car. The driver slammed on his brakes as Mitchell flew past his windshield. The driver turned to watch as Mitchell kept running. He never saw the other man run into his car at full speed.

The front bumper sent Rick flying into the ground. There was a snap as his right leg broke from the impact.

Mitchell turned around and saw Rick crumpled on the asphalt. His leg was at a funny angle. Rick was still staring right at Mitchell. He struggled to his feet and fell down. Blood spurted from where bone stuck out of the skin.

Rachel ran around the car and blew right past Rick as he struggled to get up. She never looked back.

The fear, the adrenaline, it all went numb as Mitchell saw Rachel ignore Rick as she dodged between him and the car without missing a beat.

Mitchell ran down the next service road. He immediately took a turn through another alley and towards his car. He hoped this would confuse Rachel when she got to the service road.

On one side of the alley was a wooden maintenance shack. He ran around the back of it and waited.

He could hear footsteps as Rachel raced to where she last saw him. They grew louder then passed where he was hiding.

Should he call for help now?

He reached for his iPhone then froze when he heard another sound. It wasn't as fast as Rachel, but it was definitely footsteps.

Near the entrance to the service road he could hear a footfall and then the sound of something being dragged. Step. Drag. Step. Drag.

Rick.

Mitchell decide to break for his car and call for help from there.

He rushed down the alley and on to the street where he parked his car.

He prayed that Rachel didn't decide to emerge from the service road as he ran by.

Finally he reached his car. He opened the passenger side door and slid in as he caught his first relieved breath of air.

A tire squeak made him jump. He slid away the sunshade as a parking enforcement officer pulled up in her three wheeled cart to ticket the car in front of Mitchell.

Thank god for meter maids, thought Mitchell as he got out of the car to ask for help.

7

Mitchell went to open his mouth. He hyperventilated as he tried to think of what to say. The parking enforcement officer, a middle-aged stocky Hispanic woman was typing something into her handheld computer.

"Excuse me!" Mitchell called out.

She looked up at him from the other car. It was a defensive expression she'd shown a thousand times to people who thought they could plead for a break.

She just looked at Mitchell and raised an eyebrow. No, "How can I help you" or anything resembling courtesy.

"I'm being chased by two people...I think they're trying to kill me." He made a conscious choice not to say ex-girlfriend and her boyfriend.

Mitchell looked over his shoulder. He wasn't sure if he was more frightened about seeing Rachel running towards him with murder in her eyes or Rick slowly plodding along with his bloody mess of a leg and bone poking through.

The officer walked to the driver's side of Mitchell's car and looked at him from across the hood.

She could see the terror in in Mitchell's eyes. There was a fleeting moment of humanity.

Mitchell tried to figure out how to explain what had just happened. But even he didn't understand it.

The woman reached for her radio. Then her face lost all expression.

Oh fuck, thought Mitchell.

The woman's lips pulled back as she bared her teeth.

Passenger side door still open, Mitchell leaped back in and slammed it shut. The officer jumped on to his hood and started slamming the radio into his windshield as she screamed.

"Fuck! Fuck! Fuck!", he shouted.

He looked over at the driver's side. He started to climb into it when he heard the windshield crack from the impact of the radio.

He looked back out and saw the radio break apart as it made a hole the size of a soda can in the glass. The parking enforcement officer reached a hand through the opening scraping the skin of her knuckles and grabbed Mitchell's hair.

She started to yank it.

Mitchell whipped his head back. Her bloody fingers still held on to clumps of his hair.

He leaned back out of her reach. Red polished nails flew past his face.

Did he try to start the car and drive off with her on it? Could he even drive with her trying to rip his face off through the windshield?

He fumbled his keys from his pocket and shoved them into the ignition from the passenger side. He tried to pull the car from park to reverse so he could throw her free. Fuck. He forgot he needed to press on the brake pedal to do that.

Mitchell tried to reach under her arm as it swung through the hole like an angry snake looking for something to strike.

His left hand felt a pedal. He pushed it. The engine revved up. Damn it! He pushed the other pedal as his right hand tried to pull the shifter.

Crack!

Mitchell looked up as pieces of glass began to rain down him.

The parking officer was trying to squeeze her round body through the opening she'd just made larger.

Her right shoulder and head was coming through the glass.

Mitchell pulled himself back into the passenger side.

The stout woman tried pushing through as her left hand pounded on the outside of the windshield. It was a mess of cracking glass and bloody hand prints. Her eyes kept staring at him never looking away.

Crack!

The window blew apart and showered small pieces of broken safety glass everywhere. She placed a hand on the window frame and pulled her body towards Mitchell.

His right hand found the door handle and pulled on it. Mitchell fell out of the car and to the ground.

The woman climbed all the way into the car. On impulse, he slammed the door shut and kicked it closed.

Still on all fours, he crawled backwards over the grass to the sidewalk.

The woman slammed her face against the passenger window and let out a scream. Bloodshot eyes tore into him. She began beating on the window with bloody fists as she pounded her head into the glass.

Her face was crisscrossed with lacerations. More blood was visible than skin.

Mitchell knew he couldn't stay there. He was certain she was either going to break through the glass or just open the god damned door when she calmed down for a second.

Did parking officers carry guns, he wondered?

He looked to his left and then to his right. Somewhere out there Rachel and Rick were still trying to hunt for him.

The woman in his car started kicking at the window.

Fearful of getting cornered by Rachel, Rick or the parking officer, Mitchell got to his feet and started running towards a more populated part of town. Maybe someone could tell him why people were acting so crazy.

He ran down the street and crossed several intersections without looking. He ran up another street to put him out the line of sight of the parking woman. As he bolted through another intersection a car honked at him.

That normal human reaction made him feel slightly better.

When he got to a safe place he could call the police and try to find out what was going on. How come four out of the last seven people he talked to in the last 24 hours tried to kill him? He wasn't a spy. He didn't have any secrets. *What the fuck?*

A mile away from his car he started to slow down his pace. He needed a place to think and sort things out before he called the police. He had no idea what to tell them.

Every time he tried to think about what happened he felt disconnected, like he was watching someone else's bad dream. Rachel's face was something out of a nightmare. Nothing made sense. He did the only thing he could, keep moving forward.

Up ahead he saw the mall where he would sometimes go hang out while Rachel was at work. He picked up his pace and hurried to there. He knew he'd feel much more safe in some place public. Somewhere people could help him if Rachel, Rick or the parking woman came after him.

Mitchell jogged past the half full parking lot and went through the sliding glass doors. *Safety in numbers*, he thought.

8

Mitchell headed straight from the entrance and towards the food court. Under the skylight, surrounded by a dozen different fast food places, he knew he would feel less alone. Less vulnerable.

This was where he went when Rachel told him it was over and he didn't have any friends to talk to. The mall was where he went for a sense of normal.

He walked briskly past the shops and kiosks. The smell of orange chicken and French fries told him he was getting closer.

He pulled out his iPhone and sat down at a table on the outskirts of the food court.

A few tables away, a woman knocked over her drink as she tried to reach across the table to feed her baby in its high chair. She got up to get some napkins to clean the mess.

He looked at the lines of people forming at the counters during their lunch break. Hunger began to overtake all his other instincts as his stomach let out a growl. He ignored it and stared at his locked phone screen. He'd removed the photo of Rachel after she'd broken up with him.

He tried to swipe the unlock, but his finger was still shaking from all the adrenaline and anxiety. He tried again and unlocked it. He pressed the phone icon and began typing 911 into the keypad.

His finger paused over the "call" button.

How would he explain what was happening to the calm voice on the other side?

He wouldn't tell them about the girl the night before. That would only complicate things. Should he tell them that Rick was trying to kill him and leave out Rachel entirely? His story sounded better that way.

What should he say about the meter maid. His stomach turned into a knot when he realized the woman he had just ran from was effectively the police.

"Fuck. I'm a fugitive from the police." The words slipped off his tongue as the severity of it all went way beyond the immediate implications of people trying to kill him.

Had he broken any laws in trying to get away? How fucked up would that be?

He heard another faint growl. He looked at his stomach. It didn't feel hungry at that point. He heard the growl again. It was coming from off to the side.

Mitchell looked toward the direction the sound was coming from. The baby in its high chair was staring right at him. Its mouth was wide open revealing little teeth in pinks gums. The child's tiny bloodshot eyes were locked on Mitchell. It let out another growl as it creased its forehead and squinted its eyes.

Mitchell slid his iPhone back into his pocket and just watched. The baby began to rock in its high chair letting out its animal groan. It gnashed its teeth and rocked harder. It let out a shrill scream.

Mitchell was afraid the child was going to tip over. Instinct told him to go help it. Other instincts, more primal than his protective mammal ones, told him to stay clear.

The child rocked the high chair so hard it slid a few inches across the tile floor. The baby reached out a hand and clawed at the air. It clawed again and tried to grab Mitchell from twenty feet away.

Mitchell jerked back in his seat, as if they baby was going to somehow manage to reach across the distance.

Little pearl-sized teeth tore at the air as snot and spit began to run down the baby's face and spill on its coveralls.

It rocked its chair another few inches towards Mitchell. It began to pull at the restraints and struggled to get free, while never looking away.

Mitchell remained motionless as if his very inactivity would make him invisible.

The child looked at him and growled.

Mitchell slid his chair away from the table.

In that moment, his worst fear was that if he ran or walked away the child would tip over. Then everyone would see the child sprawled out and crying on the ground as Mitchell tried to get away.

The child rocked the chair back and bumped the table in back of it. If it got much more momentum, it was going to go over.

Frozen in panic, Mitchell didn't know what to do. His social instincts told him to stay to make sure the baby didn't hurt itself. The hatred in the child's eyes as it continued to stare him down told him he had to run.

The baby was getting more frustrated. It hissed at Mitchell, then let out a shrill scream that rang out through out the food court.

The mother, who was getting napkins in front of a Chik-fil-A, looked up at her baby. The entire food court looked towards the child.

Its tiny hand reached out again clawing the air, reaching towards Mitchell.

The mother traced the path with her eyes to where the baby was reaching. Its small claw-like hand was pointing directly towards Mitchell as it convulsed and shook trying to throw the whole high chair over. The mother started running.

Mitchell slid his chair back. His mind raced for an explanation. The baby rocked and snarled. The woman knocked over another woman as she threaded through the tables towards her child.

She changed direction. He felt his blood drain as he realized the woman wasn't running to her child. She was running straight towards Mitchell.

The entire food court's attention began to shift from the furious infant and towards the mother. People dressed in slacks and skirts, ties and blouses, with little keycard IDs attached to their clothes began to ignore what they were doing and look at the scene.

Cashiers looked away from their registers. Chefs looked up from hot tables.

They looked at the mother and the angry baby. Then looked straight at Mitchell.

Mitchell could hear trays and drinks hit the floor. He looked away from the mother to the crowd.

All eyes were directly on him. Red eyes.

First the mother, who was seconds away, screamed out. Then a tall black man in a tracksuit shrieked. Then a hundred more screams let out as the entire food court let loose like a pack of wild apes in a fury.

In a wave-like motion the crowd went from a standing position to a full sprint as they started running towards Mitchell.

9

With hate in her bloodshot eyes, the mother ran past her baby knocking the table and sending the high chair on its side. The baby screamed then tried to claw at the tiles to pull itself towards Mitchell.

She was just a few yards away.

Mitchell looked at the chair in front of him. He gave it a swift kick sending it skidding across the floor and into the woman. She ran right into it. The momentum knocked her legs out from underneath her and she went sprawling to the ground face first.

Mitchell could hear the sound of people knocking chairs and tables over to get to him. He leaped to his feet and spotted three people getting close on his left. The nearest was a teenage boy in a Burger King uniform.

Without looking, Mitchell grabbed the chair he was had been sitting in and flung it at the young man. He hurled it at his face. The young man held out his hands to swat it away.

The chair bounced of his shoulder and hit a snarling teenage girl in the bridge of her nose.

On Mitchell's right a crowd of a dozen people had abandoned their places in front of the Panda Express and were only two tables away from him. He looked over his shoulder at the narrow exit from the food court to the main atrium. Rows of tables and chairs lined up the center. An old man and three blue-haired women had abandoned their bagels and coffee and were running towards Mitchell.

He looked back at the rest of the food court and decided his best chance was to go through the old people.

He ran into the old man as he tried to block Mitchell. Withered hands covered in liver spots reached out and tried to pull at him. The old man let out a yell and gnashed at Mitchell with a mouth full of dentures. Mitchell pushed the man in the chest, sending him backwards into the women.

Desperate to gain some time, Mitchell started scattering the chairs and flipping the tables into the crowd as they surged into the narrow passage. Mitchell ran into the atrium and ducked as a woman pushing a stroller ran towards him.

Three women came out of Lord & Taylor at the other end of the atrium to see what the commotion was. Their faces changed and they started screaming. Three sets of manicured hands reached out to claw at Mitchell as he got closer.

Mitchell's feet skid across the floor as he came to a stop when he realized that exit was going to be blocked. The crowd from the food court was starting to make it through the overturned tables and chairs and spill into the atrium.

The atrium opened up into two different wings. Mitchell ran towards the closest one.

A woman selling scented candles at a kiosk came at Mitchell. He jumped out of the way and hit a clothes display in a Banana Republic. Two sales girls came screaming at him from inside.

Mitchell regained his balance and ran down the mall. He felt a hand touch his backpack as someone got close. Up ahead he could see a shoe store with shoe racks in front.

As he passed it he pulled on the racks, toppling them to the ground. He looked back over his shoulder and saw the two Banana Republic girls fall over it. Behind them was the surge of people from the food court.

The first few dozen people tripped over the girls and the racks and fell to the floor on top of them. The mob in back just pushed their way through or trampled them underfoot. It was a horrific pile up of people as waves of people kept coming through. Those that fell were just treated like an obstacle by the people behind them.

There was an exit coming up ahead of Mitchell that lead to a service corridor. If he could make it in there, the narrow hallway should slow the crowd down. He prepared to make a quick turn into the alcove and through the doors.

He was thirty feet away from the alcove when two mall cops came running out. One of them was talking into a radio. He locked eyes on Mitchell and held the radio overhead like a club. The other mall cop followed suit and the two of them ran to intercept him.

Mitchell dodged to his left and ran around a toy kiosk. He elbowed the middle-aged woman as she got out of her chair to attack him. She fell back into the chair and continued going head over heels.

He moved through a rest area and jumped over a couch to the other side of the mall. One of the mall cops tripped on the toy kiosk woman and tumbled. The other was still right behind Mitchell.

Sales people and customers had begun to step into the center of the mall as the commotion got louder and the crowd's howling screams grew closer. Two young men and a girl walked out of a Hollister, looked at Mitchell and charged in his direction. They formed a wall as they closed in on him.

Looking for the weakest link, Mitchell ran straight into the girl and pushed her in the chest. Pink colored nails tried to scratch out his eyes as she fell backwards. He kept moving. From behind he heard two thuds as the young men ran head on into the crowd and their bodies fell to the floor. Mitchell could hear a sickening crack as a leg or an arm was broken.

Directly in front of him was a large department store. The front looked clear of people. Maybe he could make it in there and lose some of the crowd in the clothes racks. He pumped his arms and kept pushing himself to keep going. Occasionally he'd feel a hand grab at his backpack, then fear would kick in and he would find a little more speed.

He was dying to turn around to see how big the crowd was and how close, but he didn't dare lose a single millisecond of advantage. The sound of pounding footsteps, kiosks being toppled and wailing as people screamed at him told him enough to just keep running.

The only thing helping him was the fact that due to the law of averages, the people who could run faster than him were somewhere back in the mass of people. If they were able to break free, god help him. All it would take would be someone to grab one ankle or just loop one arm through his damn backpack and he would trip and fall to the ground. The last thing he would ever see would be a tidal wave of people falling on top of him tearing him to shreds with their hands and teeth.

Thank god he jogged. Thank god he'd lost that 30 pounds last year. Mitchell knew he'd have been fucked if he hadn't been in reasonably okay shape. He'd be dead.

The entrance to the store was deserted. He ran through it and tried to pull over a rack of coats when he moved by. Only one fell to the floor. In front of him was a perfume counter. A woman behind it with too much plastic surgery and makeup looked up at Mitchell then leaped on to the counter like a cat.

The glass counter top broke as the woman jumped into the air and tried to claw at his throat. He was already moving to the right to go around the perfume counter. She overshot and fell into a display of men's cologne sending hundreds of boxes into an avalanche to the floor.

Mitchell looked to his left and spotted the escalator. He skidded around the corner and ran up it. It was going down. *Fuck!*

Wait, this is good, he realized. Mitchell knew the secret to going the wrong way was to run up it in large steps and to not stop. It took him a half dozen strides and he was at the top. He turned around for the first time since he left the food court.

"Holy shit!", he shouted as he saw the mob.

It wasn't a few dozen people. It was hundreds of people all trying to surge onto the escalator. Two or three would try to step on to it and then get tripped up by the people in back of them. Those people would then try to step over the people in front of them. Other people were trying to climb over on the side rails. Fingers and hair got caught between the collapsing metal stairs, trapping them.

Mitchell watched in horror as a man in thick glasses pulled away a stump of a hand and tried to use it to climb over another person whose face was shoved between the railing and the escalator.

As much of a cluster-fuck of human carnage as it was, the sheer body count of people was adding up and they were making progress. Mitchell pulled a display rack of glassware in front of the escalator and shoved it down onto the crowd. He watched wineglasses and brandy snifters rain down on people before the shelving collapsed in the middle of the escalator. That was when he realized the up escalator across from him was going to be bringing a deluge of people as soon as they worked their way around.

He could see people running around the bottom of the up escalator to join the mob. He had seconds to do something. From behind he felt a hand reach out at his throat and start to strangle him. Mitchell jerked his head back and bashed in his assailant's nose. He turned to see a saleswoman topple into a rack of wallets.

Mitchell recognized her. She'd once helped him pick out a suitcase for a trip he never ended up going on with Rachel. The woman had been exceedingly polite.

All of that was gone as she made it to her feet and ran at Mitchell. He sent a knee to her face but tried to soften the blow out of guilt. She fell to the ground again. Mitchell used this opportunity to push another display over. This one he dropped on to the entrance of the up escalator to create a temporary road block.

People were half way up the down escalator. Mitchell looked around the upper level for an exit. He remembered the woman going to a store room near the bedding department. Mitchell headed in that direction.

If he could get into the storage room maybe he could block the door. If it lead to a service corridor he could hopefully find a fire exit and get out of the building. From there, he had no idea what he would do. For the moment he forced himself to disconnect his actions from anything bad that was happening to the people chasing him. In his mind the building was on fire and he had to get out.

He ran around the shaft and past the exit for the up escalator. Out of the corner of his eye he spotted a mass of people making their way through the tables and suitcases he'd dropped in front of it. Ahead of him two athletic looking men came running from the bedding section.

Mitchell reached out and grabbed a large metal pot and threw it at the closet one. It hit him in the face and opened up a gash above his eye. The man didn't even flinch.

He tried to avoid them by running left, but they cornered him in front of a display table. Rather than go around it they just climbed on to it. One of them was on all fours reaching out to claw Mitchell. The other landed on his feet and was ready to jump on to Mitchell. He knew he couldn't handle the both of them in close quarters.

The table wobbled as the two men climbing over it unbalanced it slightly. Mitchell grabbed the edge closest to him and lifted as hard as he could. The table flipped over and the two men fell off. One was trapped under it while the other fell backwards and smashed the back of his head against another display. He fell to the ground like a rag doll.

There was a snarl to Mitchell's left as luggage lady came at him. He jumped on to the overturned table and ran into the mattress section. He tried running over the top of the beds but lost too much speed as the mattress absorbed his footsteps.

He spotted the entrance to the storage area and ran to it. The luggage lady tripped and fell behind him as one of her heels broke. In back of her the mob had finally made it to the top of the escalator. Mitchell could see splatters of blood on the bodies of the people in the lead.

He felt like he was going to throw up. Somewhere a buzzer was going off because the escalator was jammed. Mitchell tried not to think what was jamming it as he bolted through the doors leading to the service corridor.

10

The doors pushed inward. Mitchell scanned the hallway for something to put in front of the doors to hold back the crowd. There was nothing. Damn.

To his left there was a break room. Further down there was a door and then the hallway went in two directions. One of them had to lead to a stairwell and out of the building away from the mob.

He ran to the end of the hallway and spotted a fire hose in a glass case. Desperate to try anything, he pulled the door off and pulled the hose free. A label on the hose warned the user to have at least two people hold on to it due to the high pressure. Perfect.

He threw the head of the hose down the hallway pointed towards the doors he'd jut ran through. Mitchell spun the wall valve until it came off the screw. The slack hose began to fill up with water as it was flooded with pressure. He watched the bulge race towards the nozzle and come gushing out. Once all the slack was free the water burst forth throwing the nozzle around the hallway like an angry tentacle.

Water flew everywhere creating chaos in the hallway. Mitchell knew people could make it through. But the water, the hose and the metal nozzle chaotically bouncing around would slow some people down and cause another bottleneck.

He felt sick to his stomach when he realized that the real bottleneck was going to be dozens of people falling down and getting trampled by the people behind them. Mitchell wanted to reach out a hand to help the people he saw fall, bloodshot eyes looking back at him with rage made him recoil. There was nothing he could do.

To his right he saw what looked like the opening to a stairwell. He ran in that direction. He kicked open the door and saw a flight of stairs leading downwards.

He was halfway through the doors when he heard footsteps running up the stairs below. Lots of footsteps. *Fuck.* Mitchell ran back through the doorway and down the corridor.

He had to jump to avoid tripping on the fire hose. Water was cascading across the floor making it slippery. At the other end of the corridor he spotted two double doors. He shoved them open with his shoulder.

This was the storeroom. He looked around for another exit. There wasn't one. Could he barricade himself in there long enough for help to arrive? What would happen when help did find him if he could make it that long?

This was no good. He looked for a place to hide when the crowd came. There were shelves of boxes and luggage wrapped in plastic. There was no place for a grown man to hide. He heard outer doors crashing open. The crowd had made it upstairs and were headed down the hallway.

Across the doorway he spotted an axe. He could use that to defend himself. But then what? There was no way he was going to intentionally crack open the skull of the luggage lady or anyone else. But what about using it to threaten people?

He went to pull it from the wall, knowing that this angry mob wouldn't be threatened for very long. If at all. He yanked it free. As he pulled back something caught the corner of his eye. He'd ignored it when he was looking for the stairs to go down.

It was a ladder leading up to the roof. Mitchell tossed the axe to the ground hoping at worst nobody would pick it up. At best that it would cause another bottleneck when people fought over it.

Mitchell pulled himself up the ladder and pulled the latch that opened the hatch above it. Daylight shot down like light into a tomb. He crawled out onto the gravel surface and quickly got up. He tried shutting the door but it wouldn't budge. From below he could hear the echo of dozens of feet in the corridor.

He tried closing it again. It wouldn't move. Why wouldn't it close? *Of course*, he realized as he spotted the safety catch. That was there to prevent people from getting trapped up there. He popped the latch with his palm and shut the hatch.

He hoped no one saw him go up. He figured he had a moment before they made it to that part of the corridor. At best he could hope for another human traffic jam in the narrow hallway. Mitchell wished there had been a better option than causing more harm.

Through the metal hatch he could hear the sound of dozens of people flooding into the back room. He could hear screaming. It felt like the roof itself was vibrating. What would happen when they all came pushing into the storage room? Would they just keep pushing and shoving to try to get through?

Mitchell had heard horror stories about people trapped in fires and stadium riots. Below him was the largest riot he had ever seen. And he was at the center of it. *For fuck sake, why?*

The animal part of his brain told him now was not the time to try to find answers. He still wasn't safe. Hundreds of angry people could erupt from the hatch at any second. All they had to do was to realize where he'd gone and pull the lever to the hatch. Even in a crowd full of people driven by rage, one or two would be able to figure out where he went.

He looked around the roof for anything to put on top of the hatch.

There was nothing but cigarette butts and a few rolls of tar paper. He looked on the latch for any place where it could be locked from the outside. There was nothing.

Not wanting to lose any more time, Mitchell decided to just run towards the other end of the mall. He would make as much distance as he could between himself and the hatch then try to find a way down.

He looked out over the parking lot. He expected to see hundreds of police cars and fire trucks by now. There was nothing.

He couldn't understand why. Hadn't anybody called the cops? Didn't anyone pull a panic alarm? Wouldn't the fire hose have sent a signal to the fire department? What was wrong with the world?

None of it made sense to Mitchell. Then he realized he'd left his table at the food court less than three minutes ago. *Fuck.* Just three minutes?

11

Mitchell reached the skylight that hung over the atrium. He wanted to walk over to it but was afraid someone would look up. He looked back where he had come from. The hatch was still closed. The sound of thumping came from under it.

He decided to chance it. He squatted low and walked towards the skylight trying to keep his body close to the roof. Through the glass he could see an overturned kiosk near the entrance to Lord & Taylor's. The ground was littered with scattered shopping bags, candles and several shoes. Off to one side he spotted an overturned stroller. Mitchell's cheeks flushed with guilt. He could make out tiny fists pumping at the air. Off to the other side he saw the body of an older man slumped over a broken planter.

Mitchell was afraid to look any more. He decided his best chance was to keep going all the way to the other end of the shopping mall and look for an exit there. In the distance he could hear the sound of sirens. He couldn't tell if it was police, fire or paramedics. The safe money was on all three.

As he ran across the graveled roof, his feet made loud crunching sounds. He panicked for a moment at the thought of attracting more attention from anybody below. It was pointless to worry about that now, he realized. He had to keep moving.

He tried to keep to the center of the roof to avoid being spotted by anyone in the parking lot. Another advantage, he realized, of running to the other side of the roof was that first responders were much more likely to go to the opposite side of the mall. What would happen when armed cops and firemen with axes came into the mall? He may have been able to outmaneuver two off-guard mall cops and a middle-aged meter maid. What about people with guns? *Was everybody affected?* He'd have to put that together later. For now he needed to avoid any human contact.

Mitchell reached the end of the mall where the other big anchor department store was located. It was a Sears, he thought. The parking lot below looked a quarter full on that end. He saw one or two cars pulling into spaces. Everything looked normal.

Sooner or later someone would make it to the roof. Maybe the cops arriving would be a good thing. Maybe it would be the worst thing. Mitchell wasn't ready to find out.

He jogged along the perimeter, exposing himself to anyone who bothered to look up. It was a chance he had to take to find a way to get down. At one end, he spotted a cluster of tall trees a few feet away from the building. Should he try to jump into them and climb his way down?

When he got closer he realized they were farther out from the building than he had thought. It was looking like a bad idea. There was no way to do it and not get hurt. He heard a bottle clink off to his right.

It sounded like it was coming from below. He walked over to the edge and peered down. There was a service dock underneath. A door shut as someone walked inside.

He could smell lingering cigarette smoke. Someone had just finished their break.

Right below him was a ladder. It had a sliding section locked in the upright position. He could climb down to the lowest rung and then drop the rest of the way down safely. *Probably.* He looked around for any other options. There was a large open garbage crusher. He could try diving into that.

He looked at the high slimy walls and decided not to. Metal hitting gravel sound made him jerk his head back towards the part of the mall he had just ran from. Someone had just knocked the hatch clean off. People were starting to climb on to the roof and sprint towards him. They were covered in red. *Fuck.*

Mitchell grabbed the top of the ladder and climbed on to it. He scurried down the rusty rungs. When his feet touched air he climbed down like monkey bars. The ground was further away then he hoped. It couldn't have been more than five feet, but his mind told him it was fifty.

Legs already bent to prevent breaking them, he let go and hit the ground. He let his body keep moving and came to a stop at a full squat. Nothing felt broken or sprained. He stood up and looked around a corner. There was nobody on foot. That was a good sign he thought.

In the distance he heard the sirens getting closer. Behind him he heard the rumble of hundreds of feet running across gravel. The sound of screaming was growing louder.

Out in the parking lot, he saw a blue sedan looking for a parking spot close to the mall. Mitchell wanted to get as far away from there was possible. Preferably on foot. Maybe he could flag them down.

He ran into the parking lot waving his hands in the air. He headed towards the car. The driver, an elderly woman, put on the brakes.

Mitchell ran to the driver's side window. She rolled it down. Mitchell started to speak. The woman let out a scream. At first he thought it was at him, but she was looking past him. Hundreds of people were on the roof looking down at him. Some of them were falling as others tried to push themselves to the front. *Oh god*, thought Mitchell. The sound of bodies hitting pavement echoed from the loading dock.

The woman let out another scream. Mitchell felt something claw at his arm. The little old red-headed woman was trying to climb out her window to get at him but her seat belt was holding her in. The car moved forward slowly as she took her foot off the brake pedal.

He needed her car. Mitchell reached down and opened her door. She tried to bite him but ended up hitting her chin on the metal door as he yanked it open. She was stunned for a moment.

Keeping pace with the rolling car, he reached over and undid her seat belt. She tried to bite him again but her head hit the horn instead. Her small hands tried to claw at his arm.

As gently as he could he pulled the tiny woman from the car. He tried not to look behind him as he heard the horrible sound of bodies hitting the pavement. When he had the woman clear of the car he ran back to the rolling car before it crashed into a parked pickup truck.

He forced himself into the small space between the seat and the wheel. He shut the door and hit the lock as his foot hit the brake. The small woman ran to the window and pounded her fists against the glass. One of her rings clicked like a dagger on ice every time it hit. Mitchell found the button to move the seat back so his chest and knees could clear the steering wheel.

He stepped on the accelerator before the woman could break the window. The car was still pointed towards the mall. As he turned around a row of cars, he saw another body fall off the roof. He headed out of the parking lot and avoided every impulse to look in the rear view mirror.

In front of him he saw a fire truck race around the perimeter of the mall, towards the first department store. Several police cars were behind it. Every impulse wanted to step on the accelerator and speed away as fast as possible. The sirens and flashing lights told him otherwise. He needed not to look like he was fleeing the scene of the crime. He fastened his seat belt and tried to focus on what he needed to do next, and not on the fact that along with everything else that had happened that day, he'd just committed a carjacking.

12

When Detective Rios arrived on the scene there were already two squad cars, three ambulances and a cluster of parking enforcement vehicles outside the yellow tape perimeter. He parked next to Detective Simmons's SUV and got out.

On the other side of the street, just inside the perimeter, were four parking enforcement officers gathered in a huddle. They'd heard the call on their radio and came to check on their fellow officer. One of them was talking in an excited manner and jerked his thumb over at a parked car near another parking cart.

The front window was completely smashed in. Several bloody hand prints were on the hood and dashboard. Pieces of broken glass reflected light like tiny green diamonds sprayed with blood. The passenger side window looked kicked in as well.

Usually when he saw a smashed in window and that much blood it was on a crumpled car in the middle of the highway. It looked out of place parked in a quiet neighborhood between two other cars. Other than a dent in the driver's side door, the body looked intact.

Rios looked over at the nearest ambulance and spotted his partner. She was talking to a young woman in a stretcher. Paramedics were cleaning up injuries and taping up her hands in preparation for the trip to the hospital. Underneath the bruises and gashes on her face, she looked like she was probably an attractive girl. Who could do a thing like that to a young girl? The answer, he unfortunately knew, was lots of people.

He walked over to his partner. Simmons was still dressed in the pants suit she'd worn to court earlier that day. Dark hair, athletic and in her early forties, she was in better shape than most of the men in the department, himself included. Rios still worked out, but was beginning to get the cop gut that came from spending more time taking kids to soccer practice than keeping in shape.

Rios waited behind Simmons as she talked to the girl. He knew not to interrupt that part of the investigation. She was good at getting people to relax and talk.

"So what happened?", Simmons asked in her most matter of fact tone. She preferred to let people talk in their own terms before drilling down for the particulars. Some cops started off with a check box kind of interrogation, which was aimed more at filling out an incident report than figuring out what was going on.

Rachel looked up from her arm where a paramedic was cleaning blood out of wounds on her knuckles. She was still in shock and not reacting to the stinging sensation. "My boyfriend...I mean my ex...he showed up and I...I answered the door..." Rachel paused for a moment and stared into space for a moment.

"What happened after you opened the door, Rachel?" asked Simmons.

"He...I don't know...it just happened you know. I don't even think I said hello. And then it was just...I was

on the ground trying to kick...I think to keep him off me."
She looked at Simmons as if she could explain what took
place.

"So you're on the ground." Simmons looked at the
metal clipboard in her hands. "So you're on the top of the
stairs by your apartment. Then what?"

"We were running."

Simmons looked at the notes. "Mitch? Mitch was
chasing you?"

"Um, I think so."

"So where was your current boyfriend at the time?"

"Rick? Where is Rick?" Rachel tried to sit up but the
paramedic gently held her back down.

"He's being treated right now. He's going to be fine."
Simmons noticed Rios behind her and handed him the
clipboard behind her back. "Can you remember where
Rick was when you opened the door?"

"Treated? He was taking a shower. Why is Rick being
treated. Did Mitch hurt him too?"

Simmons pursed her lips. Rios had noticed it was her
tell for when she was trying to make sense of something.
"He's going to be fine. When was the last time you
remember seeing Rick?"

"When he was in the bathroom. I think that was it."

"Did Rick approach Mitch? Did the two argue?"

Rachel shook her head. "No. No. I don't even think
they've ever met."

"Okay. We need to talk to Mitch. Do you have a
number where we can reach him? Maybe a photo?"

Rachel turned her head to look around. "In my
apartment. On the table."

Rios looked at the clipboard. The first officer on the scene had taken down her address. It was only two streets over. "I can get it."

Simmons turned to Rachel. "Do you mind if my partner goes into your apartment and gets your phone to bring to you? You can take it to the hospital with you if you like."

Rachel nodded.

Rios looked at the apartment number then handed the clipboard back to Simmons. "Be back in a second."

He looked down and gave Rachel a smile. He couldn't imagine what he would do if someone had done something like that to his own child or sister. He knew there were two sides to every story. In his mind though, nothing could explain the smashed up face and the scared and trembling girl. The anger turned what would have been a brisk walk into a fast jog to the apartment.

He took a shortcut and passed through a wooden gate next to a spilled over garbage can. In the middle of the alley between the two buildings there was a metal gate on the ground. It looked like it had been ripped from it mountings. There was blood all over it. Some of the bars were bent in. He made a mental note to make sure they took that in as evidence.

Down the street he could see another ambulance. Paramedics were working on the current boyfriend. His right leg looked like a bloody mess. From where he was standing, it looked like they were just trying to stop the flow of blood before they took him to the hospital. The man was screaming out in agony.

He overheard one of the EMTs mention something about trying to "save it". From the report Simmons let him look at, it looked like the man had walked three blocks on a green-stick fracture. How that was possible without being high out of your mind was beyond him. He was curious to find out what was in his blood when they took him to the hospital.

Rios reached the foot of the stairs. It was taped off as part of the crime scene. At the top of the stairs he could make out where part of the support bars had been bent in a little. There were a few drops of blood. He looked around and found another staircase leading up to the second level.

The screen door to the apartment had been ripped partially off its hinge and hung at a funny angle. The wooden door was wide open. Rios stepped inside and looked around. Well kept and in order, it didn't look like the fight started inside there. He could see wet footprints leading from the bathroom to the door. Those were most likely the current boyfriend's he assumed. Rios wondered if he was using, but didn't want to use the girl's permission to get the phone as a pretext for looking for drugs.

Angry ex-boyfriend. New boyfriend. Girl. That was all you needed for a first rate domestic disturbance. Add some alcohol to the raging hormones and testosterone and things got worse. How the parking officer figured into it was the next question. Rios would bet that she just ran into Mitch on the really wrong day.

From somewhere he heard a whimpering. His hand immediately went to the butt of his gun. He loved dogs, but dogs didn't always love cops. He heard the whimper again. This was a small dog. Rios relaxed. He spotted a large couch and leaned down.

Under the couch, two scared looking eyes looked back at him from locks of dirty blond hair. It was trying to hide behind his paws.

"It's alright." Rios patted the ground to see if the dog wanted to come out. "Your mommy is going to be fine."

The dog didn't want to budge. It just let out another whimper.

"Okay buddy. Stay there." Rios made a mental note to shut the door before he left so the dog wouldn't wander. They'd ask Rachel if she had someone to come take care of the animal. If not, the department had a person who would handle it.

Rios was a little surprised the dog was still there. Often in a domestic disturbance it would follow the owner and give chase to the assailant like a good pack animal should. Of course, other times they just hid.

He found a phone on the kitchen table and assumed it was hers. The lock screen was a photo of the dog. As he pulled the door closed he flashed the screen at the couch with the dog hiding under it. "Some protector you are."

Rios walked back to the ambulances and handed the phone to Rachel. Simmons was talking to the detective who had interviewed the parking officer. While the woman's injuries consisting mostly of lacerations, bruising and a probable concussion weren't critical, the loss of blood was.

Rachel struggled with the phone but couldn't operate it with her bandaged hands. Rios held out his hand. "Let me do that for you."

She handed him the phone. "It should just be under 'Mitch'."

Rios scanned through her contact list. No Mitch came up. He looked again. Nothing. "Would it be under his last name?"

"No. Try Dickhead." Embarrassed, Rachel looked off to the side.

Rios grinned. "Break ups are hard." He scrolled through and found a phone number next to the entry for Dickhead. He noticed there were a few other obscenities in there as well. Not his business, he reminded himself.

He wrote the number down. "What about a photo?"

Rachel shook her head. "I deleted them all." She thought for a moment. "He's still on my Facebook though. Go ahead. Do a search for Mitchell Roberts."

Rios clicked open the Facebook application and looked up the name. One of the benefits of social networking was how easy it made finding photos of people and intimate details they'd never tell the police face to face. He found the photo. He was not quite what he was expecting. It was a friendly, affable face. Not that it mattered. Faces can hide a lot.

"Do you mind if I email this to myself?"

"Sure."

He handed the phone back to Rachel. "I saw your dog back in there. He's pretty scared. Do you have a friend who can come look after him?"

"What about Rick?"

Rios hesitated. "He hurt himself chasing after Mitch, and is going to the hospital with you."

"Okay." Rachel leaned back and closed her eyes.

Rios decided to leave her be for now.

The ambulance carrying the parking officer drove off. Rios half expected the other parking officers to follow after in a motorcade in their carts like cops did when an officer was shot. A supervisor came over to explain the situation to the parking officers.

Simmons finished talking to the detective that took the woman's statement and walked over to Rios. In the background a police photographer was taking photographs of the smashed up car. He was trying to lean into the car without touching the glass. Rios morbidly wondered if he used the same camera to take photos of his family.

"This is going to be fun," said Simmons as she neared him.

Rios arched an eyebrow. "How so?"

"Like the girl, she can't give a coherent explanation as to what happened."

"That's not surprising. She's still in shock. What'd you expect." Rios would have been surprised if anyone who went through that, had at least a probable concussion, could remember much of anything.

Simmons shook her head. "She talked a little. What she says is kind of mixed up. She says she was attacked, but when they asked her where, she said while she was outside the car and he was inside."

"I'm sure she'll sort things out."

"Yeah, but when a defense attorney gets a hold of her first statement, it's going to make his job a lot easier."

Rios looked over at the smashed in windshield and the splattered blood. His stomach churned at the thought of the guy getting away with it. "So, what's our next step? Get him fast and get a confession?"

Simmons nodded. "Give him a call. See if he's willing to walk in. The computer pulled up no priors, so its doubtful he lawyered up just yet. If we can get an incriminating statement we can make the case sail through a lot easier." A voice called out on her radio. She pulled it from her waist and answered.

Rios could overhear the dispatcher say something about the mall nearby.

Simmons put the radio back down. "We need to get over to the mall right now." She looked around for the officer in charge of the crime scene.

"What's going on?"

"I don't know. Some kind of riot, or a fire. It sounds big."

13

Stolen car. That's what he was in. A car he just jacked from the woman back at the mall. Mitchell's life had just turned into one of those downward spirals he'd seen on the news. Next was the chase, then the helicopters and then it ended with him making a pathetic attempt to run away as people watched from a news helicopter. He'd make it 10 feet then he'd be tackled to the ground.

Worse for him was the possibility of what would happen next. He wouldn't be just be tased and kicked; he'd be torn apart.

He wanted to turn himself in, but he was afraid of what would happen next.

He cautiously turned on to the main road by the mall and kept driving. He tried to keep pace with traffic and not stand out. Subconsciously he sank down in the seat. As if people seeing a car with an invisible driver wouldn't notice.

At the moment he just had to keep his focus on not getting stopped. Doing that meant avoiding anything that looked suspicious.

"Fuck," he said as he drove through a red light.

He needed to pay attention to what he was doing, he scolded himself. Sirens were coming at him from the opposite direction. *Already?* Prior experience told him to pull over to the side of the road. Fear told him not to.

He kept driving and the squad cars blew past him. They were heading to the mall. Of course they were. People were dropping off the roof back there in one horrific trail of carnage from the food court to where he'd stolen the car. *Stolen car.*

He had no idea where he was going. He had no idea what to do. This wasn't the kind of thing he thought about. He was just a third rate radio host on a second rate radio station.

The radio station. The fax machine. All those police reports he'd read when they came in when he was working. He had to have learned something! Mitchell searched his mind. How do people get caught?

They get caught when they do something stupid like drive through a red light. Okay, don't do that again. They get caught when they run. Okay, don't attract attention. They get caught because they look like criminals. What did all of the men in the bulletins look like? They were either black, Hispanic or white guys that had neck tattoos and didn't look like they finished high school. They almost always dressed like thugs or homeless people.

Mitchell looked down at his ripped shirt. The collar had been pulled loose and there were tears in it. Specks of blood dotted his chest. It had criminal written all over it. He had to resist the impulse to take it off right there in the car. He looked over at the passenger side seat and saw his backpack. He still had it. There was another shirt in there. He could put that on when he had a chance.

Where was he going? A fire engine raced past Mitchell snapping his attention back to the road. He realized that his best chance of getting far away was right now. But to where? He only had thirty bucks on him. *Hell, how would he even spend money if every cashier wanted to kill him?*

He saw an ATM in the middle of an empty parking lot. Should he go empty out his account? It had to be then or never. If he used it further away from the crime scene they'd know what direction he was going.

Direction. Mitchell realized that if he wanted to go North and get as far away as he could he was going the wrong way. He needed to go back where he came from and past the mall. *The mall.* Was that stupid?

He realized it didn't matter. He didn't want to go towards Miami where it was more populated and he had less familiarity. If he was chased down there, there was nowhere else to go unless he felt like swimming to Cuba.

Mitchell got into a turn lane and took the car back in the other direction. He spotted the ATM and pulled into the parking lot. He couldn't help the fact that the camera on the ATM would see him, but if he parked in back of it he could avoid the car getting seen. For whatever that was worth.

He looked around the parking lot to make sure it was empty. Pulling up at an ATM in a stolen car was bad enough. He didn't want to have to deal with the fear of someone getting between him and the car and try to murder him.

He put the car in park but left the keys in it. He walked briskly around to the ATM looking over his shoulder every few seconds. His hand trembled when it tried to pull out his wallet. He took a deep breath and put in the card.

His mind went blank for a moment as he tried to remember his pin code. He closed his eyes and took another deep breath. It came to him. He keyed it into the touch pad and withdrew the $500 maximum. There was still another $300 in his checking account. He had no idea what he'd use it for or how, but it would have been better to have it.

More sirens were coming towards him. Out of the corner of his eye he saw three ambulances in a row heading to the mall. *Oh man,* he thought, *that's a lot of emergency personnel.* All because of him.

Mitchell heard brakes squeal. A bus was coming to a stop at a bus top in front of the parking lot twenty feet away from him. There was no point in waiting to see if anybody got off. By then it would be too late.

Mitchell hurried back to the car. He shut the door and belted himself in. *The card!* He'd left it back in the machine. *Christ,* he was not good at this, he reminded himself.

He saw three young black men get off the bus with backpacks. He felt guilty for thinking they were just going to steal the card. More guilt. Then he realized that wouldn't be a bad thing. If someone stole it and used it, it'd put the card far away from him. *Damn,* if he'd thought of that earlier he could have wrote his pin number on the card.

Maybe they'll take it, maybe not. The card was gone for him now. Now he needed to get as far away as he could and think of his next step. He also had to figure out how to get away from the car sooner than later. It didn't look expensive enough to have tracking in it, but it was a hot car and the license plate could be traced. He either had to ditch it or change the license plate for another one. He didn't know which was the smarter idea.

Mitchell waited for the bus to leave then entered the road from the parking lot and headed back towards the mall. Once he was past it he would take some side streets and just keep going north until something came to him.

As he neared the intersection by the south end of the mall another row of ambulances drove past and into the mall. He could see squad cars and unmarked sedans with magnetic blue lights on their roofs pulling in as well. That made him even more anxious for some reason. Maybe it was the thought that those cars contained detectives and not just beat cops.

He tried not to look, but all the other cars had slowed down as they passed the mall. It was hard to ignore the flashing lights from the fire trucks, ambulances and police. He allowed himself one glance, although he was afraid he was going to get sick from all the anxiety.

Two of the fire trucks had their ladders against the roof as firemen carried people down one by one. Mitchell tried not to count, plus it was hard to see from where he was, but it looked like a hundred people were up there. He didn't want to think how many fell or were trampled.

Pangs of guilt seared into him like hot pokers. He knew he had to do something. Even though he felt like a victim in all of this, he hated being the fugitive. He had to do one more thing before he flat out left.

Mitchell pulled his iPhone from his pocket and dialed 911.

"911 Emergency services. How can we assist you?"

"People are trying to kill me."

"Slow down sir. Who is trying to kill you?"

"The girl. My girlfriend. Fuck, the people at the mall. Everyone."

"I see."

"Are you in a safe place now?"

"Are you fucking kidding me? What is safe about everyone trying to kill you?" Mitchell knew the flood of emotion was making him sound like he was insane.

"Do you need the police?"

"So they can fucking shoot me?"

"Calm down sir. I want to help you. It says here you're calling from a cell phone. What's you exact location? Are you near the mall?"

Mitchell's heart skipped a beat. *They can trace those things. Stupid. Stupid. Stupid.*

"Sir, are you near the mall now? If you're hurt, one of the paramedics there can help you. Just find a place to sit down."

Oh man, they thought he was one of the people. One of the victims back at the mall. "Thank you." He thought for a moment. "I know this won't make much sense, but when you watch what happened, really watch. You'll understand that they attacked me."

"Yes sir. We need to keep this line available for emergency calls. If you need assistance, just ask for one of the paramedics or talk to a police officer. We have more coming." She paused. "Lots more."

Mitchell hung up then powered off his phone so they couldn't track it. Maybe he had more time. They still didn't know what happened at the mall. He practically tried to confess and she didn't understand.

A car honked behind him. Mitchell jumped. He'd been standing still for so long he was holding up traffic. He sped up and moved away from the mall as fast as he could without causing an accident or getting stopped by the police. *In his stolen car.*

14

When Rios pulled into the mall parking lot, the first thing that came to his mind was a circus. The fire trucks and police cars with flashing lights were all laid out in a ring around the mall. On the inside, he could spot ladders where firemen were helping people off the roof. He looked for smoke. He couldn't see any. A riot? At that mall? Was it some kind of Justin Bieber autograph thing that went out of control? He looked at all of the people standing on the roof waiting to be helped down. Why would people be up there from a riot? Unless there was a fire, it didn't make any sense to him. Between two fire engines, past a row of cars, he could see a sheet on top of a body. It looked like it fell from the roof. *Fell? Jumped? Pushed?*

He put his radio on an open channel. He heard first responder teams go back and forth with clipped chatter.

"Found twelve more in the upper corridor"

"Have three in the food court."

"Six in the stairwell."

"Three on escalator one."

What were the numbers? *Injured? Dead? Alive?*

He spotted Simmons's SUV and parked next to it. She was already jogging towards the mall. She had her first aid kit under her arm.

Rios grabbed his and chased after her.

He caught up with her as she passed the first row of fire engines.

"What the fuck?" he asked.

"I have no idea. I thought we were here to get statements but," she gestured to a row of forty people sitting on the sidewalk. They looked banged up, but not as bad as the people in the stretchers they saw scattered around near different ambulances.

A van came to a stop in front of them. A dozen doctors and nurses came piling out with first aid kits of their own. A female doctor pointed to the line of people, and half the group went towards there to help them. She lead the rest into the mall through the front of the department store.

Rios looked over at Simmons. "It's like one of those terrorism drills we used to have."

"I know. But these people aren't actors and community college volunteers paid to wear red colored Karo syrup for a few hours."

They found another detective who'd been called on to the scene early on. He was talking to a mall cop on a stretcher. The left half of his face was covered in bandages and his right arm was wrapped up.

Simmons called out to him, "Brooks!"

Brooks walked over to them. Tall and thin, just over fifty, he looked seventy that day. His thinning red hair was in total disarray. His white shirt and tie were covered in blood.

"Where can we help?" asked Simmons.

Brooks rubbed a hand on his forehead. "The paramedics will pull us in if they need to patch someone up. Right now the fire fighters are pulling through the bodies and trying to find who needs what kind of attention."

"What happened out here?" asked Rios.

Brooks turned around and looked at the front of the department store then back at Rios and Simmons.

"Here? This is nothing." He waved his arm from one end of the mall to the other. "We've got people falling off the roof here." He pointed towards the center. "People trampled in the food court." He pointed to the far end of the mall. "And people crushed in escalators and crammed inside a corridor and storage room. We can't even get up there yet there are so many people stuck inside."

"Fire?" asked Simmons.

"No fire. No smoke. It just looks like all out panic." He nodded to the mall cop in the stretcher. "As soon as one of them is up to it or mall management gets here, we're going to look at the security tapes."

Simmons looked at the row of people lined up on the sidewalk being tended to by paramedics. "What are they saying?"

Brooks shook his head. "Nothing that makes sense. Most of them have no idea why they panicked. A couple said they were being attacked. A few other said to 'get him'."

Rios looked around. "To get who?"

"They haven't a god damn idea who, Rios. Not a clue."

Simmons looked towards the entrance. The doors were being held open. Inside she could see more people being treated. "Can we get in there?"

"Yeah. We should start investigating now. Keep your first aid kits if any of the medical personnel need any help."

Inside the mall entrance the paramedics had set up a triage area. EMT's treated the people who came down from the roof, or those that fell and survived the fall. Their first goal was to get the seriously wounded to the hospital and treat the rest on site.

Rios saw over two dozen people leaned against walls or laying on the floor. Most of them were dressed in casual work attire and looked like they had come to the mall from nearby businesses to get lunch. Their shirts and blouses were ripped. Many of the women were missing one or both of their shoes. Few were talking. They all looked shell shocked.

Simmons noticed some and pointed it out to Rios and Brooks. "I see a lot of scratch marks and ripped clothing." She gestured to a team of paramedics applying antiseptic onto the backs of several people who were leaning forward with their skin exposed.

Brooks nodded. "There's a lot of that. People in back were trying to pull their way through."

Simmons thought it over for a moment. "Yes, but whenever I've seen people panic to leave a place like a club or a movie theater after a shooting, they might have bruises, but never this much...clawing."

They passed by a woman in her late thirties, with chestnut hair and freckles whose neck was wrapped in white gauze. A bright red blood stain was soaking through. She leaned against the wall cradling herself.

"You take their cell phones away?" asked Rios. So far he hadn't seen anyone talking into one.

Brooks turned around. "Huh? No. Why?"

Simmons looked around the entrance. She couldn't see anyone with a cell phone out either. That was kind of odd. Usually the first thing people did in a crisis was pull their phone out. She lost track of the number times she had to ask people to put down their phone so she could ask them questions.

"People mostly dropped everything. The women let go of their bags." He pointed towards the slacks of a young Hispanic man. They were ripped along the sides. "A lot of pockets got pulled open as people tried to claw through."

As they left the first triage area Simmons took one last look. In some ways it looked like a brawl had taken place, but with a few differences. There were lots of bruised and broken noses from flying elbows, but there weren't that many facial scratches. Necks and shoulders to be sure, but it looked like people were violently trying to inflict damage only as they moved through the crowd. There weren't a lot of injuries that looked like retribution for not letting someone pass by.

Past the entrance on the interior of the mall, there was a small field unit where a cluster of doctors and nurses were working on the more seriously wounded. Through huddled shoulders they could see a woman with both legs completely fractured. On another stretcher was a man with his face was caved in.

They heard the sound of a helicopter fly overhead and land somewhere on the roof.

Brooks pointed towards the other end of the mall where they were headed. "They're medevac'ing people out via helicopter on the far end." He pointed to the small medical unit. "This isn't the worst of it."

They walked further down the mall towards the center atrium. Most of the shops had lowered their gates. Simmons assumed that the clerks were being sequestered elsewhere. That part of the mall looked relatively normal besides the shuttered doors in the middle of the day. There was a group of people towards the back in a cordoned off department store watching them. They looked unharmed.

"This end of the mall, the part under the roof, didn't know what was going on. They just heard the commotion and then saw the people falling," said Brooks.

Simmons walked over to a young sales clerk in front of a woman's clothing store. She had tears streaming down her face as she watched the people being taken inside and treated. Mascara ran across her delicate cheekbones.

"Excuse me miss," said Simmons. "Are all of your salespeople here?"

The young girl shook her head. "Phil and Steve are still gone."

"Who are Phil and Steve?" asked Simmons. "Did they work here too?"

The girl nodded. "They heard the screaming from the food court and ran down there to see what was going on. Nobody can tell me if they're okay."

Simmons clasped the girl on the shoulder. "Don't worry. We'll find out." She turned to Brooks. "When are we releasing people?"

"As soon as we get a head count and contact information." He looked over at the girl. "We'll have someone come get you to go home soon."

The girl nodded.

Brooks continued to lead Rios and Simmons towards the food court. When they rounded a bend, the atrium came into view. Overturned kiosks, shopping bags, food trays and drinks were thrown all around. Simmons could see three bodies under sheets. It looked like a plane crash minus the plane.

"Holy crap," she exclaimed.

"We haven't even got to the bad part," said Brooks.

The Naked Man in the Forest had been feeling uneasy. He let the Otherself do what he was supposed to do, but he was having second thoughts. He stole away from where he was supposed to be and came to the forest place.

A light rain had made it damp. Mosquitos swarmed and kept biting him, but he ignored them. He had to speak to the Earth mother.

He sat there staring at the oak tree as large red welts began to cover his naked flesh. He ignored the urge to scratch and waited. He had another Ziploc bag in his pants. His Otherself pants, he corrected. If she didn't show herself, then he'd take a blotter to let him see what his mind was denying him.

He looked over at the khaki pants folded on a nearby rock. Should he?

From the corner of his eye he saw something move on the oak. He sat upright and put the thought out of his mind.

Vines and leaves began to form the familiar face. Oh, how he wanted to touch it, to kiss it, to be part of it.

What is wrong my child?

He tried to find the words. "The Otherself. He...he may have made a mistake." Yes, the Otherself did it.

What has he done? My eggs?

"Your eggs are fine for now. They're safe. It's just that I fear the ones who trust the Otherself may grow suspicious. They may know that he plots."

The Otherself is so important to us right now. You must make sure that he doesn't lose their trust.

"I know Earth mother. It's just that the Otherself made choices. Some of them hasty ones. He has powerful friends. If they find out what he's done..."

My eggs, child. My eggs are all that matter. When the Otherself is no longer useful to us, then bring them here.

"Yes Earth mother."

15

Mitchell avoided the freeway and drove along US 1 for a few miles. Although it was much slower with the traffic lights, he had more potential exits if he thought he was being followed.

He'd seen how the police set up roadblocks on exits and parked police cars with spotters on overpasses when they wanted to stop someone on I-95. Once they spotted you there, they could close down whatever they needed to pin you down. Game over. At least on US 1, he had a sliver of a chance of losing a police car if they decided to follow him. Or at least he hoped so.

When he began to get nervous about staying on the same road for too long he decided to drive a few miles to the west to catch up with State Road 7. Waiting to make the turn, he saw a helicopter flying by low overhead. His knuckles clenched the wheel until he saw it was a medivac chopper. He relaxed. When he saw it head towards the mall he felt anxious again.

He hadn't seen as many ambulances racing towards the mall, which he took as a good sign, until he realized that they might have run out of them. In the distance he could see another helicopter. It belonged to the local news station. The scale of what had just happened was starting to build.

Mitchell looked at the radio in the car but was too terrified to turn it on to his station. He'd have to find out what was going on in the rest of the world, but not at that moment. Especially when he was out in the open in a stolen car, already panicked.

He had no idea where to go. He couldn't drive forever. He needed a safe place. There wasn't a chance in hell he'd try calling one of his friends. From reading the police bulletins on the fax, he knew the two fastest ways to get caught were to get reported to the police when you scared someone or to have a scared friend report you when you went to them for help. Besides, he realized, he really didn't have any friends that he trusted enough to count on.

He knew calling his family was out of the question. The last thing he needed was to send his mother or sister into a panic. They both lived in California and wouldn't be of much help anyway. He hadn't talked to them in weeks. He could deal with them later.

Going back to his apartment was out. That'd be the first place the police would come looking. But what if he barricaded himself in there? He shook his head. The SWAT team or whoever they sent after him could be in there in seconds and then...He didn't want to think about that part.

He knew he'd have to turn himself in at some point. There was no way he could make it for long as a fugitive. But in order for him to surrender, he needed to be sure that whoever arrested him wasn't going to tear him to shreds. To be sure of that, he had to know why people were attacking him. Was it some kind of conspiracy? Was it some weird psychological thing? Had he become such a loser that people were turning on him like a wolf pack on a wounded dog?

Worry about where to go next, he reminded himself. Nothing came to mind so he tried to break down what he needed.

It had to be devoid of people.

He had to be able to hide the car.

He had to have an exit.

Finding an out of the way motel was useless if he couldn't check in without the clerk murdering him. He also knew he couldn't barge into someone's house and hold them hostage. Besides the moral problems of that, he couldn't imagine how he would restrain said person if every moment they were focused on killing him.

What about an abandoned house? South Florida was filled with empty houses that were either for sale or foreclosed by the bank. He'd have to break inside. From there he could open the garage door and park the car.

That reminded him of something. He thought for a moment. Of course! When Rachel had kicked him out, one of the station interns had told him his grandparents were looking for someone to rent their house. Mitchell had even gone out to look at it before deciding it was too far. He still knew the code for the door.

It was forty minutes from where he was and not too far off from two main highways. It was also two cities over and in the next county. He didn't know how much that would help him evade the police, but it had to at least buy him some time.

It was a quiet neighborhood where most of the houses were owned by people who lived out of state. Mitchell remembered that almost half the houses had 'For Sale' signs. That meant he was less likely to be confronted by neighbors.

He knew staying there wasn't the best idea. But for the moment it was the only idea. Mitchell tried to remember how to get there.

Even if just for the night he could hide out he would have some time to at least plan what to do next and hopefully figure out what the hell was wrong with him.

Mitchell saw the sign that said "Sunny Acres" and pulled into the community. It was a planned development from the 1970's where all the streets were laid out in a grid. Palm trees and flat lawns in uniform rectangles lined the streets. There was a community center and a pool towards the middle. The single-story houses were built from three basic designs and painted from a limited color palate.

They all looked the same to Mitchell. Only the random rust stains from the sprinklers differentiated them. He couldn't remember which one was the right one. The last thing he wanted to do was barge in on an occupied house. He drove down one road and then up another.

There were cars parked sporadically in different driveways. It seemed like there were even more 'For Sale' signs than last time. One house looked vaguely familiar. He pulled into the driveway and tried to figure out what to do next.

If he knocked on the door and somebody answered, that could be messy. His best bet was to knock and then run back into the car and wait to see if someone answered. It was a coward's plan and he knew it. It was all he had.

Mitchell turned off the car and walked up the walkway to the house. It looked very familiar. He got to the door and looked at the keypad. He decided to just try the code and open the door and look. He knew he could run back to the car if he heard anyone.

Fortunately, his mind didn't blank like it did with his ATM card. He keyed in the code. The door unlocked. From behind he heard a car pass. Mitchell almost pissed himself.

The car kept driving. Mitchell relaxed and looked inside the house. It was completely empty. He'd expect that, but wanted to be certain. He shouted, "Hello." His voice echoed through the house.

He looked back at the car in the driveway. The sooner he hid it the better. He stepped into the house and walked through the barren kitchen and into the garage. He fumbled for the switch and opened the door.

Mitchell remembered the intern, Mike, telling him that his grandparents had kept power to the house so the air conditioning would keep the moisture low. Apparently, other people didn't do that with their empty property and that caused mold and other damage. Mitchell was just glad he didn't have to figure out how to open the door by hand.

He pulled the car inside the garage and lowered the door. He was reasonably certain that no one had seen him and felt safe for the moment.

But for how long?

If they cast a wide enough net, would they find him there?

His name wasn't attached to the house, not directly at least. Mitchell walked back into the house and peered through the front blinds and looked down the street. What next?

16

The entire mall was essentially a crime scene. A narrow path had to be cordoned off with yellow tape to show people where they could and couldn't walk. To Rios, it felt like the line through a haunted house. Only this one was filled with real bodies and stretched the length of the shopping mall.

They followed the path to the front of the food court. Tables and chairs were flipped over. Spilled drink cups covered the floor mixing with food and puddles of blood. Rios could spot two places where fire fighters had to put out grease fires on unattended grills.

Brooks motioned for them to follow him. He pointed to the other entrance to the food court. "That's where it looks like everyone came through."

Bloody footprints lead away from the narrow corridor between the coffee shop and the cookie store. Overturned chairs and tables were shoved to the sides. Some from the looks of it, pushed aside by first responders trying to make a path. Others, from the trails of blood, by the mob of people rushing through there.

Rios could make out three outlines of bodies on the ground. Blood was so thick someone had to lay down floor mats so paramedics and fire fighters didn't track it into the mall and leave their own layer of bloody footprints.

"We think this is where it started. There was some kind of disruption and everyone came out of the food court and into the atrium."

"A disruption?" said Simmons. "Do we have any idea what kind of disruption could cause this kind of panic?" She looked at one of the restaurants that had scorch marks where the fire fighters had put out a small fire. "Was it over that?"

Brooks shook his head. "I don't think so. We think the small fires happened after the fact. We won't know until we get a look at the security cameras." He pointed down the mall. "After they left the atrium they went down that way."

"Shit." To Rios it looked like something out of National Geographic. The bloody footprints marked a path straight down the mall tracing out a path of destruction. There were more overturned kiosks, scattered shoes and clothes. Planters were knocked over leaving piles of dirt and palm trees in the middle of the floor. Pieces of broken window glass were scattered around. And then there were bodies under sheets. *Lots of bodies.*

The bodies seemed to be clustered near choke points at places where people had run into obstructions or had been too slow and just got overrun by the crowd.

Rios tried to imagine what could cause that kind of panic. He looked over at Simmons. She just shook her head.

They followed the path down the mall. Since most of the destruction was on the right side, the path stayed mainly on the left side of that wing. Forensic techs were scattered around taking photographs. Others were putting down numbered markers and gathering blood samples.

Rios looked into a beach wear shop on their left. Several clothes racks were overturned. He looked across the way into a jean shop and saw more overturned clothes racks leading from the back of the store. He pointed it out to Simmons.

"Was there anyone on this side of the mall who didn't join the crowd" she asked Brooks.

"When I first came in here I didn't see anyone." He looked at the overturned racks. "It sure looks like they ran out of there in a hurry. We found three babies still in the strollers their mothers had left them in."

"You had mothers abandoning their children?" As a father, Rios couldn't understand that. "I could see one, maybe. But three?"

Brooks pointed to the covered bodies and tracks of blood. "It's a good thing they did. I can't see a stroller surviving that."

Rios shuddered. Bodies under sheets were one thing. The thought of crushed infants unsettled him to the core.

They kept walking. There were more bloody footprints and covered bodies at bottlenecks. Rios and Simmons noticed more knocked over racks and spilled clothes inside the stores beyond the reach of the crowd.

Up ahead they could see the department store everyone had ran into. Displays were smashed to piece along the front. Makeup racks and jewelry cabinets were trampled under foot. The perfume counter that faced the front of the mall was half caved in. Broken shards of glass stood out at wicked angles. He saw blood splattered over a white dress that looked like one his wife had.

Rios felt his mouth go dry when he saw what looked like a decapitated body. He was about to speak up when he realized it was just a mannequin. Nearby there were two other mannequins that had almost been flattened.

They entered the department store. The entire right side looked like a hurricane had gone through there. Counters were smashed. Piles of clothing lay in heaps. Entire departments were leveled. And everywhere were footprints in trails of blood.

Brooks took them the long way through the relatively unscathed mens section. Rios wondered why that side was spared and the other wasn't? Was a panicked crowd as random as a tornado that destroyed two houses but left the one in the middle? Hopefully the security footage would have some answers.

"This is where it gets pretty ugly," said Brooks.

Now it gets ugly, thought Rios? What had they just been looking at?

Brooks took a deep breath and pointed towards the escalators. "They all came in over there and tried to go up the down escalator." Brooks took another breath. "I have no idea why. But three hundred people tried to go up there at once. People fell. Then more people fell on top of them. It got worse from there. They tripped on the up escalator too. It's almost as bad."

The escalator looked like the chute from a slaughterhouse. Dozens of bodies were laid out near it in a row along the aisle. Jackets and dresses taken down from the racks were used to cover the heads.

Brooks looked down at the ground. "I was nearby when the call came in. I was one of the first ones here. We had to pull the bodies apart as quickly as we could. There were people suffocating under them. We found some survivors. And then..."

His voice cracked and trailed off.

The blood drained from Rios' cheeks. For the first time he noticed that Brooks was still in shock. He hadn't realized how soon after the scene he had got there. As a detective he'd become used to arriving after the body count had been tallied and not being someone responsible for trying to keep it from climbing.

Rios looked over at the lined up bodies. He couldn't imagine what it was like to arrive when they were piled on top of each other with people screaming while trying to claw their way from underneath. Just the thought of it made him want to gasp for air.

Ever the professional, Brooks continued. "There's a stairwell at the far end. They've cleared the bodies and the wounded from there. It was a much smaller number of people than here, but not a pretty sight. We're still trying to sort out the storage room at that end." He looked at Simmons and Rios for an answer. "There were over a hundred people trapped in a room smaller than my bathroom." He looked at the escalator and shook his head.

Simmons spoke up. "I can understand panic. I can understand people following the pack. But why did everybody try to go up?" She pointed to the far end of the store where light was pouring in from two propped open doors. "We're on the ground floor. Who goes up unless there's a fire?"

Brooks shrugged. "I guess they do if they're chasing something."

He lead them to an elevator. The doors opened and two paramedics came rushing out pushing a stretcher with a middle-aged woman whose head was covered in bloody bandages.

The second level was filled with people too hurt to be moved just yet and those with lighter injuries that could wait for medical treatment. Paramedics were using the mattresses in the bedding department to hold all the people.

Rios looked around the floor. He counted over a hundred people in various states of injury ranging from claw marks and sprains, to what looked like broken arms and legs. Most of them were sitting or laying by themselves as medical workers moved around from person to person trying to figure out who needed the most help.

A fire department captain called over to them. "Over there." He pointed to a cluster of mattresses with people laying on them with untreated wounds.

Rios remembered he was still holding on to his first aid kit. He followed Simmons as she ran to help the people the captain had signaled to. Until they had some answers, it felt good for him to be able to do something besides being a ghoulish spectator.

17

Mitchell tore off his ruined shirt and threw it into a corner. He looked at his reflection in the master bathroom mirror.

"What's wrong with me?" he asked as if he expected his reverse image to have the answers. On one side the right handed, frightened and confused version, on the other the left handed, confident one who knew what to do.

The sight of his own image only added to his sense of despair. There were claw marks on his chest and back. He had bruises he had no idea how he got. His hair was a sweaty mess of brown. He looked exactly like how people look in the their mug shot photos.

Was this how people look after they are apprehended, or was falling apart so much what made them easy to spot and capture?

Mitchell turned the faucet and thanked Mike's grand parents for not disconnecting the water. He splashed cold water on his face and smoothed back his hair. For a moment he didn't feel quite like the state of constant panic he had been feeling before. He splashed more water on his face then caught his first unhurried breath.

He turned the faucet off then looked back in the mirror. His reflection had changed. He felt different. With his hair slicked back and no longer out of control, the effect the water had on relaxing the tension in his face and calming his burning cheeks, he didn't look like a man in the middle of a panic attack.

He placed his palms on either side of the counter and brought his face in close to the mirror. The face he saw was more composed, less apprehensive. It was the face of someone who could figure out what to do next and manage whatever the world threw at him.

He was looking at Mitch. Not Mitchell. Mad Mitch, the man in control.

Part of it he knew was the trick of the sunlight coming through the window giving his cheekbones and jaw a more masculine look, but he also knew that somewhere deep inside him was someone who wanted to survive. He'd seen horrific things that day. Even though a part of him just wanted to fall down and let the nightmare roll over him and bring everything to a close, something told him to keep running. Something told him that his life was worth fighting for. Fighting for. He repeated those words in his head. *Yes*, he decided, *he would fight to survive*. He'd never intentionally hurt someone, but if they got in his way then he'd have to go through them.

Whatever guilt he was feeling he could deal with later. When it was time to surrender he would do it only when he knew he would be safe. Until then, he had to do everything he could to protect himself.

"What the fuck," he said to his reflection.

"What the fuck," Mitch replied.

In broadcasting school he'd learned the quickest way to feel confident was to assume the posture of someone who looked confident, even when you were alone. He turned around and hopped up and sat on the counter. For a moment he would try to think of a reason why certain people were trying to kill him.

If the girl by the side of the road hadn't attacked him he would have thought that something happened to him at the radio station. But she had. If he'd been attacked by Rookman or Bonnie or the old man at the gas station things would make more sense. Why not them but everyone else? It couldn't be proximity. He was much closer to most them than anybody else.

Mitchell looked at his reflection in the medicine cabinet mirror, hoping for the more confident version of himself to give him an answer.

It did.

"Rookman, Bonnie and the gas station dude were behind glass, dumb ass," said Mitch.

Fuck.

Mitchell thought back over the last two weeks since he'd been sick. When was the last time he'd actually been face to face with anyone that wasn't behind glass or on a Skype screen? *He hadn't.*

What was the most significant thing that happened between the time when people just ignored him and when they wanted to murder him on sight?

Getting sick.

What did he come down with? Reverse rabies? Could there even be such a thing?

It was stupid, but it made the most sense for the time being. It gave him something to think around. Rather than thinking it was something so far beyond his understanding or involving a cosmic level conspiracy, that hypothesis was something he could deal with on a rational level.

Seeing him wasn't what made people want to kill him. It was something in the air. Something he gave off, either his scent or something else like a fast acting virus. Maybe it was like the pheromones bees gave off when it was time to attack? Did getting sick mess up his pheromones and tell people to kill him?

It didn't matter for the moment. Knowing that it was scent or something else he gave off allowed him to focus on the problem. They key to his immediate survival was going to be to avoid having people smell him or breathe the air near him. Handing out gas masks or finding a spacesuit weren't practical solutions. Until the authorities understood what was going on, he had to avoid them as well.

Mitch hopped off the counter and walked through the house checking the windows and doors again. Everything was locked down. Not that it mattered if the police surrounded the house. They'd have no trouble getting inside.

Mitch walked back into the bathroom and splashed some water under his arms and on his chest. He dried off using toilet paper. No time for a shower, he just wanted to get some of the sweat and smell of fear off of him.

He looked back at the reflection. "What now?"

"Find out what's going on and move to some place else."

He pulled out his iPhone. It was still turned off. Could they locate it when he powered it on?

He knew they could trace phone calls, but what about just the phone? There was a "Find my phone" function that used GPS and WiFi spots to find iPods and iPads. All he had to do to use that was to log into his Mobile.me account and click a button to see where the device was.

Fuck. His iPad. Mitchell put his phone into his pocket and ran to his backpack. He pulled out his iPad and pressed the 'Home' button. It was on.

He quickly powered it down.

He knew the odds were against them having gotten a search warrant and accessed his account to trace him. But there was that small chance. He could take a risk or he could assume the safe house was blown.

The scared Mitchell wanted to just stay there, or better yet, go hide in the attic. The Mitch he caught a glimpse of in the mirror knew it was a bad idea to stay. The more he tried to guess the risk on things like that, the more likely he was to put himself in harm's way.

Something Mitchell had put at the back of his mind finally made its way forward. When he turned off the iPad, for the first time he got a look at the time. For some reason he thought it was almost night fall. It was only 1 PM. He'd left the mall just a little over an hour before. He'd left his car and the mess at Rachel's less than twenty minutes before he got to the mall.

He had been on the run for less than two hours. All hell was going to break loose very soon and a lot of angry people were going to be looking for him. However he still had time to get more distance. He had time to find out what the rest of the world was saying.

Mitch shoved the iPad back in his pack. He sat down with his back against the front door so he could listen to the street outside while keeping an eye on the backyard through the sliding glass doors. He pulled out an analog radio he kept tuned to the radio station and turned it on.

18

Mitch pushed one ear bud into his ear. He left the other one open to listen for anything suspicious. He half expected the station to have switched over to a full time talk format dealing with the mall events like they did on 9/11. Thankfully, no. The station was playing its normal afternoon lunch time mix of 80's pop. For a moment Mitchell felt a sense of calm from the normalcy of it. New Order's Blue Monday was playing. He listened to the song a little bit longer than a man on the run should have, but he could feel his heart stop beating so fast.

He flipped the dial over to AM and went to a local news station. In his mind he expected to hear someone say "...in other news" and then go right to talking about the mall. But they didn't. It was a car commercial. Then a commercial for a life insurance company. Then a commercial for an accident attorney. I bet that guy has a boner right now, thought Mitch.

Finally the station's afternoon newsreader came on.

"We've got an update on the incident at Park Square Mall. The fire department has said that it wasn't a fire that caused the evacuation."

Evacuation. That's what they were calling it right now?

"We're getting more reports that a riot took place inside the mall and lead to a chase of the person who instigated it."

Was that a riot or an attempted massacre? *Instigator?* They didn't understand.

"Although official numbers haven't been released, news helicopters on the scene have spotted what look like at least six bodies on the outside of the mall. It's not clear yet if they fell from the roof as some people reported or if they were injured inside the mall or outside in some other manner."

Six bodies. And that was just on the outside. He'd heard the sounds behind him as he ran. He knew a lot more people were hurt than that. *Seven? Ten? Twenty?* Lots of people died because he ran. Mitchell's knuckles were beginning to whiten as he squeezed the radio. He switched hands before he cracked the plastic.

Should he have just stayed there in the food court? If he had known then what he knew now, would he have just sat there and let them get him? Part of him thought that would have been the moral thing to do. Sacrifice himself so that other people wouldn't be hurt.

He thought about the bloodshot eyes looking at him in the food court. The horrific way people stretched their hands out at him and bared their teeth. The shrill screams. The rage.

Could he have sat still for that? It was one thing to put on a blindfold and take a bullet or to have a doctor administer a lethal dose. Those things were quick. What would it be like to be scratched and bitten until you lost so much blood your heart gave out? He knew the crowd wouldn't have wasted any time killing him, but it would have been an agonizing death.

No matter the moral calculation of his pain versus those of others, nothing could make him want to go down like that. He'd die for someone else, but not like that.

Not that way.

The newsreader was still talking.

"Police have told us that they'll be making a statement in approximately a half hour from now. We're hearing now that they may have a person of interest they'd like to speak to."

Fuck.

"In other news an area man is wanted for questioning in the assault of a parking enforcement official and two other people."

Double fuck.

"Police would like to speak to Mitchell Roberts who was last seen on foot near the scene of the altercation."

Trifecta fuck. They had his name. Of course they had his name from what happened with the parking officer. They had his damn car and they had Rachel and Rick. They had everything about him at that point.

Everything except that he was also the 'person of interest' at the mall. Person of interest. It was such a silly way to say 'guilty' without saying it. Nobody had any doubt what made this person so interesting.

At this point it was reasonable to assume that there was some kind of low level manhunt and APB put out for him for what happened that morning. If it hadn't been for the mall, he bet that would have been the story of the day. Unfortunately for his pursuers, he'd created one horrific distraction. From the news, it was a distraction they were still trying to pull bodies from. Once they connected him to that, everything would escalate. He'd become a really fucking interesting person at that point. It wasn't just cops waiting for him at his apartment or work place. It'd be people looking for him at train stations and airports. When they talked to the old lady whose car he took, they'd throw the license plate and car make up on every electronic sign on the highway. Every cop would have his face on the computer screen in their cars.

"Unofficial reports from Park Square Mall are coming in that Department of Homeland Security officials are on the scene. Officials are downplaying that this was a terrorism related incident, but haven't ruled it out just yet. As we pointed out earlier, police are expected to give us an update in 30 minutes..."

Terrorism? Holy Christ. Had he just gone from fugitive of the day to Unabomber and DC Sniper status? Was he in Osama bin Laden's league now?

Mitch shut off the radio. He'd check back in later to find out what they knew. For the moment he needed to get proactive. He looked around the empty house. He couldn't stay. He also needed to figure out how exactly he was going to go into hiding. Right now he was on the run. Full-on hiding out meant being able to spend days or weeks without getting caught. That meant survival. Food, shelter and ways to protect himself.

In the house it was only a matter of time before either the police found it through Mike at the radio station or someone else came to check up on it. It was also totally empty of food. He could make it a day or two without eating, after that he knew he would get weak and make stupid decisions.

He looked at his backpack. He had his iPad, radio, comics, some notebooks, a charger and another shirt. Was there anything else in the house?

He remembered the door to the attic in the garage. He went back in and pulled the ladder down and climbed up. He found the light switch and turned it on. There were boxes of Christmas decorations, luggage and a box of old clothes. He took the box down from the attic to rummage through it.

He pulled out all the men's clothing and went back to the master bathroom. He didn't have to try on the pants to know that they were too small. There was a golf shirt and a pair of shorts that fit. He also found a blazer and a golf cap. A pair of cleated shoes were going to be useless unless he wanted to hide out on a golf course and play the back nine, thought Mitch.

Mitch put on the blue golf shirt. He decided to wear it instead of the t-shirt he had in his bag. It made him look slightly less like a person of interest in his mind. The more upper middle class he could look, the better.

He decided to shove the blazer and shorts into his bag. He couldn't remember ever seeing a manhunt from a helicopter where the bad guy ran away in a suit jacket. In a pinch, he could throw the jacket on and look slightly different. That might be the difference between getting stopped and making a clean getaway.

To make a getaway he needed to know where to 'get.' He wanted to turn on his iPad and just pull up Google

Maps and see if anything came to mind. The risk of having it give up his position was too great.

The car in the garage. Old people still used maps. Mitchell ran back to the car and opened the glove compartment. It was filled with pill bottles. He started to throw them on the floor but decided he should see what was in them. If he got an infection or some other injury, he wasn't going to be visiting a pharmacy any time soon.

Most of the bottles were for various old age conditions. He did find a bottle of painkillers. Those could be helpful. He didn't want to take them with him and add 'junky medication thief' to his growing rap sheet, but he knew survival could mean the difference between being able to keep moving despite pain and being crippled by it.

The pill bottle was mostly full. He looked back at the label. 'Beatrice Stein'. Mitchell stared at it for a moment. Beatrice, with her bright red hair and gnashing teeth was the first person he consciously did something wrong to unprovoked. It was one thing to try to stop people from chasing you. It was another to take an innocent person's car. Mitch put the bottle in his pocket. If roles were reversed and he'd pulled into that parking lot and seen her running. He'd given her his car if he knew she was seconds away from being torn apart.

Under the bottles he found three maps. One was of South Florida, the others were for the entire state and Georgia. He put the other bottles back and then put the boxes back into the attic. The less it looked like he had been there, the better.

Mitchell walked back into the living room and gathered all his stuff back into the backpack. He needed to be ready to go in an instant. He opened up the map of South Florida and laid it on the floor. He sat down over it and looked at it in the sunlight filtering through the venetian blinds. It was just a piece of paper, but looking down at it like he was god looking down at earth, gave him a sense of control. He could imagine a miniature Mitch and miniature pursuers trying to capture him. As long as he knew where he was going, he could be a step ahead of them. *It was a fucking board game.*

Rather than be some loser who tried to rob a cashier and was shocked by how fast the cops caught up with him and had to make a pathetic attempt to run, he could be a mastermind and plot this out like a heist. He looked around the floor and noticed a dime near the impression of where a couch had been. He traced the map and located where the house he was in was at and placed the dime there.

Mitchell looked around the map. How could he get that dime as far away as possible, as safely as he could?

19

Simmons and Rios bandaged up people who needed less immediate attention while paramedics worked on the more seriously injured. They moved through the crowd and helped out wherever the fire captain pointed them. Mostly they were there to reassure people. Rios watched as Simmons went from person to person and gently prodded them for information as she sprayed disinfectant on scratches and found pillows for sprains and bruises. It wasn't an official questioning, just her way of getting some facts and trying to understand what happened.

Rios sat down and leaned against a check out counter next to where Simmons was wrapping a woman's ankle. He hadn't trusted himself to ask questions in that situation outside of an official capacity. Sooner or later his supervisor would come to them and tell them what to look for. Until then he just told people they were working on it and did what he could.

Simmons finished taping the woman's ankle and leaned back against the counter next to him. The entire second floor was a mixture of the wounded laying on mattresses pulled from displays and storerooms, stretchers and emergency personnel trying to make sure the living were being taken care of.

She brushed a lock of dark hair out her eye and readjusted the band holding her ponytail. "Every situation is different. I know that. But this is just really odd." She shifted a little closer to Rios. "This many people, I get that they are still in shock, but with this many people you'd expect a lot of different stories. People should be begging to tell you something. Not here. They seem just as baffled as we do."

"What are they saying? Do they know how they got up here?"

"Some of them say they were trying to catch up with 'him'. When I ask who 'he' is, they don't know. They just say that they felt threatened and they felt attacked."

Rios looked at the turned over displays and wrecked merchandise. "Well I don't think 'he' did this by himself."

Simmons shook her head. "No. No, he didn't."

She pointed towards a middle-aged Hispanic woman leaning against a bed frame. She was wearing jeans and a blue blouse. She was looking at something in her hand that wasn't taped up. From where Rios was sitting it looked like the chain to a crucifix.

"A few people like her, mostly religious, say that they weren't chasing after a man. They say they were chasing after the devil."

"The devil?" repeated Rios.

Simmons pointed out a heavy-set girl with too much eye make-up crying next to a shelf full of towels. "She said the same thing." She pointed out an elderly man in slacks and dress shirt leaning against a mirror. "He said Satan. Crazy, I know."

Rios remembered something at the back of his mind. "My grandmother was from Chile. Before she died she told me a story. I guess because she was too afraid to tell her priest, but thought a cop was second best. I know, it's a stretch.

"She was from a real small town. They were very poor. To get to the market they had to rely on the one man who had a truck. Mr. Carlos. Anyway, she said Mr. Carlos was a mean man and used to take advantage of the fact that he was the only one in the village that had a truck.

"He'd make them pay more money than they could afford. He once refused to take an old woman to the hospital because she didn't have any money for gasoline. The town hated him, but they needed him. He was more important than the mayor who only had a horse.

"One day a young girl was coming back from visiting her cousins in the next town. She was a pretty girl and sang very beautifully in the church choir. My grandmother said they wished they could be that girl because they knew some rich man would come marry her and move her away to a big house with an automobile.

"Mr. Carlos sees the girl walking on the road. He offers her a ride but she refuses because she has no money to pay for it. He says that was okay. It would be a free ride. So she got in.

"Nothing with that man was free. He drove her a little further and then forced himself on her. He then left her on the side of the road and drove back to town. He went to the one bar in town, my grandmother says it was just two tables and a man with a bottle of whiskey, and he sits there gloating.

"When the girl got home she told her mother. Her mother ran out to the bar and confronted the man. He just sat there and laughed and waved the key to his truck.

"Soon the whole town gathered to see what was going on. When the girl came out to get her mother, they saw her ripped clothes and her tears. They knew.

"Mr. Carlos held up the key to his truck and laughed at them all. What are you going to do about it? He asked them.

"A woman threw a rock. It hit his glass of whiskey. He laughed at them all. Then without a word all of the women and then the men ran to him. They attacked him with their fists, their teeth. My grandmother said they tore the man to pieces. There was nothing left that looked like a man to bury.

"She was just a little girl, but she said she was part of it. I asked her how she could have been a part of it? This was the one woman in my family that never hit me. She said it was easy. Mr. Carlos was the devil. To her and the rest of the town they weren't killing a man who had raped a little girl. They were sending the devil back to hell. This was what god wanted.

"When I asked her if she wanted to talk to the priest for forgiveness. She told me no. She didn't need forgiveness for putting the devil back in his place in hell. She just wanted to know that like me, the policeman, she'd seen evil, she'd seen the face of the devil."

Rios looked across the room at the dead and confused injured covered in the blood of the people around them.

"Between you and me, does this look like the work of a man or the work of the devil?" he asked.

Simmons shook her head. "It looks like the work of a lot of angry, scared people Rios." She looked at their faces. "People more scared by what they saw inside themselves."

Simmons's cell phone began to vibrate. She answered it then hung up. She stood up and dusted off her slacks. "Brooks in the security office. They got someone to pull up the mall security footage. He wants us downstairs."

The security office had a wall of 20 screens showing different parts of the mall centered around one large screen. When Rios and Simmons got there the office already had a dozen people inside and dozen more outside looking in through the glass. Rios didn't recognize most of them. He looked around and saw state and federal ID badges from various departments.

A detective from the police department, Jeff Oliver, was operating the control board. On the largest screen they were looking at footage of people running down the main corridors of the mall. Although he couldn't make out individual expressions, the first thing Rios noticed was the posture of the people. This wasn't a crowd running away from something. This was a crowd chasing someone. Their hands were outstretched and their fingers curled into claws.

Detective Oliver spoke up. "The department store footage is in its own system. Someone bringing those drives here. This is the sequence for now. I can show you different camera angles for some of the shots." He pressed a button.

On the large screen they saw an overhead shot of the food court. Toward the lower right they could see the back of a man's head. He was seated at the farthest point away from the main area. From out of frame on the upper right side of the screen they saw a woman running in the direction of the man. The tables and chairs prevented her from making a straight line but they only slowed her down a little bit. Rios thought she looked angry as hell.

"Watch this," said Oliver. He pointed to a spot in front of the seated man. A chair came skidding out and towards the woman. She tripped over it. The man jumped to his feet.

"Now you can see the crowd react to what happens." All of the people in the food court turned to the man and began running towards him. The detective changed to another view. From that angle Rios could see the man running from the crowd and push an older man over as he tried to block his exit. He clicked another button.

A wide shot of the atrium showed the man running towards a group of women in the department store then changing direction. A kiosk got knocked over. The man ran out of frame.

In the next shot the man was running down the main corridor as more people started chasing him. The next camera, looking towards the atrium showed him knocking over displays and throwing things in the path of the people behind him.

"If assaulting a woman and the elderly isn't enough, check out this one." He clicked another button. The screen showed the man running towards a group of teenagers and knocking down a young girl to get through them. On the last camera angle the man ran into the department store and the entire mall following him in.

"So what caused this panic?" Oliver had a rhetorical tone to his voice. He pressed another button. "How about mob justice?"

On screen they saw video of a furious child screaming at the man and rocking its high chair back and forth.

Oliver turned to the people watching the screens. "Some asshole starts yelling at a kid. The mother comes running and he knocks her down with a chair. He takes off and the rest of the mall decides to catch him. The guy keeps knocking people down and the crowd only gets more angry." The detective leaned back in the chair with a smug look.

"There's your devil," whispered Rios.

Simmons wasn't convinced. Technically everything the detective said was true, but it just didn't feel that way. That wasn't a crowd that wanted to catch somebody. They had blood lust.

She spoke up, "Can you show us the part right before he kicked the chair at the woman?"

Oliver nodded then pressed a button. Rios looked at the screen and tried to see what Simmons was looking for. All he saw was the man kick the chair at the woman.

"Do you want another angle?" asked Oliver.

Simmons shook her head. "Forget the chair and the woman. Roll it back before she ran. Now look at the screen and tell me at what point the crowd turns on the guy?"

Rios saw it too. The crowd was already beginning to move towards the man. Throwing the chair at the woman may have tipped them over, but they were already focused on him.

"Alright," said the detective. "They saw him yelling at the kid." He pressed another button.

For the first time they got a good look at the man from the front as he sat at the end of the food court. Several tables away the child was having a fit. To Rios it didn't look like the crowd even noticed the child. They were just looking at the man.

"Can you go back to when he sat down?" asked Simmons.

Oliver clicked another button. On screen they saw the man hurry into the food court and stare into space. The mother spilled a drink and ran to get napkins. The man looked at his phone, but otherwise just sat there. The child started screaming and then the man finally looked over at him but never said anything. He looked away when the mother came running and kicked the chair towards her.

"I don't see him yelling," said Simmons.

Brooks spoke up. He was still wearing his blood stained shirt. "Whether or not he instigated this, he didn't handle it in an appropriate manner and we need to speak with him." He paused. "A lot of people were hurt today because of him. And someone has to answer for that." Brooks turned to the room. "Do we have any leads yet?"

Rios finally spoke up. "His name is Mitchell Roberts. He's our guy from the assault on the parking officer earlier today." He reached into his pocket for the photo on his phone he'd gotten off of Rachel's Facebook. He handed it to Simmons.

Simmons looked at the photo and nodded. "Well that makes things interesting."

"Looks like we have a one-man rampage here," said Oliver.

"Let's bring him in," said Brooks. "Assault on an officer and....and now this. Let's put everyone we can on getting him sooner than later."

20

It took 20 minutes from the time Detective Brooks said it was a priority they find Mitchell Roberts to when a uniformed police officer walked through the doors of WQXD where he worked. Meanwhile, other uniformed police were showing up at his apartment and back at Rachel's house.

Unmarked cars were parking further out from his apartment to see if he came by on foot.

Since it was normal business hours for the station, most of the daytime staff was still there. The station manager, Philip Dunlap, left his office in a hurry to meet the officer at the front desk. The afternoon news producer had already put an item on his desk about a person of interest with the same name as their late night host. Odd, he thought, he'd always imagined that when the police came for one of his hosts it would be Rookman.

"Mr. Dunlap?" asked the officer.

"What can I do for you?" he answered, although he already had a pretty good idea what this was about.

"We're trying to locate one of your employees. A Mitchell Franklin Roberts. Does he work here?"

Not anymore, thought Dunlap. One host fighting a cocaine rap was enough. "Yes. He's our nighttime host on the weekdays. Would you like his home address?"

The officer looked down at his notebook. "Is it 1221 Pass Ave, apartment 32?"

Dunlap turned to the receptionist, sitting at a desk next to a fake plant. "Kayla, could you check on that?"

The dark skinned young woman who was listening attentively pulled up Mitchell's contact information on her computer. "That's it."

"Do you have any other contact information for him?"

Dunlap shook his head. "I don't really know him that well. Let me see who else is here who might know. Kayla, could you page Mike?"

Kayla called for the intern on her desk phone then offered up, "I know he was apartment hunting a couple weeks ago."

The officer wrote that down. "Is he friends with anybody here at the station who he might try to go to for help?"

"Like I said, I don't really know him. To be honest, he's a bit of a loner." said Dunlap.

The officer wrote down 'loner'.

Dunlap regretted calling Mitchell a 'loner'. He'd written enough news items to know what kind of context people always put that term into.

"He did have a girlfriend," said Kayla. "Pretty girl."

The officer referred to his notes. "Yes, it looks like he beat her up pretty bad."

Kayla made a face. "Mitchell? Are you sure you got the right guy?" she asked with a high pitched tone.

The officer ignored the question.

Mike the intern walked in, saw the police officer, and almost pissed himself.

"Are you Mike?" asked the officer.

"Yes....."

"I just want to ask you a few questions about Mitchell Roberts. Do you have any idea where he might be?

Mike's normally blank face went blanker. "His house?"

The officer shook his head. "Besides there. Is there any other place he might go? A friend he trusts? Family that live in the area?"

"Not that I'm aware of. When he broke up with his girlfriend he didn't have any place to stay."

"Do you think he might try to contact you?" asked the officer.

"Gosh, I don't think so. I don't know him really well. He's a nice guy and all."

The officer pulled some business cards from his chest pocket. "Some detectives will be coming by to ask some more questions. In the mean time, if anything comes to mind, you can call us here"

He gave a card to each of them and walked towards the door.

Mike looked down at the card. "Sure thing. I hope Mitch isn't in trouble. He's a good guy and all. When his girlfriend broke up with him I tried to help him find a place to stay."

"Pardon me?" asked the officer as he turned away from the door.

21

Mitchell was in the attic when he saw the police pull up. He'd wanted to wait for nightfall before he moved on to his next hide out. The police were going to complicate things. Overhead a police helicopter was hovering to provide support in case Mitchell ran. Up in the attic, looking at the street, he didn't notice the thumping of the rotor until it grew louder.

Two blocks over, a retired broker and his wife were ushered back into their house by the SWAT team leader when they went outside to find out why the large van was parked in their driveway. The SWAT team had been on alert since the crisis at the shopping mall. Once the officer got the address from the intern at the radio station, they got a warrant to arrest Mitchell at that location.

There were five men on the SWAT team, plus their commander, who was in the van along with the driver. The plan was to send three men in through the back and have two approach the front door. They were going to do a 'no knock' search in case Mitchell was armed.

The three men assigned to the back of the house ran through the adjoining backyards and took up a position right behind the fence that separated the yards between the two houses.

One man popped his head up and looked into the backyard and sliding glass windows.

"Back yard clear. Back interior clear," he whispered into his radio.

From the van the commander gave the command, "Go."

One man went left while the other went to the right. Their plan was to scale the fence at the far ends and then approach the house at a diagonal angle. That would put them in the blind spot if Mitchell looked out the window.

Despite their gear and body armor, they both swiftly climbed over the fence and were at the opposite sides of the house in seconds. The third man climbed over the same spot on the fence as the man on the right had. He joined them at the corner of the building.

He whispered into his microphone, "Back of the house."

The commander tapped the driver on the shoulder. Fast but not recklessly so, he drove around the block and brought the van to a stop in front of the house.

Two men in the back jumped out and ran to the front door. One of them had a 'knocker', a heavy metal cylinder used for knocking doors open at the knob. He held it back at the ready. The other man gave the commander a hand signal.

The commander spoke into his microphone. "Red team go."

The man with the knocker slammed it against the door handle. The door flew open inwards sending a shower of splinters from where the lock had been. Both men pulled their bodies away from the door frame.

"Mitchell Roberts, we have a warrant for your arrest," shouted the man to the left of the door.

There was silence in the house. Red team leader gave a signal to the commander. He spoke into his microphone, "Red team proceed."

The two men entered the living room. As one man stepped in the other would follow. Each one kept his gun trained on a different part of the room.

"Living room clear," said red team leader. "Proceeding to hallway."

The two men stepped into the hallway keeping their backs firmly against the wall. From that position they could see the back sliding glass doors and backyard. Out of sight, but waiting, were the other three SWAT team members.

"Unlocking the back door," said red team leader. He darted over to the sliding glass door and unlocked it with a shim, faster than the original owners ever did with the key. He pushed the door open then pressed his back flat against the wall to the side of it.

"Blue team go," said the commander.

The three men in the backyard entered the house through the open glass door. The joint five man team proceeded to check all the rooms and closets in under twenty seconds.

"First level clear," said the red team leader. "Checking the garage."

The blue team from the backyard kicked open the door that lead from the kitchen. They entered with their guns pointed at all the corners.

"Garage clear."

"How's it look inside there?" asked the commander.
"Like nobody lives here. There's no sign of anyone having been there. What now?"
"Proceed to attic," said the commander.
The red team leader pointed to the attic door. He pointed to another man and gave him a hand signal telling him to look for another entrance to the attic. The other man nodded and went back into the house with another member of the SWAT team following. They checked all the bedrooms and found another entrance in a hall closet.
"Hall closet," he said into the microphone.
"Hold steady," said the red team leader. He reached into his pack and pulled out a periscope that extended almost two feet. Since there was no way to open an attic door quietly, all three men stepped clear of the opening. The man closest to the rope handle pulled it down. It made the inevitable creek.
"Mitchell Roberts! Surrender now."
Mitch stayed calm as he heard the team leader shout out his name.
From below, the SWAT team could see the attic was completely dark. One of the men pulled several light sticks from his pocket and threw them into the attic. The team leader lifted the periscope into the attic and looked through it.
The attic was filled with lots of dark corners but nothing was moving. Off to one side he could see several boxes and what may or may not have been a man laying down. He whispered into his microphone, "Blue team go."

Using a ladder from the hall closet, which saved one of them a trip to the van, the first man in the hall closet pushed open the hatch covering the entrance and threw in three more light sticks. He then ducked back down. The red team leader handed the periscope off to another man. He called out into the attic, "Mitchell Roberts, surrender now or we'll gas you out."

Although that was an option, at this point it was meant as a means to intimidate him. If he was a known felon assumed to be armed they'd go straight to tear gas and not risk it. In this situation the commander had the discretion to take him peaceably first. The last thing he wanted to do was to send one of his men into a dark space with a bad guy with a gun.

The team leader spoke into his microphone. "No response."

"Proceed with tear gas," replied the commander.

The three men in the garage put their gas masks on. The team leader pulled a canister from a pouch and threw it into the attic. He heard it pop and hiss as the smoke started coming out filling the attic. The three men stood back for the entrance to avoid getting attacked by any animals that tried to escape the smoke.

The team leader was going to give it another minute then climb into the attic himself with his night vision and compact assault rifle.

After counting out a minute, the red team leader climbed into the attic holding his rifle in front of him as a shield. His night vision goggles revealed the attic interior in bright green light. The shape that may or may not have been a man was just a pile of clothes. To confirm it he pushed the barrel of his rifle between the boxes and pushed them apart.

It was an old pair of slacks and some golf cleats that had spilled out of a box. He gave the attic another look then hopped back down to the garage.

"All clear," he said into his radio.

While he was relieved that his men were safe, it was frustrating not to get the guy. He hopped out of the van to take a look himself. He walked over to the front of the house and looked at the broken door. He called over to one of the men, "Do we have a temp we can fix that with?"

With cooperative home owners they tried to fix things as best they could. In the van they had kits to fix doors they had to break open. He looked through the back glass doors and was glad they didn't have to break those. That was always a mess and a pain to have to fix.

22

When Mitchell saw the SWAT van he knew his only choice was to wait it out. Besides the hovering helicopter, he would guess that there were several police cars at the entrance and exit to the development blocking anybody from entering or leaving. The entire neighborhood was on lock down. Running or surrendering was suicide for him. He had to just lay still.

He had an uneasy feeling about the house once he decided it was going to be his hideout. The problem was that it was the best choice he could think of but not the best possible choice. The difference being his total lack of experience in being a fugitive from justice.

After he had put away the map and came up with a tentative next step, he decided the best place to wait was the attic. It was hot, but tolerable. He could also look out through a vent and see the street outside.

The SWAT van seemed inevitable to him once he realized how eager the intern was going to be to make the police happy. From there it was only a matter of time before they followed up on the lead and showed up on the doorstep of the house. Fortunately for Mitchell, his heightened paranoia paid off.

While Mitchell was waiting for night to come in the living room, he kept obsessively checking the street in front. That's when he noticed the house across the street.

It looked a lot like the house he was in, as did most of the other houses in the neighborhood, but it also had several newspapers piled up on the porch. Someone lived there, but they had been gone for the last few days. To Mitchell, it seemed like a safe bet they were going to be gone for a while longer. At least the next few hours.

It was impulsive, but he figured his odds were better waiting there than in Mike's grandparent's house. Plus, he could find things like food in there as well. Mitchell decided it was a good idea to move across the street.

He'd gone over there and did a quick check for a hidden key underneath a rock or along a ledge. When he couldn't find one he went around the back of the house and looked for a way to get into it from there. That's where he noticed the sliding glass doors like his parents used to have. Whenever they would get locked out, his father would just grab one end of the door and give it a tilt. The door would slide open from there.

Before trying the trick on the door he did a quick search for an alarm system and found none. Few of the homes had them in that area since they were mostly summer homes with little in them or houses put up for sale.

After he got the door open he checked to make sure the garage was empty, it was, and moved the car and removed all traces of himself from the first house. He then locked up that house and abandoned it for good.

The new house was sparsely furnished, but he found some plastic cups of apple sauce that he wolfed down. In the bedroom closet he saw several blouses and skirts. It looked liked an older woman lived there by herself.

Remembering that old people tended to use things like calendars, he went back and looked at the kitchen refrigerator. Sure enough, there was one. There was a long line going from four days before to the day after tomorrow. Mitchell's best guest was this was how long the woman would be gone. Although he didn't plan on staying more than a few hours, it was comforting to know he wouldn't be found out right away.

Having accepted the fact that this was his second breaking and entering, he did a search for anything useful that he could take with him.

In a drawer by her bed he found an old iPod Touch that was completely drained. While not as powerful as his iPhone, he was confident he could take it and it would never be missed. That way he could surf the web or make a phone call using Skype if he found WiFi somewhere.

The mere possibility of being able to connect with the world electronically made him feel immensely better. The first thing he did when he climbed into the attic was look for a place to plug it in and charge it. It was only a few minutes after that when the SWAT van pulled up.

Up there in the attic, he couldn't see much of what was going on because the SWAT van was blocking the front door. As he watched the masked men jump out of the van and enter the house, he got a perverse thrill. He knew they could only be seconds away from finding him, but watching them go into the wrong house gave him the feeling on the back of the neck after you realize the car heading for you didn't hit you or when you really were about to see her breasts. Mitchell was confused by the feeling to be sure, but it made him feel better knowing that deep down he could be motivated by something other than pure fear.

His gut impulse to get out of the house had proven right and confirmed for him that he needed to move quickly when his instincts told him to. He knew that now was not the time to run, but as soon as the pressure slackened enough for him to leave, he'd have to get on it.

The SWAT team commander walked around the living room and looked at the floor. There were impressions on the carpet where it looked like the furniture had just evaporated. He looked for any foot prints, but the carpet fiber was too resilient to hold them for very long. There was a dime in the middle of the floor. He bent down and picked it up. He tossed it into the air and caught it.

He checked all the bedrooms and the kitchen for any sign that somebody had been there. There was nothing. He walked into the master bathroom and looked around the sink and into the toilet.

He called one of the men over. "Gentry."

Gentry, the red team leader, walked into the bathroom. He still had his helmet and gear on. "Yes sir?"

The commander pointed at the toilet. It was an easy thing to overlook.

"Huh," Gentry finally noticed it too. In a house that was unoccupied the water in the toilet bowl would evaporate over time. This bowl looked like it might have been flushed in the past few days. The water level was still high.

"What do you think? Was he here?" asked Gentry.

"I dunno. We'll tell the detectives it was possible someone was here in the last few days. They can decide what to do with that. Either way, he's not here now."

The commander walked back outside the house and looked at the neighborhood. There were a lot of empty houses. There were dozens of places for Mitchell to hide. Getting search warrants on all of them would be impractical. The best they could do would be to keep at least one marked car in the area to look for anything suspicious. Maybe Mitchell would come back or do something stupid.

From his hiding place Mitchell got his first clear view of the SWAT team commander as he walked out the front. Over six foot tall, with a bald head, he looked like a former college linebacker. Pure testosterone.

The commander looked at the house across the street and walked over to it. Mitchell tried not to piss himself when he looked right in his direction. He slowly leaned back from the vent and remained still.

He heard the doorbell ring. Mitchell slowed his breathing. There was a knock. Mitchell almost passed out from not breathing at all. He allowed himself a slow breath. He became suddenly aware of every itch and sore muscle. The door bell rang again. Mitch tried to ignore the feeling as sweat tickled the back of his neck. He focused on just breathing slowly. He tried to ignore everything else.

The commander pulled his business card from his pocket and scribbled a note for the occupant to call him or one of the detectives. They needed to let them know that there was a possibility Mitchell might be in the area and could be coming back. A tip from a neighbor could be all that it took to get the guy. He turned back to the van and went to see what they needed to finish up.

Mitchell watched the commander walk back into the street and then stop.

Halfway to the van the commander felt something strange. It was a flash of anger that just lasted a millisecond. He looked down and his fingers were curled up in claws.

What the hell was that? He wondered to himself. He guessed he was more pissed about not getting the guy then he realized.

As soon as he saw the man turn, Mitchell pulled away from the vent and swore at himself silently. Just because people couldn't see him, he realized, didn't mean they couldn't smell him or be effected by whatever was going on. For a moment the commander looked like he was going to hulk out in the middle of the street.

Mitchell wondered what would happen if the man had full-out freaked out. While Mitchell was nowhere to be seen he feared that when that animal side of people took over, deeper senses were used. If dormant instincts involving scent and sound took hold, nothing would help him.

The commander's hands relaxed and he felt his head clear.

23

Steve Baylor, PhD, looked out the 8th floor window of his office located in an industrial park on the outer edge for the Center for Disease Control in Atlanta, Georgia. His employer, Athena Biomedical was ostensibly one of scores of satellite businesses that provided services to the agency that was the United States front line against infectious disease. The truth was a little bit murkier. The company was a de facto government agency unto itself. Created under a presidential order that had been renewed under the last three administrations, the purpose of its charter, the actual one kept inside a locked safe no one saw, was to take proactive measures against the creation and distribution of biological agents that may pose a threat to the citizens of the United States. Those proactive steps included everything from developing rapid vaccines outside the normal channels of government approval, to recommending targets for predator drone strikes. As Baylor liked to describe it, it was the medical equivalent of a SEAL team.

He was in the middle of typing his comments concerning a research paper on which he'd been asked to be an anonymous referee. Baylor had convinced himself the reason he was asking the journal to reject the paper wasn't because he was co-author of a forthcoming paper dealing with a similar subject, but because the evidence was lacking. Petty, perhaps, but when he controlled the largest off-the-books budget for biomedical research, he was entitled to some of the privileges that came with that. Besides, he told himself, if he spent less time dealing with the political side of science, he'd have more time to do actual research.

When he clicked 'send' one email in his flooded inbox caught his eye. It was from a mailing list with only a few dozen recipients. All of them involved in different agencies that dealt with biological and chemical warfare threats. The purpose of the list was to bring potential "patient zero" incidents to their attention. If a Pakistani man checked into the hospital after arriving at JFK with strange spots on his body that looked infectious or an elementary school in Chechnya came down with an extremely virulent form of the flu, these cases would be forwarded to the list if they had a friendly health worker on the scene. The CDC had official channels for those kind of reports. This list was a back channel one.

It was the headline that grabbed his attention first. "Rigor mortis symptoms similar to Factor 9."

Baylor opened up the email. An attachment contained several cell phone images of people who were killed earlier that day in a riot at shopping mall in South Florida. There were close ups of their hands and faces.

The peeled back lips baring teeth like fangs and the hands curled into claws, sent a chill down his spine. He'd seen lots of horrific imagery, on an almost daily basis; bodies didn't concern him. He'd lost any fear of that after his first dissection. What worried him here was the familiarity of it all. He'd seen those expressions and the twisted cruel fingers before.

He read the rest of the email. It was sent by a doctor who was a first responder for the Department of Homeland Security. The responder thought the circumstances of the riot were unusual and the physical condition of the deceased worth passing on to the list. He didn't know what Factor 9 was other than a few slides he'd been shown at a seminar on different things to look for in the field.

Factor 9 was a code word for the symptoms of a condition caused by what was known to only a few people as the Mongolian Flu.

But it couldn't be that, thought Baylor. They made sure of that. He'd pushed for extraordinary measures to be taken to prevent an outbreak of Mongolian Flu. He looked at the images again. They were identical to Mongolian Flu.

Baylor had read the report of the mall riot as it went national. Nothing about it sounded like what an outbreak of Mongolian Flu would cause. He'd just dismissed it as panic and ignored it. He opened up his web browser to read the latest reports and made a note to ask his assistant for the field reports as soon as possible.

Ten minutes later he'd read enough to know this wasn't Mongolian Flu, or at least not exactly the same thing. For starters, the crowd in the mall didn't attack the first responders. The deaths appeared to have been caused by people getting trampled and not intentionally. He couldn't find any examples of direct violence between the crowd. It was just a violent outcome.

Baylor felt relieved. He leaned back in his chair and looked out the window again. Mongolian Flu was one of the many nightmare scenarios he had to deal with on a daily basis. It was horrific in that it affected a lower part of people's brains and switched on the 'fight' reflex. It was dangerous because all evidence indicates it was man made.

The first case was brought to their attention by a Red Cross worker in Mongolia. His team was immunizing children in a yurt village when they told him about a 'wild man' that chased them back to the village. When the worker went with two other men to look for him they found his body with a bullet to the head. An old woman said she'd seen a military helicopter in the area. When he asked the local military commander he said he didn't know anything about it, but oddly came back later that night to seize the body. Fortunately, the aid worker had taken blood samples before soldiers in masks took the body away.

The blood samples sat in a refrigerator in the CDC until a Chinese defector passed along some documents including a video of a gruesome experiment apparently performed in a Chinese controlled prison in Mongolia.

Baylor had used the video to get funding and push through programs that otherwise saner minds would have said 'no' to. Shot with a handheld camera, it showed forty Asian men in prison uniforms led into the center of a prison yard wearing blindfolds. Six men in green hospital gowns injected the kneeling men with a handful of syringes and then quickly left the yard. At first nothing happened. The men sat there obediently awaiting further instruction. Then a handful began to make growling sounds and pull away their blindfolds like animals. The camera zoomed into bloodshot eyes and the claw-like way they held their hands. Within moments it was pandemonium as men leaped to their feet and attacked one another with teeth and claws. They opened up huge gashes in throats and clawed at each other's eyes. Two men would attack another and then attack another when he was down. The camera tried to capture as much of the blood frenzy as was possible, but it was all over in under four minutes. The dead laid there with their fingers held out like claws and their lips pulled back in an angry expression. Calm dispassionate voices spoke in Chinese making clinical observations.

When the blood samples from the 'Wild Man' were examined they discovered a new pathogen. Rapid genetic sequencing revealed a simple virus that pulled an interesting trick. When the body's autoimmune system went to fight it, instead of just reprogramming it to make more copies of itself, like retroviruses did, it had a payload of genetic information that tricked an older immune system, one we shared with reptiles and sea animals. This system is what researchers believed evolved into the 'fight' part of the 'fight or flight' reflex.

Instead of just causing the body to fight off the infection and inadvertently make copies of it, this virus actually caused a physical fight response. A fight response so powerful and primitive, it overpowered all the higher brain functions.

In the Mongolian prison the men didn't discriminate, they tried to kill their best friends. They went after anything that moved and didn't stop. The mall panic subsided without anywhere near the high mortality rate of the prison. The fact that it subsided at all was more evidence this wasn't the Mongolian Flu. From later experiments with the pathogen, off the books experiments, Baylor oversaw, they discovered victims wouldn't stop trying to kill other people. They kept going until physical fatigue stopped them or they underwent cardiac arrest.

The version of Mongolian Flu they obtained from the 'Wild Man' was transmissible through an open wound but not airborne. Baylor had to explain to his oversight panel that could be changed with just a few keystrokes on a genetic sequencer. If someone had malevolent intent for the virus, they could infect a lot of people very quickly.

Baylor tapped his fingers on his desk. Although this wasn't the Mongolian Flu they were familiar with, there was nothing saying that the people who made the first version hadn't come up with a variation. If they'd found out about the preventive measures Baylor and his team had taken, they may have tried to engineer a work-around.

China was the obvious guess for the creator, but there was credible evidence to suggest the virus was something they had accidentally discovered and the prison experiment was just their own cruel way of finding out what it did. The problem of trying to have indirect communication with the Chinese was that each branch of the military kept secrets from the others. It could have been a project by a group like his own.

Cold War political machinations aside, Baylor had second thoughts and decided the photos were enough reason to take precautions. He picked up a secure line and dialed the research center.

30 miles away in a 60,000 square foot building that said 'NitroFertilizer Inc.' on the front, a phone rang. A 52-year-old molecular biologist with curly grey hair and a well manicured beard answered the phone.

"Ari, you followed the mall thing down in Florida?" asked Baylor.

Ari Steinmetz replied, "Not really. What's up?"

"I'm going to have some blood samples sent to us. I need you to stay late to look at them. I'll have a courier waiting at the CDC for when they get their batch."

Steinmetz looked over at two of his lab assistants who were leaning over a piece of hardware while referring to a manual. "Hey guys, we've got to stay late."

They nodded then went back to trying to figure out how to get the new automated sequencer to work.

"Anything I should be on the look out for? I can get some lab tests ready to go," asked Steinmetz.

Baylor paused for a moment. "It's just a precautionary thing. Nothing we need to worry about. And it'll be a good exercise for your team." He tried to make his voice sound as matter of fact as possible. "I just want to follow up on something relating to Mongolian Flu."

"The virus or the vaccine."

"The virus," replied Baylor.

"No problem," inwardly Steinmetz swore.

"Thanks Ari." Baylor hung up then dialed another number. "What's the current prep time for one of our go teams?" he asked.

"Three hours," said the voice on the other end.

"Okay. What if we need site containment in South Florida? Say five hundred people?"

"Six hours."

"Thank you. Just updating my files." Baylor hung up then called over to the executive airport they used outside of Atlanta and told them to keep a plane ready.

24

Mitchell watched the front of the other house for another two hours after the SWAT team left. Periodically a patrol car would pass through the neighborhood. Mitchell suspected this wasn't their usual beat. Although he wasn't experienced at how the police tracked down fugitives, he would bet that there was probably another car, maybe an unmarked one, parked near the entrances or worse yet, hiding in plain sight in a driveway; masquerading as one of the neighbor's cars.

For a moment he thought he was being too paranoid, then realized that was the whole point. He had to be extra paranoid. Getting out of the house was going to be tricky. He needed to make it from there to his next location while avoiding whatever surveillance there was. At least they would be looking for someone heading to the house and not away from it. Maybe there was something to that.

The attic was starting to feel more claustrophobic. He was tempted to go down into the house, but didn't want to take the chance of being seen through a window or have the owner come home early. He needed to sit tight for another few hours.

Mitchell pulled the pocket radio from his bag and put in an earbud. He used one ear to listen to the street and the other to find out what was being said on the news. He hoped in vain that he'd hear newscasters explaining that the manhunt was all a mistake and that he was in the clear.

He found an all-news AM station, catching the middle of a broadcast.

"...while the search continues for South Florida radio personality Mitchell Roberts after an apparent one man rampage that lead to a riot at Park Square Mall where at least 18 people are believed to be dead, authorities have downplayed rumors the riot was caused by some kind of unknown chemical or biological agent. A Department of Homeland Security spokesperson said that their personnel on site are there merely as a precaution.

"Meanwhile, news outlets have continued to press for access to security camera footage, hoping it could shed some light on how the actions of one man could lead to such a tragic event."

While the news overall was depressing, hearing the phrase 'chemical or biological' made Mitchell feel like there was a chance of finding out some kind of explanation that didn't involve him being a sociopathic mass murderer.

The newscast came back from the commercial break, "...earlier today we spoke with University of Miami psychology professor Jeff Keating in a phone interview."

Keating spoke with a precise tone. "What we may have here, may be a case of mass hysteria. We see this all the time in news footage from the Middle East and places like India and Pakistan where crowds of people are so angry by what they see, that in the comfort of the crowd, they feel empowered to take actions that otherwise morally they'd never do.

"Ultimately, they're not responsible for their actions. The man who caused the riot, by threatening a mother and her child, is the one who has to pay the price for these actions and be brought to justice."

"Go fuck yourself," Mitchell replied to the radio.

Sick of hearing people who weren't there, describing something they did know anything about, Mitchell turned off the radio. He decided to try to catch a nap in the attic before he departed.

To keep on the safe side, he set the alarm on the stolen iPod for two hours. He used his backpack as a pillow and placed the iPod inside of it. Wedged between old boxes and itchy insulation, he somehow managed to fall asleep.

Two hours later he almost cracked his head on the ceiling when he woke up startled and confused. It took him a minute to find the iPod and shut off the alarm. He was terrified a passing patrol car was going to hear it and know where he was hiding.

After he turned off the iPod he took a look out through the vent. It was dark out. There were a few more cars in driveways, but the neighborhood still looked deserted.

Mitchell decided he should wait to see it there was a pattern to when the police car drove through the neighborhood. Knowing that could help him plan his escape out of there.

In the meantime he needed to occupy himself. After a lot of internal debate he decided to turn to WQXD to see what they were saying. He was also strangely obsessed with the thought that they were going to give Mike the intern his late night spot. It was a stupid thing to think about, but the idea that Mike would rat him out for the opportunity nagged him. Everybody for himself.

Mitchell heard the opening music to Rookman's show. It was some Neil Diamond meets the Doors send-up that Rookman had recorded in his garage with a few of his buddies. Imagining Rookman playing guitar next to an ex-cop playing a drum set in front of a half-put-together Camaro and beer bottles strewn about the place, made Mitchell feel like things were back to normal.

Rookman's gravelly voice came in over the music, "Man on a rampage! Watch out! Our own Mad Mitch a wanted fugitive folks! It doesn't get any more exciting than that. Tonight I'm going to give you the inside scoop into this criminal mastermind. This dark loner who sat just a few feet from where I am now earlier this morning.

"I've got a special last minute guest on the line whose going to tell us how the authorities are going to catch this dangerous menace before he murders us all!"

Mitchell shook his head, *what the hell?*

"Please welcome former police captain Dick Miller. Dick just wrote a book about the search for the DC Snipers and is an expert on how manhunts work. I brought him on the show so he could explain how the authorities are going to catch our Mad Mitch and bring him to justice. Dick, how are you?"

Mitchell's stomach turned. Despite all his fight the power talk and what he thought was mutual respect if not friendship, Rookman was ready to pounce on him like everybody else. Mitchell wanted to turn off the radio, but his sense of self loathing wouldn't let him.

"Great Rookman, thanks for having me on here," Miller.

"Thank you for agreeing on such short notice. Just for background for our syndicated listeners and those of you living under rocks and in your bunkers, an arrest warrant was issued today for Mad Mitch, aka Mitchell Roberts, the kid who plays that emo music here after I go home to get drunk. Run for your lives folks!

"So Dick, first I have to ask you, is it clear to you why there's this manhunt for Mitch? I've looked at the bulletin they've sent out and I can't find any mention of a gun, a rifle, a knife or even an angry t-shirt."

"Well...", Miller hesitated. "I think that since he's the one person who seems to be at the center of the tragic events at the Park Square Mall, I can understand why police want to talk to him. That plus the events earlier in the day when he assaulted, allegedly, his girlfriend, the boyfriend and threw the parking enforcer into a windshield."

"Have you ever seen Mitch?" asked Rookman.

"I saw the photo. But no, I've never met him."

"I guess you never really know a guy until he beats up on two people at once and then picks up an overweight parking cop and throws her five feet into the windshield of his car. I'd never have believed it myself if the cops hadn't told us that's what happened."

"So Dick, you're an expert on the what happens when police decide who public enemy number one is and have to go after them. What's going on right now?"

"I'm not part of the search so I really couldn't tell you," replied Miller.

"Just give me your best guess. I know a lot of my listeners would feel safer knowing what steps are being taken."

"Well, the first 24 hours is critical. Although there's a coordination between the different city and county police departments, the further away he gets from here, the harder he's going to be to catch."

"Why is that?" asked Rookman.

"As much as they try to cooperate with one another, you're not going to be as concerned about something that didn't happen in your own jurisdiction. Dade County and Palm Beach County, which surround Broward County, have their own problems and have to figure out how much of their own resources to expend in trying to apprehend Mitchell Roberts. So the further he gets away from here, the harder he'll be to catch."

"I see," said Rookman. "So he needs to get as far away from here in 24 hours if he wants to avoid getting caught."

Mitchell's ears perked up. He couldn't help but notice the way Rookman said that. It wasn't even a rhetorical question.

"Now, what are some of the ways fugitives can travel that allow them to avoid getting caught?" asked Rookman.

"The first method is a car that hasn't been reported stolen. Or a stolen car where they've switched out the license plates for a car that the owner might not realize they've gone missing."

"Like a long term airport parking lot?" asked Rookman.

"Yes, that's one place."

"What if they don't have access to a car or don't know how to steal one?"

"That makes it harder. In populated areas it's difficult to travel by foot and not go noticed. Public transportation is heavily monitored as well," answered Miller.

"So if he sticks to side roads and places like railroad tracks and travels by night it would be harder to catch him?"

"It would make things more complicated."

"I've heard that one of the things that some fugitives have used is police scanners to listen for police presence," asked Rookman.

"It's not a common thing, but a lot of departments use open frequencies. Especially when they're doing coordinated activities with other agencies."

"Let's just hope that Mitch doesn't get one of those. Mitch might be able to stay hidden for days..."

"I agree," said Miller.

"As a public service announcement to any truckers out there listening to this show who might think about leaving your police scanner on your seat when you went into a diner to get something to eat, think twice. Our Mad Mitch might just put a brick through your window and steal it."

25

Rookman spent the rest of the night using his guest to covertly offer Mitchell helpful advice. Mitch paid close attention. When it was time to leave he put the radio away and gathered all of his belongings together. In total darkness, he carefully climbed down the attic ladder and raised it back into place. Being extra cautious, he fished the apple sauce containers from the trash can and placed them into his bag to throw away someplace else. He threw them back out when he realized the mysterious car in the garage was probably going to be a bigger tip-off that somebody was there than a few empty containers of Mott's.

He'd heard the police car roll by three more times, roughly an hour apart. The last time was ten minutes before. He knew he couldn't count on that being a reliable estimate, but it gave him an idea when he should avoid the street entirely.

After doing a last pass through the house, Mitchell carefully slid open the sliding glass door enough for him to pass through. He then pushed it back into place and gave it a tilt to lock it into position.

He looked up at the moon. It was half full. He couldn't decide if he'd prefer no moon so he wouldn't be seen, or a full moon so he could see where he was going.

There was a tall wooden fence between the house he was at and the house in back of him. He looked over the fence and could see into the darkened living room. There was a light coming in from the hallway. It looked like somebody was living there.

Mitchell climbed over the fence at the far left corner away from the part of the house with activity in it. He kept his body down low and moved along the left fence to the front portion of the backyard. He popped his head over the fence and looked.

The street was empty except a few cars parked in driveways. His plan was to cross the street and move to the next back yard. Mitchell was getting ready to climb over when something touched his leg. He froze in panic. Something touched it again.

Mitchell looked down and saw something shaggy beneath him. He hoped it was a friendly dog and not a confused raccoon. He knelt down and gave the furry thing a pet. He heard happy panting.

"What's going on boy?" he whispered not knowing if it was a boy or a girl. He was just happy to know that not all members of the animal kingdom were out to get him.

Mitchell squatted down to give the dog a scratch around the ears. He felt a tongue lick his face. He gave the dog a few more scratches figuring it was a good idea to win over the locals best he could.

The dog gave him another lick then marched off into the backyard to go about important dog business. Mitchell looked back over the fence for a spot to drop his bag. An alarm went off inside his head.

Three doors down across the street there was a car with a spotlight attached above the driver's side door. The car was facing the street. *Unmarked cop car.* Inside he could see the glow of what looked like a computer. Definitely a surveillance car. Mitchell felt like he owed the dog a French kiss.

If there was one unmarked surveillance car, there could be others. His idea of just walking out of the neighborhood looked less plausible. They were waiting for him to show up, effectively trapping him there.

He looked back towards the house he just came from. He knew he couldn't stay. He couldn't take the chance that they would start going door-to-door tomorrow and peak into people's garages. It had to be tonight.

For a moment he allowed himself the fantasy of busting through the garage door in the tiny compact and tearing off down the street blowing by the cops. Then he went back to reality. He could try to steal a car from a house he was near. That was if he magically figured out how to hot-wire a car in the next five minutes.

He could try to break into a house and steal keys to a car, but with a cop literally around the corner, one 911 call from a frightened homeowner would have him caught before he turned the ignition. He needed a better strategy.

That strategy came back over and licked his ankle. Good idea, stupid idea, it was the only idea. Mitchell went back into the yard and looked for a piece of rope. He almost walked right into a clothesline while looking at the ground.

Keeping an eye on the living room, he took down the clothesline and rolled most of it up. His furry friend came over to help. Mitchell tied one end to the dog's collar. The mere thought of a walk sent the animal into ecstasy. It began prancing around his feet. Mitchell had to give him a soft shush to not wake its owner.

Mitchell went around the other side of the house and found a latch to the gate. He carefully opened it and left it slightly ajar. He passed what he was sure was the bedroom window. Through curtains he could see a flickering television and hear snoring.

Before he stepped in front of the house and in plain view of the cop, Mitchell made one last adjustment. He pulled the blazer from his back backpack and put it on with the backpack under his arm. He put the golf cap on too. From a distance he hoped he just looked like another retiree out walking the dog.

He leaned over and gave his accomplice a pat on the head. His hope was to step out to the sidewalk and go in the opposite direction of the police car without notice. Worst case scenario; the cop would see an old guy out walking his dog at night.

Mitchell took another step and heard a click. He was surrounded by light. He almost dropped the leash and bolted down the street. Then he realized that it was just a floodlight on the corner of the house with a motion sensor.

He resisted the urge to look over at the cop car. He was already a few feet in front of the house. There was no way he wasn't in plain sight. Mitchell leaned down and gave Mr. Barks a pat on the head.

Mr. Barks? He had no idea where that name came from.

Acting as if this was his normal routine, Mitchell and Mr. Barks walked out to the sidewalk and headed away from the cop car. He tried not to walk too fast. Mr. Barks made that easy by stopping to smell everything.

When the dog stopped to take a leak, Mitchell panicked that the dog might go number two and the cop would get out of the car to give them a citation. It was a million silly things that filled his mind. He pushed the thought out and just tried to focus on making it to the development's exit.

They reached the end of the street with no sound of doors opening or tires squealing. That was encouraging. He had two more streets to go before he came to the entrance. Mitchell was convinced there would be at least one more car near there waiting to see if he drove in.

Mitchell reached the end of the last street and sure enough, there was another unmarked car waiting inside the entrance parked on the grass behind a hedge. It was the only thing separating him and Mr. Barks from freedom. There was another entrance he could try, but he was certain that one had a car waiting there too. It had to be this one.

Mitchell took a step forward. Mr. Barks began to pull at the rope. He thought the walk was over. He was ready to go home.

"Not yet buddy." He kept walking and the dog followed after.

The sidewalk wrapped around the the entrance and onto another sidewalk that ran along the main road in front of the complex. He remembered a convenience store and a strip mall located off to one side, near where he was going.

If he played it casually enough, the cop in the car would just assume he was taking a walk down to the store with the dog. He assumed they were looking for someone driving a stolen car or walking in on foot. But that was only an assumption. One that could get him killed.

Mitchell kept walking on the sidewalk with Mr. Barks trotting alongside him. It would take him on a path directly across from where the cop car was parked. He could already see the glow from the computer screen inside. He imagined his face was on it in full color.

Trying to stay casual, he gave the car a quick glance while keeping the hat low, and rounded the corner opposite where it was parked.

His ears tried to pick out every single detail. There was nothing to indicate the car was moving. Mitchell kept walking and he and Mr. Barks rounded the entrance and came to the sidewalk along the main street. Car headlights came around a corner and moved in his direction.

Mitchell shielded his eyes from the light while Mr. Barks did his part to blend in by taking another leak. A real method actor, thought Mitchell.

As the car passed, Mitchell could see that it was a police squad car. It kept going behind him and pulled into the complex.

Mitchell tried to keep the same pace and not avoid breaking out into a run. He walked several more blocks on the sidewalk. Mr. Barks stopped more frequently and looked back.

Mitchell had to figure out what to do with the dog. He couldn't let him go just yet. If the dog ran back into the development, there was the chance one of the cops would notice and wonder what happened to the owner.

Mr. Barks let out a soft whimper as he looked back towards the development.

"Sorry buddy. You volunteered to be my hostage."

26

Somewhat reluctantly, the dog followed Mitchell as he continued traveling away from the housing complex. Until Rookman had mentioned the police scanner, the plan was to make his way over to a marina two miles away and try to steal a small boat. While Mitchell knew nothing about hot-wiring cars, he knew something about boats. He'd spent a summer working in a marina that belonged to his mom's boyfriend at the time. In South Florida there were five ways to go north and south. There were three major highways, I-95, US-1 and the Turnpike. The other ways were via rail or the Intracoastal, a waterway that lead from Miami all the way up to Georgia.

Besides giving him a way to travel that didn't involve major roads, being out in the open water would give Mitchell a safe distance from people getting too close.

He remembered an all-night diner was right off the main highway that ran near the marina. Mitchell decided that Rookman's hint about the police scanner was worth paying attention to. He walked another half mile with Mr. Barks.

He came to the other side of the street across from the diner. In the distance he could hear the low rumble of trucks on the highway and smell the exhaust fumes.

Several tractor-trailer trucks were pulled up at the diesel pumps or parked in the large lot in the back. He looked down at Mr. Barks. The dog stared back up at him. The animal had enjoyed the adventure at first but was now scared by the unfamiliarity of everything. Mitchell tied the dog to a pay phone near a darkened strip mall and walked back towards the diner. He could hear whimpering behind him.

He's just a dog, Mitchell told himself and kept walking. The dog let out a sad whine.

Mitchell stopped. *For fuck sake*. He turned back to the dog, not believing himself. After everything that happened that day. The horrific human tragedy he partially caused, the god damn dog was now making him feel bad?

He sat down by the dog and looked at its collar. He found an old tag and a new tag with the same phone number. He pulled one off and put it in his pocket.

"Listen buddy, when I get away from here I'm going to call your parents so they can come get you. I just can't do that right now." He looked at the rope. "If I let you go I don't want you to get hurt and well, I can't let you go running back home and have the cops see you."

Mitchell looked at the pay phone he'd tied Mr. Barks to. Should he make one more effort to call 911? He picked up the receiver and started to dial. He hesitated over the last number. What would happen if he called? They'd send a cop car out to get him for sure. None of the cops he saw so far had been wearing any kind of protective gear. That meant that even they didn't know what was going on. Calling for help was an invitation for suicide.

"Damn," said Mitchell as he hung up the phone. They'd think he was crazy. They got dozens of calls a day from paranoid lunatics. There was no reason for Mitchell to think they'd treat him any differently.

He dialed a different number and made a collect call. A gravelly voiced answered. Mitchell hesitated to think about what to say. He knew Rookman was a security nut.

"Um, is this poison control? Cause I think I ate too many dicks." said Mitchell.

"Asshole." said the voice then he hung up.

There went that plan, thought Mitchell. He looked over at the diner to see what the best way to get in and out of the back would be.

Mitchell jumped when the phone rang behind him. Mitchell stared at it, afraid to answer. Mr. Barks looked up at him.

Mitchell picked up the receiver. "Hello?"

"Looks like a pay phone number and not a burner. That's a mistake man. Always have a burner cell phone." said Rookman.

"Yeah, um I'm new at this."

"No shit. Do you have a plan? I mean, don't tell me. But do you have a plan?"

Mitchell looked at the diner and the row of trucks in back where he hoped to find a police scanner. "I think so. Part of one. I got an idea for a hideout."

"That's good. But keep moving. So tell me, what's really going on?" asked Rookman.

"I don't know. People try to kill me when they see me. Their eyes go all bloodshot. They look like fucking vampires or zombies." Mitchell's voice started to crack. "I just want it to stop."

"That's some scary shit man. Sounds like it might be some kind of rage virus or something. Is there anything on you that might be making people go bat shit? Like a high frequency transmitter? There have been experiments on ultra high and low frequencies that make people loose their shit."

"No." said Mitchell. "I searched everything I have. Nothing unusual. I thought maybe my iPad or something. But that was in my car when I first got attacked. I think there's something wrong with me."

"There's nothing wrong with you man. Something happened to you. Don't forget that. You're just trying to do what you can to survive. You're a good kid Mitchell. I see a lot of assholes everyday and I know you're not one of them. Right now you need to stay alive. I'll ask some of my spook connections if they know anything. If I can get you some help I'll try, maybe through them. But you got to know sooner or later they're going to start tracking me to get to you. So don't fall for it."

"Yeah man. Thanks."

"Stay safe. Stick with what you know. Don't do anything stupid. Stay away from people. Especially stay the fuck away from me."

Mitchell thanked him and hung up. *Stick with what you know.* Mitchell knew two things; broadcasting and boats. He'd have to avoid broadcasting for the time being. Boats were his next stop.

Mr. Barks had watched the conversation trying to understand. Mitchell gave him a hug then walked over to the diner. Behind him, the dog laid down to take a nap and wait for his new friend to come back.

It would be a long wait.

Mitchell avoided the streetlights that illuminated the parking lot in bright patches and worked his way to the rear of the diner. He was certain all kinds of shady things took place back there; from drug deals to prostitution. He kept a careful eye for anybody lurking in the shadows.

He heard the loud roar of a tractor-trailer start and then watched one pull out. From where he was standing, he could see the front of the diner. It didn't look like anyone was on their way out so he approached a cluster of six trucks.

Through the large glass windows he could see drowsy men in baseball caps drinking huge cups of coffee and eating more carbs than Mitchell would in a week. A waitress, who looked like she belonged in a nursing home, would shamble around filling cups then go back to a stool behind a register and watch the clock. This was no SWAT team.

His plan was to scope out the trucks and look through the windows to see if he could spot a scanner. He had no idea how common they would be, but at least he'd give it a shot here. If he came up with nothing, then he'd just head over to the marina.

Mitchell approached the first truck from the side furthest away from the diner. He climbed up on the running board and looked inside. It was too dark to be sure, but it didn't look like there was anything on the dashboard or seat that looked like a scanner.

He hopped down and was about to walk around the front of the truck when he noticed something; all the trucks had been parked in a staggered fashion. If he walked around the front he would be visible by the people in the diner. He guessed it was a strategy to make it easy for the drivers to keep an eye on their rigs while they ate.

Mitchell decided it would be prudent to take the long way around and avoid being seen. He passed around the back of the truck and walked up to the cab on the next one. A quick look inside showed nothing like a scanner.

He hopped down and walked towards the back to look at the other truck. Doubts about Rookman's advice were starting to settle in. Mitchell would look at two more then give up the whole idea.

Mitchell climbed up on the third truck's running board and looked in. He couldn't see anything in there either. He was about to hop back down when he noticed an antenna sticking out from under a map on the passenger side door.

Alright, we're in business, he thought. The next step was getting it. He tried the door handle with no luck. That left the next option. Mitchell undid the zipper on his backpack and pulled out the tire iron he'd taken from the back of the stolen car.

Through the windows of the cab, he looked at the diner to see if anybody was coming. It looked like he had the all clear. Mitchell had no idea what kind of sound the broken glass would make. He decided to wait for a truck to pass by before he broke the window.

Two minutes went by, then a truck roared by on the road in front of the diner. Mitch struck the window and it shattered. Without hesitation, he grabbed the scanner from under the map and hopped down off the running board. He moved towards the back of the trailer and caught his breath.

He heard a door open. *Fuck.* Mitchell looked to his left and saw a large figure climbing out of the other rig he'd just looked into. He was holding onto something metal in his hand.

Christ, these guys sleep in their cabs, Mitchell remembered.

"What the fuck are you doing?" called out the man.

"Just broke my beer bottle," said Mitchell.

The trucker was in the shadow of his own trailer. "Come here for a second," he called out.

Mitchell was in the process of thinking of something clever to say when he heard the trucker make a familiar low pitched growling sound. The silhouette lunged toward Mitchell. A shot went off.

Mitchell didn't feel like he'd been hit, so he ran. From behind he could hear the trucker's footsteps as he chased after him. Afraid to get caught in the open where the trucker could take another shot, Mitchell ran around the back of the nearest trailer, hoping to put it between him and the raging man.

Even though Mitchell didn't get a clear look at the man, he could tell he was large by the sound he made as he ran. It was like a locomotive heading towards him.

Mitchell passed around the back of the trailer and ran towards the rig in the front. The trucker was still in pursuit.

Out of the corner of his eye he could see more men pile out of the diner to see what was going on. Mitchell made a bee line from the parked trucks to the street. If he could make it across the street maybe he could lose his pursuer in the trailer park he'd seen back in there.

As Mitchell passed by the diner he realized that the men coming to see what the commotion was were going to be too close. He made a quick jag to the right and headed towards the pumps.

A trucker was standing outside his truck filling it up. He looked up to see Mitchell running in his direction. Confusion turned to rage. He charged towards Mitchell.

Mitchell heard more footsteps behind him as the men who stepped outside the diner to see what was going on joined the chase. The man from the pump was getting close. Mitchell didn't want to get caught in the middle.

The pump man held out his hands to claw at Mitchell's face. Mitch ducked down to the right and slammed the tire iron he was holding onto into the man's shin. The man fell over. Mitchell could hear the men behind him getting closer.

He wasn't sure if he'd make it to the other side of the street, let alone the trailer park.

He looked at the open cab door that belonged to the man that he had just hobbled with the tire iron. Mitchell jumped between the pumps and hopped inside. He closed the door just as the first trucker slammed into it.

Mitchell locked the door then locked the passenger side.

A man began beating on the door with his head and fists. Mitchell could hear a loud clanging as the hand holding the gun struck the metal exterior. The men from the diner started to pound on the truck as well.

It was a horrible racket. Foreheads and fists began to split open and blood began to cover the outside of the cab. The windows were going to break at any moment.

Angry faces stared at him with bloodshot eyes.

Mitchell looked at the controls. The rig was still running, but the shifters were in different places and he had no idea where the brake was. The driver's side window cracked.

He'd seen trucks started up a thousand times in movies. Mitchell searched his memory. He reached out with his right hand and unlocked the parking break then put it into gear as his left foot popped the clutch. Mitchell hit the gas and the truck jerked forward.

One of the men who was trying to climb on the hood fell away. Mitchell stepped on the gas again and got the shifter into the groove. The truck rolled away from the fuel pumps.

Outside the cab the men kept slamming their fists into the metal sides. Mitchell pushed the accelerator all the way and angled the truck towards the road. He overshot and the trailer clipped the side of a parked pick up truck dragging it into the road.

Mitchell had no choice but to keep going. In the blood splattered rear-view mirror he could see the men were still chasing him. Mitchell passed the pay phone where he had tied up Mr. Barks.

The animal gave him a woeful look as Mitchell roared by. In the passenger side mirror he could see the dog barking at the men as they chased after Mitchell.

The truck built up speed and the men eventually weren't able to keep up.

They faded into the distance, but he didn't need the scanner he stole to know the police would be on him in minutes.

27

Charging down the road in a stolen tractor-trailer truck, Mitchell racked his brain what to do next. Far from keeping a low profile, the giant rig made it difficult for him to slip into the night. There had to have been a better way to get a police scanner. He knew he needed to stay away from people, but he'd acted stupid. Just because he couldn't see someone, didn't mean there weren't people around.

He had to get rid of the truck and fast. He wished he was a movie hero and could just head it towards a convenient cliff and fake his death by jumping out before it went over. He didn't have the convenient cliff or athleticism to pull that off.

His next best option was to pull off the main road as soon as possible and park the truck somewhere it wouldn't get noticed for a while. If he could do that, he might be able to buy enough time to get away from his pursuers.

In his head he played out the fantasy of just keeping going in the huge rig. Screw roadblocks and chase helicopters. Driving an out of control tractor trailer truck on a televised police chase was a much better way to go then getting stopped in a beat up old Hyundai and getting tackled five feet from the door.

Up ahead he saw a strip mall next to a car lot. If he could park the rig in the back alley behind the mall, he might have an extra few minutes. Mitchell accelerated. Hopefully the cops would drive right by before they realized that he'd taken a side street.

Mitchell jerked the wheel to the right to go down the narrow street between the car lot and the mall. The truck skidded into the turn. As soon as the truck pointed down the street, Mitchell stepped on the accelerator again liked he'd done a thousand times in his little car.

Only his little car never had a 10-ton trailer behind it with its own inertia. The back end of the trailer jackknifed into the center of the road and kept going. Burnt rubber smoke came from the wheels as the trailer swung past the rig like a pendulum.

Mitchell felt the back of the rig suddenly jerk behind him.

"Oh fuck," he gripped the wheel and braced for impact.

The trailer skidded across the street and flew up onto the sidewalk in front of the car lot. It knocked down a street lamp and a power line. It kept going and bust through the chain barrier that ran around the entire lot. Mitchell heard the trailer make a loud 'boom' sound as the force of the impact ripped open riveted sections.

The truck itself began to tip over as the trailer smashed into a row of new Toyotas and pulled it over with it. Mitchell watched the back of the trailer make a shower of sparks in the driver's side mirror before it was crushed between the street and the weight of the rig. He felt pain in his shoulder as he was thrown against the driver's side door when it became the new down.

The trailer and rig slid a few more feet, sending cars flying before it came to a stop. Mitchell heard hundreds of car alarms go off all around him.

That didn't take long.

He lifted himself up off the door. Nothing felt broken or cut. While the back end of the trailer had been moving at 50 miles per hour, the truck cab was at the pivot point moved more slowly when it rolled over. That was something to be thankful for, Mitchell thought half-heartedly.

The police were going to be on him even faster now. Mitchell had to get out of the rig. The windshield was still intact so the only way out was the passenger side door.

Mitchell grabbed his backpack and stood up. He pulled the passenger's side handle and pushed. The door didn't want to move. Mitchell shoved again. The door opened a few inches then fell shut again.

Mitchell looked around the cab interior and found his tire iron. He gave the windshield several whacks and it fell apart in thousand tiny pieces of glass. Mitchell stepped out onto the street and looked back at the damage.

The front part of the car lot was a complete wreck. A street light was crushed between the side of the trailer and row of smashed in cars. Nearby he saw another broken pole being held up by two thick power cables. There was a loud crack as one of them gave out and the pole collapsed. The entire lot was thrown into darkness as the power went out.

Mitchell looked around, the entire neighborhood had just lost power. For several blocks in either direction the street was covered in total darkness as the lights went out one by one.. The only illumination at all was the flashing lights of the smashed cars as their car alarms went off. Over the racket they made, in the distance Mitchell could hear sirens.

He guessed a blackout maybe was a good thing. It'd make it easier for him to hide if there were no street lights. Good parking job or not, Mitchell had to keep running either way.

Although the blackout could help him hide or least provide a distraction, he now had to worry about the people coming outside to have a look as they left their houses and trailers behind the strip mall. Running into them would only make things worse. He'd had enough human contact for the night.

Mitchell put his other arm into a backpack strap and ran down the dark street between the car lot and the strip mall. He wanted to go another two blocks then take a side street and head towards the marina. It was still the best plan he had. If he couldn't find a boat there or near there, he didn't know what else he do; other than literally find some sewer pipe to crawl into and wait for a better idea.

As a defensive measure, he kept a tight grip on the tire iron in his right hand. It'd saved his life twice in the last few minutes. He felt safer knowing that it was ready at his side.

28

Mitchell kept a brisk pace as he headed towards the marina. He would move down one street then go up another. Heading there in a diagonal pattern. If anyone noticed him and thought he looked suspicious, he hoped moving street-to-street like that would make it difficult to peg down his position.

The blackout extended several more blocks then everything returned to normalcy. Although he was in a quiet residential neighborhood, he took extra effort to make sure that he didn't walk right into someone else out for an evening stroll. A few times cars passed him, but none of them slowed down.

As a precaution he gripped the end of the tire iron in his right hand and shielded the bulk of it with his right arm. That way he wouldn't look too suspicious if anyone caught a glimpse of him through an open window.

The car lot was over a half mile behind him, but he could still hear the sound of fire engines and police cars. He hoped they would be too focused on the chaos to spread out in a larger search. When he stopped for a moment to look back he could see a police helicopter shining its spotlight in the area around the car lot.

The hundreds of cars in the lot provided a lot of hiding spaces for someone on the run. The more they focused their attention behind him, the better his odds of getting away would be.

In between some of the houses he could see the canals that ran all around this part of South Florida. The marina was only a few blocks away. He kept an eye out for a potential boat behind the houses in case the marina didn't work out. The odds weren't as good targeting a single boat, but it was preferable to have some kind of back up plan.

One of the things he looked for was any house that was up for sale and looked unoccupied that had a boat in the backyard. That usually meant the owners lived elsewhere and either kept their boat berthed there or rented it out to someone else. A boat from a house like that could go missing for days before anyone noticed.

His ideal boat would be a small one no more than ten feet long, with a small engine. A bigger boat would be faster and could give him a cabin to sleep in. The problem was keeping it hidden and refueling it.

Mitch needed a boat with a gas tank that he could fill with gas siphoned from cars. There was no way he would be able to comfortably fill a large boat's gas tank at a marina gas pump. He needed something small that he could dock without notice and make his way up the Intracoastal without anyone calling attention to himself.

The next two blocks went by without incident. Finally he came to the marina. Across an almost empty parking lot he could see the docks. He could make out several tall masts and a few luxury yachts. A slightly more upscale marina was a good thing.

When he worked at a marina, during one college summer he got a pretty good understanding of boaters and what life was like around a marina. Many of the larger boats were lucky to get used more than a weekend a month. Owners bought them for the prestige and the potential for adventure but then grew bored with them and frustrated by the expense.

Smaller fishing boats tended to get a lot more use. The bigger luxury yachts often had at least one crewmember who lived on board to take care of the boat. The kind of boat Mitchell was looking for would either be tethered to one of the larger boats or tied off at the far end of the marina.

Within the ecosystem of a Marina you had people who rented berth space for their pleasure craft or charter boats. Then you had people who rented smaller slips for boats they used to provide services to the bigger craft like boat detailing and servicing electronics.

The marina he had worked at owned two small 'john' boats they used to navigate around the marina and go up and down the waterway to run errands. They were usually tied off on the dock and secured with a cable that went from a metal loop attached to the boat and around a support. Often the key for the lock would be somewhere on the boat itself.

Mitchell stood by a palm tree and watched the marina for movement. The docks were separated from the parking lot by two gates. Near the closest one there was a single story building that served as the office.

It was a toss up if there was anybody in the office watching the boats. The most common kind of crime in a marina was people pulling up in small boats and stealing things off the deck like rod holders and any kind of gear left out in the open. Boat owners tried to keep everything of value fastened down or in lock boxes.

The good thing for Mitchell was he could pop open a fiberglass lock box pretty quickly with his tire iron. First he had to find a boat and make sure it started. There was little point doing a smash and grab if he couldn't make a clean getaway.

Mitchell waited another few minutes and saw two men carrying fishing gear and heading down one of the docks towards the parking lot. They were on the opposite side of where he wanted to go and could possibly serve as a distraction as they unlocked the gate to leave.

Staying close to a low wall at the far end of the marina, Mitchell walked towards the sea wall. He tried to stay in the shadows behind the lights that illuminated the parking lot. He got to the sidewalk and looked out at the boats in the marina. On the side of the dock closest to him he saw a 14 foot Boston Whaler. It was bigger then what he needed.

Mitchell wrestled with the idea of just trying to take that boat and switch it out for a different boat later when he noticed that tied up next to it was a smaller aluminum boat with a dark green hull. It had a 20 horse power engine and an exposed gas tank. It also had a center console, which would make steering a little easier.

That could be the one, he thought. The trick was getting to it. Mitchell looked over the edge of the sea wall. It was near low tide. He could see a small concrete ledge below the rocky wall. It was only a few inches, but enough for his toes to stand on. Worst case scenario, the water was probably only three feet deep. He'd just have to keep his bag above the water if he fell in. He put the tire iron in his bag and got ready.

Mitchell looked down the sidewalk and saw the far gate swing open. The sound echoed across the quiet marina. Using that as cover, he got on all fours and lowered himself on to the lower edge.

He could feel the rough edges of the rocks on the sea wall against his knees. His finger tips held on to the concrete lip as he ducked his head out of sight. His feet found the small ledge and he lowered his weight on to it.

Sliding one foot after the other, he moved his body towards the ramp that lead up to the gate. He stopped for a moment when he realized he'd never bothered to check if the gate was unlocked to begin with.

He craned his neck to look up at the gate. That was when he saw a surveillance camera for the first time. The camera was aimed at anybody walking through the gate. Mitchell felt a little better about taking the indirect route.

If he could avoid being seen walking onto the dock and hopefully never be observed at the marina at all, it made his chances of a clean getaway that much better.

Mitchell slid over to the underside of the ramp. The boat he was after was about ten feet away tied to a pylon. A wire cable went from the steering wheel, through a rod holder and through the rung of a ladder that lead down to it and the Boston Whaler.

The original plan was to climb up onto the dock and walk over to the boat like a civilized person. Because of the camera, Mitchell had to hang from the edge of the dock and scramble like a monkey while trying not to get his feet wet.

Halfway to the boat, Mitchell could hear footsteps on the dock. He froze. They sounded far off but getting closer. Should he stay where he was and leave his fingers in the open?

The ladder was only a few feet away. Mitchell decided to hurry towards it and hide underneath the dock behind it. He shimmied along and almost fell into the water when his hand hit grabbed an unexpected rope cleat.

He pulled himself behind the ladder and waited. The footsteps grew louder on the wooden dock above. He could also hear the sound of something being rolled. Probably a cart with gear in it.

A few tense moments later he heard the sound of a key going into the lock on the gate. It opened then closed. Mitchell waited another minute to see if he could hear any other footsteps. The dock sounded empty.

He lowered himself into the boat and looked around. The gas tank felt at least half full. That would give him a couple hours. He made a note to find an extra gas tank and fill it up when he could so he could avoid having to go ashore whenever possible.

Mitch examined the cable lock. There was no way he was going to be able to just pry it open. The ladder it went through was made from aluminum and was bolted to the dock. It was doubtful he'd be able to rip it free and just take it with him.

He looked around the boat for a likely spot to hide a key. He reached under the wooden center console and tried to find a hook or a peg where the key might be hanging. Nothing. He looked under the console and saw a few cables and a beer cozy. Still nothing. He looked around the floor. Other than two oars, there was nothing that said 'key'.

Mitchell checked the gas tank and the outboard motor. The motor was also locked to the boat. There wasn't anything that looked like it hid a key.

Mitchell moved to the front of the boat and opened up the small compartment at the bow. Inside was the legally required life vest, some cushions, a rope and anchor and more beer cozies. He was about to close the hatch when he got the urge to stick his hand underneath the back edge. He slid it along the smooth inside then felt something in the space between the hull and where the top of the compartment connected. It was a plastic hook with a small key ring.

Mitchell pulled it out. There were two keys. One for the cable lock and one for the outboard motor lock. Mitchell unlocked the cable and stowed it in the compartment.

There was still something else he needed. First, he had to make sure the boat would run. He figured it would be better to start the boat further away from the dock and just glide in when he spotted the right boat.

Mitchell pushed off on the pylon and the boat gently glided away from the dock. When he was twenty feet away he pumped some gas into the engine using the hand bulb on the fuel line then pulled the starter cord. He was expecting a small battle with the engine but it started right up.

Mitchell steered the boat in a giant arc and went around the front of the marina. He wanted to get one more thing. He knew it was silly, but it would make him feel a little safer.

He spotted the type of boat he was looking for and aimed his little boat towards it. Mitchell killed the engine and drifted towards the boat. He moved to the bow of the boat and caught the other boat with his hands.

Trying to keep the boats from hitting, Mitchell moved the boat towards a dive platform at he stern of the large boat. He tied the smaller boat and then peered into the back of the boat. There were two large gear boxes.

Feeling like a pirate, he climbed aboard the boat with his tire iron. *Fuck*, he told himself, *he was a pirate at this point*. Mitch pushed the flat edge near the lock of one and pried it. The fiberglass around the lock snapped and the lid opened. Inside was a pile of life vests and cushions.

He closed the lid and pried open the other box. This time the lid made a much louder crack as it opened. Inside he was a flare gun, an emergency radio, diving masks and some other gear. He took the flare gun and a few other things and dropped them into his boat.

Mitchell was about to climb in when he heard footsteps again. Still in the back of the larger boat, he squatted down behind the box he had just opened. He waited for the footsteps to pass him by.

Only they didn't.

29

Mitchell stayed down as low as he could trying to keep his body out of sight of the person on the dock above him. Did they stop because the saw or heard something? Or did they stop because they sensed something like everyone else who attacked him?

He decided to try to wait the person out. Rather than attract their attention and leap into his boat and make a getaway, he wanted to avoid having anybody know he stole the boat at least until morning. And even then he hoped nobody would make the connection right away between him and the boat.

Mitchell waited. He heard shifting feet, but the person wasn't moving. This was bad. If it had been a security guard, or at least one that didn't have the rage, he'd probably see a flashlight beam poking around.

This person was using his more basic senses to try to find him. Mitchell could hear a snort as the man took in more air. *How did it work*, Mitchell wondered? Did they get a small amount of his scent and try to zero in on him? Just one more question to add to the list.

Frustrated, Mitchell poked his head around the edge of the box and looked up on the dock. He saw a black man with a beard in a windbreaker who looked to be in his mid-fifties standing there. His face was curled into a snarl as he twisted his head around smelling the air. The man's head jerked towards Mitchell.

Damn! Mitchell cursed himself for not pulling his head away sooner. The man leaped from the dock and into the boat. The floor made a huge crack sound as the man landed.

Mitch shot up and threw himself over the stern and onto the dive platform below. He felt hands reach out and grab at his neck. The man was trying to choke him.

He tried to use his fingers to pull apart the man's fingers but couldn't get them to budge. Black spots began to form at the corner of his vision as his brain was cut off from blood. He felt something hot near his right ear as the man opened his mouth to bite it off.

Mitch pulled his knees into his chest putting his full weight on the man's hands. The man's grip didn't let go as he was pulled further over the edge. Mitch kicked out against the platform and brought the back of his head against the man's nose. He heard it crack and could feel the warm trickle of blood on the back of his his neck.

The fingers slackened. Mitch wrenched his neck free and collapsed into his stolen boat. Blood returned to his head and the spots faded. He could hear the man behind him climbing over the edge of the larger boat.

Mitch's hand was on one of the oars. He gripped it like a baseball bat and turned around swinging. The narrow edge of the paddle hit the man in the side of the head. The oar made a loud thwack as it connected.

Mitchell's attacker went slump and fell over the edge of the boat and into the water. Mitchell leaned out and looked at the man as he lay face down in the water. Unconscious, he was about to drown.

Damn it! Self defense was one thing, but leaving a man to drown was another. Especially a man that apparently had no control over his actions.

Mitchell set down the oar and grabbed the back of the man's shirt. He pulled him towards the dive platform. Mitchell stepped out of his boat and dragged him out of the water and on to the platform.

He felt for a pulse. His hands trembled at the thought of the man regaining consciousness at any moment and biting off his fingers or face. Not any expert by a long shot, he felt something he thought was a pulse. That would have to do.

Mitchell pulled him into the back of the larger boat. He was tempted to try to lift him on to the dock in the hope that when the man awoke no one would notice that Mitchell had broken open the boxes. The risk of having the man come around didn't seem worthwhile.

Mitchell climbed back into his little boat and shoved off. He started the engine and drove away. He wished he could just head off into the night and drive until dawn, but there was one more thing he needed to do.

30

Detective Rios parked his police car in back of an evidence van near the car lot. He'd just finished taking statements at the diner and come to take a look at the mayhem. Fire fighters had cordoned off an area around the down power line while works tried to get power back on.

Mobile work lights hooked up to generators illuminated the damage the out of control tractor-trailer truck had caused. Laying on its side on top of a row of crushed cars, it looked like a giant sea creature that had been beached. The shadows of balloons and waving flags on the building behind made it look like one of the accidents his son would stage with his toys.

Rios walked over to the cab of the truck where Simmons was kneeling. "What the hell did the kid do now?" he asked.

"The people at the diner confirm it was him?" asked Simmons.

"The ones inside did. The ones outside that chased him away are a little confused."

"Like the people back at the mall?" she asked.

"Yeah." Rios stood back and looked at the lot from a different angle. He looked at where the trailer had ripped open. There was another row of smashed cars in front of it not visible from the street. A utility worker in a bucket at the end of a crane arm worked to unhook the power cables from the broken pole.

Simmons stood up. "Any idea what he was doing at the truck stop, beside planning the world's worst joy ride?"

Rios shook his head. "I don't think he was after the truck. One of the other rigs was broken into. It didn't look like he was trying to steal it though. The driver is a bit disoriented right now and can't tell if anything is missing."

Simmons waved an arm at the rig. "If all he was after was petty theft, then why go through the trouble of stealing a tractor trailer truck, driving it a quarter mile and then causing a million dollar's worth of property damage?"

"He's a one man doomsday machine. It's what he does," said Rios.

Simmons shook her head. "I don't buy it. The kids got no priors. No history of domestic abuse. Nothing even marginal. Unless some Facebook photos pop up of him wearing women's underwear while reading Soldier of Fortune, I think we're dealing with a person who is just reacting to everything that happened today."

"Sometimes people just snap," said Rios.

"I don't buy that. People with erratic behavior sometimes go way out of line and do something horrific, but there's almost always signs there before."

"The break up with the girlfriend," replied Rios.

"What about it? Everybody goes through break ups. I think we're just looking at it as a convenient explanation." Simmons paused for a moment. "I saw his girlfriend's face, but I also saw the boyfriend too. I don't know if its what it looks like. We've been so focused on the mall we haven't even done any proper forensics."

Rios folded his arms, "What about the parking officer?"

"I don't know. We just don't know yet. When you talked to the people at the diner, the ones inside, did they say anything different than what other witnesses have said?" asked Simmons.

"They could identify him. Not much else."

Simmons bit the edge of a nail as she thought. "What did they say about the people who chased after him?"

Rios pulled a notebook from his back pocket and looked at it. "They said it looked like they wanted to kill him. Which is understandable."

"Did they say 'kill' specifically?"

Rios looked back at his notes. "One of them said 'murder'. Another said 'tear apart'."

"Those are some pretty harsh words for someone doing a smash and grab."

"I think after what happened at the mall today half this city would like to murder him."

Simmons held up a finger. Something just came to her. "You said the people chasing him didn't know who he was?"

"Yeah, but they saw the other man chasing after him."

"The trucker with the gun? They didn't know him either?" asked Simmons.

"Yeah, he was the one who caught him breaking into the other truck."

"Wait a second." Simmons looked down the street towards the truck stop. "If you hear a gun go off and look out the window and see a man running away from another man with a gun, who do you think the victim is? Assuming the guy with the gun isn't a cop?"

Rios arched an eyebrow.

Simmons continued. "The men in the diner who went outside, automatically, without hesitation, go into vigilante mode and decide to chase after Mitchell Roberts? They ignore the man with the gun and decide that have to murder the guy trying to run away? That's messed up. It doesn't make sense."

Simmons walked over to hood of the truck. She kneeled down to look at a bloody smear near the driver's side door. "Did the men who chased him have any injuries?"

"A few. I saw some cuts on their faces and a lot of bloody knuckles."

"From what?" asked Simmons.

"Trying to get him out of the cab according to the people in the diner."

"Who uses their forehead to try to smash open a window?" She pointed to a bloody print on the metal bracing around the windshield. "Or beats their hands into a pulp smashing a steel frame?"

Rios shrugged. "I've seen that lots of times."

"On someone who wasn't psychotic or on drugs?"

"Well..."

"Me neither. Let me ask you another question. When you saw the men back there, what made you think it was Mitchell Roberts? Was it the statements from the people in the diner? And I'm not talking about the fact that we're only two miles away from one of the stakeouts."

Rios got her point. "The injuries on their faces. They reminded me of this morning and the mall."

"What can we say about the injuries here and at the mall as far as cause?"

Rios nodded. "For the most part, they were self inflicted while they were pursuing the suspect. He paused for a moment. "So you think the injuries this morning were self inflicted as well?"

"It would seem to fit the pattern. All of the injuries were the result of chasing Roberts," said Simmons.

Rios shook his head. His mind went back to the grisly scene at the escalator and the people who fell off the roof. "You saw what happened back at the mall. Who in their right mind would let that happen?"

"Someone scared, Rios. Someone running for their life who can't stop to look back."

Simmons pointed to the bloody knuckles prints on the hood then took a step back from the wrecked tractor trailer truck. "These people weren't chasing the devil. He was running from it."

31

Steinmetz looked up from the computer display and wiped his eyes. He hoped it was just the fatigue. He knew that was wishful thinking. He looked over at the 30 year-old man with thick dark hair and a perpetual five-o-clock-shadow sitting next to him.

"You've double checked these Nick?" he asked him.

"I checked four times and seven samples. All show the same kind of elevated peptides." He leaned over and touched tip of his pen to the screen. "You can see the spike on Neurokinin C here."

Steinmetz took off his glasses and wiped his eyes again. As was his habit when he felt stress. He'd been doing it a lot lately.

His lab assistant, Nick Arturous, hesitated to speak. Finally he couldn't hold it in any longer. "It looks like..."

"I know what it looks like Nick," Steinmetz came across much harsher than he meant to.

"But Great Wall was supposed to stop this."

"Great Wall was rushed."

"Maybe, this is what it looks like when it works?" asked Nick hopefully.

"Maybe. Maybe. I got to call the big man. Go back and ask Selena to help you run everything through the sequencer. I want to send it through our internal gene bank."

Nick nodded then closed the door behind him..

Steinmetz picked up the phone and called Baylor.

After going through a forwarding center he picked up after two rings.

"What is it Ari?" asked Baylor.

"It's not good Steven."

"It can't be Mongolian Flu."

"It's not. We couldn't find any variant there. We're looking again. It's just that it shows all the symptoms of Mongolian after it recedes. All the elevated peptides. Neurokinin. It's all there."

"Fuck," said Baylor. "Is it a variant of some kind?"

"We're looking right now to see if our screener was too imprecise and miss called it. But I'm skeptical," said Steinmetz. "We have to consider the possibility that..."

"No," said Baylor interrupting him. "That's technically impossible."

"Well..."

"Ari, listen to me. That's not an option. For all we know this could be Great Wall doing what it's supposed to do." Baylor paused. "One of the things we looked into was the possibility of using the same mechanism that Mongolian Flu did in an airborne solution. For crowd control."

This was news to Steinmetz. "Good lord Steven, what kind of crowd would you be trying to control?"

Baylor ignored the question. "We have to consider the possibility that someone else had the same idea. You could bypass the virus altogether and create a biological agent that would cause the same reaction as long as people were exposed to it. Turn it off and the reaction stops."

"Do we tell DHS about this?"

Baylor thought for a moment. "I'm going to send a containment team down there. We'll hold off for now so we can protect the integrity of Great Wall for now. Since we have no reason to think it's an infectious agent, it's not that serious."

Steinmetz had seen the news reports of what happened in the mall earlier that day. He was afraid to find out what Baylor thought was 'serious'.

"We need to be there when they apprehend this man and make sure the right precautions are taken with whatever kind of dispersant he was using," said Baylor.

"Is there a chance we could get a blood sample from the man?"

"After we catch him, certainly."

"No, I mean is there one now?" asked Steinmetz.

"Not that I'm aware of. Why?"

"I just wanted to cross check something involving Great Wall."

"Forget about Great Wall Ari. I need you to look at those blood samples and find some kind of evidence of a dispersant. We need to figure out how it got into their systems. I'll call back in a couple hours. I'm going to take a jet down there to meet up with the containment team." Baylor hung up.

Steinmetz put the phone down and walked back into the lab. He called one of the assistants over.

"Selena, can you do a search in the blood database for Mitchell Roberts? I'd like to see if we have access to a sample anywhere."

"The official one? Or Backdoor?"

The Backdoor database was an index Steinmetz had helped develop for Baylor. Using genetic fingerprinting it matched blood samples from known donors with anonymous donors and had a prediction algorithm that could calculate the likelihood of someone being related to other individuals in the database. Even if someone had never given a blood sample, they could often trace a drop of blood back to a specific person if their family members had ever donated blood. The database was not only a secret know to just a few people outside the lab, it was highly illegal. Steinmetz only used it sparingly.

"Use Backdoor, Selena."

32

Mitchell drove the boat for a half hour up the Intracoastal then down a canal. He tied it off to a tree next to a highway. He climbed out of the boat and looked over the concrete embankment that separated the highway from the canal. Across the road he could see the twenty four hour box store, Super Center, that he was looking for.

Before he went into total hiding, he needed a few more things. It was a calculated risk, but one he needed to take if he was going to avoid human contact until things sorted out. Whatever that meant.

He waited until there were no cars coming or going on the road then ran across it. He came to a small hill that ran along the front of the parking lot and looked over the hedge that topped it. He counted fourteen cars in the parking lot. Usually there was some kind of rent-a-cop driving a car around. Mitchell spotted him at the far end of the mall parked near the other entrance.

If Mitchell walked normally past the car he could get inside without too much trouble. Just as long as the window wasn't down.

Before he went shopping he needed to take care of something while he was in the parking lot. Mitchell found an opening in the hedge and walked over to one of the cars. Making sure that nobody was looking, he knelt down by the license plate and pulled out a fishing knife he found on the boat.

Using the flat edge he unfastened the screws holding the license plate onto the car. Mitchell tucked the plate under his jacket into his back waistband. He walked over to another car and did the same thing. He wanted to get as many license plates as he could, but settled for one more.

He had no plans to use them. He just wanted to give his pursuers a strong reason to believe he'd stolen a car. The multiple missing plates would frustrate their search for him.

He tucked the third plate behind the others and stood up. The security vehicle was still in the same spot. Mitchell looked to make sure that there was no one else in the parking lot and walked towards the nearer entrance. If he saw anyone coming through the doors towards him he readied himself to run around the side of the building.

Through the glass doors he could see an old man in a red vest working as the Super Center's door greeter, their polite term for shop lifting deterrent. Mitchell knew there was no way around the man. He was counting on the fact that once the man noticed him he'd abandon his post.

Mitchell tried to remember the layout of the store so he could get everything he needed as quickly as possible. Mitchell took a deep breath, smoothed back his hair then walked through the main entrance. Mitch entered the store.

He tried to pass as far away from the old man as he could, but it didn't matter. Two seconds after Mitch walked through the door the man's teeth were bared and his eye's narrowed on Mitch .

Mitch kept walking. "Take it easy old timer, I don't want you to have a heart attack."

The old man lunged towards him. Mitch walked faster, easily outpacing the old man as he tried to move towards him as fast as his arthritic legs could take him. Mitch kept going straight down the aisle then darted to the right in the hardware section. He searched the shelves for what he needed. The old man rounded the corner as Mitch found it.

Mitch jogged around the shelves and headed back down the aisle towards the back. He ripped open the container and pulled out what he needed.

When the footsteps grew fast behind Mitch he broke into a light run. He didn't want to attract attention from anybody else in the store. From behind him he could hear the old man let out a low pitched groan. Mitch increased his speed and headed for the men's bathroom at the back of the store.

Down an aisle he caught sight of a young couple with a shopping basket looking at DVDs. Mitch didn't know how far whatever made people attack him worked, but he was sure he was going to have to deal with them after the old man.

The footsteps were getting closer. Mitch reached the bathroom and pushed the door open. He quickly ran around the back of the door and waited. The old man ran in after him a few seconds later and charged into the center of the bathroom.

Mitch slipped around the door and pulled it shut behind him. The old man started to pound on the door. Mitch couldn't hold it shut forever. Somebody was going to come sooner or later when they heard the noise the man was making.

Mitch pushed the door open slightly and a clawed hand came at his face. He slid a zip tie around the hand then attached it to the one he'd fastened to the door handle. He cinched them both tight fastening the old man to the door. It might hurt the man's wrist if he fought it, but it would keep him at a safe distance.

Mitch walked back towards the sporting goods section and grabbed a few things; a wooden baseball bat, a paint ball gun and extra ammo. He found a large duffle bag and shoved them inside. He ran over to the camping section and started shoving freeze dried food packages into the duffle bag. He grabbed a few other camping tools then went to another aisle.

From behind he could hear the sound of two pairs of footsteps running towards him. Mitch looked over his shoulder and saw the girl and her boyfriend going full speed.

Mitch ran away from them and turned down an aisle that lead to the toy department. He turned into what he thought was the right aisle but realized he'd made a mistake. He ran down the aisle and turned around the next end cap.

Mitch scanned the shelves for what he needed. He knew it was a borderline stupid idea. He just wanted to try it before he used the baseball bat. He'd hurt enough people that day.

The couple came around the corner filled with rage and closed in on him. Mitch ripped open the bag of marbles and threw them on the floor. The man and the woman tripped and skidded across the smooth tile. The man's head smacked into a metal shelf. The girl fell face first. Mitch ripped open two more bags and scattered them around the couple as they tried to get up.

He shoved some more bags of marbles into his bag and ran back to the hardware gun section of the store. Mitch found a shelf filled with pepper spray canisters and began shoving them into his bag. He popped the safety off one and held on to it.

Mitch ran back to the hardware section and grabbed a few more things. At the other end of the store he could hear the sound of merchandise being dropped and footsteps hurrying in his direction.

It was time to go. Mitch headed back to the center aisle and ran towards the exit the old man had abandoned. A heavy-set woman in a t-shirt, shorts and flip flops was running at him, rolls of body fat shaking like a hula skirt. Behind her was her pig-tailed seven year-old daughter in hot pursuit. Both pairs of eyes were bloodshot.

He ran to the right into the clothing section and started weaving through the racks. Another man in a red vest came running at Mitch from behind a row of shelves.

Mitch sprayed the man in the eyes with the pepper spray. The man let out a roar but didn't stop coming after him. He was blinded but kept swinging his arms around. Mitch knocked over two clothing racks to trip the man up.

He looked to his left and saw the mother getting close. Mitch aimed a cloud of pepper spray at her then tipped over a rack in her path. She went sprawling across the ground.

Mitch looked around. He couldn't see the little girl because she was shorter than the racks. There was the sound of little footsteps coming from somewhere, but he couldn't see where.

Mitch moved away from the man and the little girl's mother and headed towards the exit. Suddenly he felt a searing pain in the back of his thigh as the little girl bit him.

"Fuck!" Mitch jerked around and tried to kick the girl away without being too harsh. She just attacked his leg. Mitch looked at the can of pepper spray. He couldn't do it.

From the moment he entered he knew there were surveillance cameras watching. At some point authorities would see everything he did in the store when they watched the recordings.

He couldn't bring himself to hurt the little girl anymore than was necessary. Mitch kept pushing her away with his leg. He pulled a zip tie from his pocket and grabbed one of the girl's wrists.

He yanked her into a clothes rack before she could bite into his arm. He wrapped the zip tie around her tiny wrist and strapped her to the metal curtain bar on the clothes rack. Once he was confident she wouldn't chase after him as he left the store, Mitch ran towards the exit. The little girl snarled and spit.

He could hear more footsteps behind him. He caught a glimpse of two cashiers and four customers running at him. Mitch pulled out another bag of marbles and ripped it open. He tossed the bag over his head.

He could hear the sound of several bodies hitting the ground. There were still more footsteps. He threw down another bag of marbles. A pair of footsteps still came after him.

Mitch didn't want to be followed back to the boat. He turned around the corner that lead to the exit and pulled the baseball bat out of the duffle bag.

As soon as he was around the other side of the wall he knelt down and stuck the baseball bat out to trip whoever was behind him. He man in a sheriff's deputy uniform ran past the corner and tripped on the bat. He skidded across the floor on his face.

Not another cop, thought Mitch. He had no choice. He took the can of mace from the bag. Mitch walked over and sprayed the man at point blank as he tried to get up. Mitchell started to sneeze from being so close to the spray.

The deputy screamed out and tried to claw at anything he could. Mitch ran through the automatic sliding glass doors and into the parking lot. He saw the deputy sheriff's car parked up on the curb.

Christ, that guy got here fast, thought Mitchell. He looked out at the parking lot. It still looked the same as when he came in with the exception of the flashing blue light from the empty police car. Mitchell ran towards the far end of the lot.

As he reached the hedge on top of the hill that separated the mall parking lot from the highway he saw three police cars racing towards his direction with their lights flashing. Mitchell ducked down behind the hedge and tried to figure out what to do next.

The police cars pulled into the parking lot and headed towards the front of the store. While they're attention was on the front of the store, Mitchell decided now was the best time to make the break for it.

He climbed over the hedge and looked for traffic. The road was clear. Mitchell ran across the highway and climbed over the concrete wall. He found the spot where he tied his boat to a tree and threw the duffle bag filled with stolen goods inside.

Mitchell untied the rope from the tree and shoved off. He didn't want to get caught next to shore as he tried to get the engine going. He'd be too vulnerable like that.

When the boat was ten feet away from shore he gave the starting cord a pull. It took him three tries. Finally it started. Mitchell aimed the bow away from the store and headed up the canal and back towards the Intracoastal waterway. It wasn't uncommon for police to call in a police boat unit when they thought a suspect might be on or near water. Mitchell kept the boat going as fast as he could without attracting too much attention.

As he entered the main waterway he looked back and saw the police helicopter over the Super Center shining its spotlight into the parking lot below.

Mitchell reached into the back of his pants and pulled out the license plates. He looked at the numbers and letters then tossed them into the water where they sank to the bottom.

Mitchell steered the little boat towards a large draw bridge that connected the inland part of the city to the beach. There was one more errand Mitch had to do that night.

33

When Detective Rios got home he had trouble sleeping. His wife and two kids were already sound asleep when he got there. He crawled in to bed and stared at the ceiling for an hour. He couldn't get the idea out of his head that Mitchell Roberts really was a victim. Certainly someone who left a wake of destruction in his path, but someone just as scared as everyone else.

When he saw the paper the next morning he texted Simmons that he was going to check on something before coming into the office.

The headline read 'Mad Mitch Rampage' and described the events of the previous day using lots of convenient 'allegedly's in a way that made Roberts out to be some kind of domestic terrorist. To be fair to the paper, this was how law enforcement was proceeding at this point. Anytime you have bodies and someone running from the scene, it's hard not to conceive of that person as being guilty of something heinous.

Rios drove over to the neighborhood where the first incident took place. He parked his car and walked to the spot where Mitchell had allegedly attacked the parking enforcement officer. The car had been towed away to evidence. Yellow spray paint marked out on the street where the car had been.

If it hadn't been for the incident at the mall, Rios and Simmons would have canvased the neighborhood for witnesses. That had been put on the back burner while they dealt with the larger crisis. The problem with waiting was that people forgot things or moved away.

He looked around the street to see what houses or apartments had a view of the where he was standing. There were at least half a dozen. He walked up the steps of the nearest house and knocked on the door. The house faced the street and had a large living room window with open curtains.

Nobody answered. Rios was about to walk away, then decided to be a little more thorough. He pulled out a business card and wrote a quick note on the back to call him. He moved on to the next house.

There was no answer there either. He tried an apartment after that and found a young woman getting ready for work. She told him she'd already left for work the day earlier. Rios thanked her and left.

Back in the street he looked around for other places to look. Across the street to the right he saw a second floor apartment he'd missed before. Rios walked over and climbed up the flight of stairs the lead to the second level.

He knocked on the door that faced the street. From inside he could hear someone coming to the door.

The door opened, a short old woman with platinum blond wig answered.

"Hello?" she said from behind the door.

Rios showed her his badge and introduced himself.

"Is this about that boy?"

"The boy?" asked Rios.

"Yes, the young man those people were trying to hurt. Is he alright?"

"Did you see what happened out here?" Rios pointed through the apartment to the street below.

"I always knew that meter maid woman was a bitch. Gave me three tickets this year. When she attacked the young man I felt so sorry for him."

"Did you tell anybody?" asked Rios.

"I called 911."

Interesting thought Rios. Nobody had told him about the 911 call. He'd have to look into it.

"So when you say she attacked him, attacked how? How did the window get broken?"

"When that cow climbed on the hood and started bashing her head into it. I've never seen someone so angry."

Rios got a few more details then told the woman he would be in touch. She insisted he let her know as soon as he could if Mitchell was okay. Good to know that the kid has at least one friend in the world, Rios thought as he walked back to his car.

34

Mitchell was about to get a lot more friends. Before he made it to his hiding spot for the night he made one more stop. The effects of which were rapidly changing at least some people's minds.

In a back alley between a highway and a canal where he'd parked his boat Mitch made a video and uploaded it to YouTube on his iPhone.

When he turned on the device for the first time since that morning the screen was filled with a barrage of text messages and voicemail. Some familiar, others weren't. He didn't have enough time to check them and could already imagine what they said anyway.

He launched the video camera app. He wanted for people to at least hear his side of things. Up until then the police had been telling everyone what was taking place. Mitchell suspected that even they really had no idea.

Mitch took off the hat and jacket he'd been wearing and combed back his wild hair with his hand. He took a deep breath and tried a relaxation exercise so he wouldn't come across too excited or crazy. He knew that no matter what, he was going to sound crazy to most people, but if he could just reach a few, then that could make a difference.

He thought out what he needed to say. He didn't want to come across as too paranoid or too glib. He also reminded himself that there were people who suffered a lot worse than him. Mitch pressed record.

"Hi, I'm Mitch Roberts. As you know, I am on the run. Let me make it very clear that I am ready to surrender. All I have to know is that I won't be harmed and the people who I surrender to won't be harmed directly or indirectly by my surrendering.'

'There is something strange going on that I don't understand. Since yesterday, anybody who comes near me that's not behind glass tries to kill me. Not approach me. Not stop me. But tries to kill me.'

'According to the news they haven't released the video from what happened at the mall. I understand that it's disturbing. I was there. But you need to see this video. The public needs to see all of the video that's available. You'll understand that I'm not trying to harm anyone. I'm only defending myself, the same as you would do.'

'For me to surrender I need to know that the people I'm surrendering to are properly protected and that I can be safely isolated from contact with other people until they find out what's happening." Mitchell paused for a moment and looked off screen. He had been holding up so far using his radio voice. It was beginning to crack.

Mitchell's eyes began to get moist. "If I had known today what would have happened, when I ran from the food court to all of those people. To the people in the department store. To the people that jumped or got pushed from the roof by other people, I'd like to think I wouldn't have ran."

Mitchell's voice quivered. "I...I don't know if I could just sit there and let everyone attack me. I'd never been so scared in my life...but I'd like to think that if I could go back there and do it all over again I would have let them."

Mitch clicked the stop button. He wanted to check the video again but didn't have time. He pressed the button to upload it to his YouTube account. It would take another hour before it went live. As he was about to shut off his iPhone an instant notification message popped up from twitter.

@MadMitchFM Your not the monster they say you are.

#runmitchrun

He didn't recognize the person who sent the message, but it was comforting still the same. He opened up his Twitter account just to see how people were reacting. There were thousands of @replies to him. Many calling him a monster, others showing support. He saw the hash tag #runmitchrun used a lot. Not everyone was buying the story that he was the public menace the press and authorities had made him out to be.

A number of people using the hash tag were offering him advice that ranged from ridiculous to almost helpful. He scanned through and found a couple things to keep in mind. If he could have crowd sourced his escape earlier on he could have saved himself some trouble.

Mitchell decided it was worth the risk to send out a tweet. He didn't want to be flippant, but he also just wanted to feel a part of something bigger than himself for the moment. Trying to figure out what to say took him a minute. Finally he managed to types something out and clicked 'tweet'.

Ask for the truth.

Think of those who have been hurt.

If you see me coming, please run away.

Mitchell's YouTube video inevitably went viral later that night. The morning papers had already been sent to bed, but the television channels were filled with news anchors and commentators parsing through every frame of the video. Public officials were flooded for requests for the mall video and the Super Center robbery.

Although people were having trouble accepting Mitchell's claim that people were attacking him without provocation, the discussion shifted from the manhunt to the root cause of what had happened. There was the growing feeling that the government wasn't telling people everything.

Far away from Mitchell, The Naked Man in the Forest was in his own clearing of woods. He'd come again to the Earth mother for advice. Only he'd taken longer than he should.

He couldn't wait much longer. He needed her guidance. He took a small piece off the blotter from the Otherself's pants and sat down on the rotting log. Dark thunderclouds were forming overhead. He felt cold and afraid.

He placed it on his tongue and stared at the oak tree. It took a few minutes but the familiar face began to form. Only this time the lips weren't supple and inviting, they formed a cruel sneer. The eyes looked at him accusingly.

What have you done foolish child!

The Naked Man in the Forest cowered in her presence. He felt shameful in his nakedness.

Her eyes burned with green fury. Vines writhed around her head like Medusa's snakes.

My eggs? Are they safe?

"Yes Earth mother! They're safe. I'd die for them."

And you just might! What is that you've done?

"The Otherself Earth mother! He made a mistake. There's a man, a dark man, I'm afraid he may bring harm to your eggs. To me."

Then you must kill this man!

"I will try. But killing him may expose the Otherself. They may know that he plots."

Green leaves flicked from her lips like a forked tongue.

My eggs! All that matters are my eggs! If the Otherself can be spared for now, then do it. But kill this man!

He'd wanted the man dead. He just had to know that was what the Earth mother wanted as well.

The Naked Man in the Forest saw bees flying from an empty tree stump several yards away. Was the Earth mother giving him a sign?

"Should I punish myself Earth mother?" He walked towards the hive. His hand was outstretched.

She said nothing. He brought his hand closer to the stump. An angry bee buzzed past his head. He looked back at the oak. Bright green eyes stared back at him. He reached into the log.

Stop it you fool! The Otherself can't be punished like that. Over there instead.

Her forked tongue pointed to a vine of leaves on a nearby tree. He pulled his hand away and walked over to the tree.

Grab the leaves.

He did as she commanded. His right hand grabbed a cluster of the green leaves.

Rub them on yourself. Rub them where no one will see.

He rubbed the leaves on his testicles. They felt cool at first like mint. They then began to itch. His scrotum was on fire. He kept rubbing. His genitals still felt distant from himself.

Her green eyes stared right through him. The leaves began to fall apart. He could feel welts forming on his balls.

Stop it fool. That's enough.

"Yes Earth mother."

Now go. Go stop this man. Stop him from hurting my eggs.

Her angry face withered away and The Naked Man in the Forest was all alone again.

The Otherself whispered to him that he needed to do something about the poison ivy on his balls before the acid completely wore off.

35

Simmons and Rios were in a conference room with Brooks looking at surveillance video from the Super Center robbery. Rios removed a DVD from the player and put another one in the tray.

"This camera is all the way at the other end of the store. Look at this woman and her little girl here." Rios pointed to figures in the cereal section.

The mother pushed the cart down the row then reached up to get a box. Suddenly her nostrils flared then her face changed expression. She turned her head towards the center of the store and starts to run. The woman's daughter looked confused then followed her mother a few steps. Just like her mother, her expression changed and she started to run in the same direction.

"Tell me what's happening here?" asked Rios. "That's not somebody who heard a disturbance then decided to check it out. That's somebody who smells something, like a dog getting a scent, then goes to chase after it leaving her child behind."

Brooks waved his hand. "What are you asking for Rios? When we catch him we can look for an explanation."

Simmons spoke up, "That's the problem Brooks. Would you want to be caught by us if that's what happens when we get near you?"

"No one wants to get caught. But its our job to see that they are. We can handle it like professionals," replied Brooks.

Simmons pointed to another DVD. Rios put it into the player. The screen showed the sheriff's deputy walking through the far entrance. He took three steps in before his face took on the same contortion as everyone else and started running towards the other exit.

Rios put in another DVD. This one showed a view looking down the aisle along the front end of the store. Mitchell was running towards the camera throwing bags of marbles on to the floor. Rios paused the video.

"Marbles. The guy has a baseball bat and he's throwing marbles on the ground like a kid trying to ruin a parade. This is a person who just wants to get away from people," said Rios. "But look at them." Rios pointed to the faces of the people chasing Mitchell and the animal-like way they held out their hands to claw at him.

Simmons spoke up, "I showed some photos to my husband last night after he got off from the pathology department at the hospital. I didn't tell him what they were from. I just showed him some stills of people's faces and posture, without any context. Besides making reference to zombies, his opinion was that these people were on something. Something that was giving them a bad trip."

Brooks shook his head. "We already tested for that. Nothing."

"Nothing we know to look for," replied Simmons.

Brooks finally realized that Simmons and Rios had put a lot more work into their questions and were trying to sell him on something. "Level with me." He looked at Simmons. He knew the crafty way she would get people to reach conclusions she already had.

Simmons gave Rios a glance then looked back at Brooks. "Something else is going on here. We don't think our culprit is a man or these people. We think there could be some kind of chemical agent that Roberts was exposed to. Something that's causing this reaction."

"We had Homeland Security personnel on the scene. They haven't said anything like that," said Brooks.

Simmons shook her head, "Would they know? What if they only suspected? Would they tell us?"

Brooks leaned back. "I can tell you this, they're about to release a statement. They're going to call it 'contagious hysteria'."

"It's contagious alright," interjected Rios. "But this isn't hysteria. This isn't some kind of Pokemon thing or a Justin Bieber sighting." Rios pointed back at the screen. "Those people weren't reacting to anything they saw or heard."

"Whatever," said Brooks. "Once we catch him we can find out."

"Who ever catches him is going to kill him." replied Simmons.

Brooks shook his head. "I think trained law enforcement professionals are going to handle this differently than average people."

Rios stood up and pointed a finger at the image of the deputy frozen on the screen. His face was in a snarl and his hands were reaching out trying to claw Mitchell. "Like that guy?"

Brooks checked his watch. "So what are you guys asking for? That we let him go?"

"Of course not," said Simmons. "We need to make sure that who ever apprehends Roberts takes the proper precautions. If there is something chemical or biological then we can't have people interacting with him without the right kind of protective gear. We also need to make sure that we have the proper facility to put him into. We certainly can't put him in the county lock up." She paused to think about the consequences of that. "That could be disastrous."

Brooks held his hands up in surrender. "Okay. I'll speak with our Homeland Security liaison about your concerns. If they think its necessary, there are precautions they can take."

There was a knock at the door. The Detective Oliver entered.

"Guess what genius forgot to turn his phone off after he made his little YouTube video?"

Brooks looked up. "You got a trace?"

The detective nodded. "Yup. I used the warrant to get into his personal account and activate the GPS. He's in Martin County headed North near the ocean."

"We need to call them," said Brooks.

"Already did," said Oliver. "They're sending out their chopper and SWAT. I gave them the account info so they could track them from the air."

Simmons looked at Brooks. "You need to tell them."

"Fine. Fine. I'll let them know to be cautious," he said reluctantly. "We can call them from the car."

36

When the Martin County Sheriff's department was informed Mitchell Roberts was in their jurisdiction they locked down the highways within minutes.

Police cars were dispatched to all of the major intersections. A fleet of marked cars came in from the south while another fleet came in from the north on the main highway, US 1. Each time they passed a major artery the last car in line would pull off to block traffic.

The sheriff's department aviation unit dispatched an American Eurocopter AS350 with a map tracking system to zero in on the location of Mitchell. It flew down the Intracoastal waterway just above the tree tops as a deputy at a console plugged in tracking information. As the system got a lock on the GPS signal he gave the pilot and deputies on the ground minute-by-minute directions.

"Heading north bound on US 1," said the deputy. He zoomed into the map. "Heading towards route 401."

"Going to intercept," called the pilot. He turned the stick to the left and flew the helicopter over the highway at over 100 miles per hour.

The deputy in the back of the chopper looked at his console then at a video screen showing the ground below. There were a handful of cars on the highway, but few clusters. He clicked a button and the mapping system superimposed what the camera underneath saw and the tracking point from the phone.

"3 miles and closing," said the deputy. "Still heading northbound towards 401."

Five sheriff's cars heading south bound crossed the route 401 intersection and created a barricade with their cars. Two deputies ran out in front of the wall their vehicles made and threw a metal track across the highway. If the car kept going it would rip the tires to shreds making it a very short chase.

The deputy on board the mapping console watched has the helicopter headed right over the blip. "Bingo," he shouted over the microphone. "Looks like last night was just a test run."

The pilot swung the helicopter in a wide arc. He turned on the bullhorn and spoke. "Driver of the tractor trailer truck, pull over and turn off your engine."

The truck came to a screeching halt. The helicopter pilot lowered the helicopter so that he was almost eye level with the driver. Diesel exhaust stopped spewing from the mufflers.

"Throw your keys out the window."

There was a pause then a key ring flew onto the street in front of the cab.

"Place you hands against the front windshield," instructed the pilot.

The driver placed the palms of his hands against the window.

Three northbound police cars caught up with the rig. Two cars pulled in front of it while the third guarded the rear, boxing the truck and trailer in.

Two deputies ran over to the truck cab with their guns drawn. One pulled the door open while the other kept his gun pointed through the window at the driver.

The truck driver was pulled out of the cab and asked to lay down flat. He was quickly handcuffed and searched. Finally he was rolled over.

The arresting deputy looked at a printout and back at the man. "What's your name?"

"Michael Holland," said the scared 42 year-old.

Then deputy spoke into his radio. "The driver isn't our suspect."

The deputy on the circling helicopter looked at the overlay on the computer screen. "The signal is coming from within the truck."

The arresting deputy looked down at Holland. "We have probable cause to search your truck. Do you have the key to open it?"

The man looked up at him. "No. Of course not. You have to ask the Postmaster for the key."

Twenty minutes later a police escort brought the nearest United States Postmaster with a key to unlock the trailer. When Simmons and Rios arrived the sheriff's deputies were going through bins of mail in the middle of the highway under the Postmaster's supervision.

"I can tell you how this is going to end," said Simmons as she watched from the driver's side of her SUV.

"You think we should tell them what we told Brooks?" asked Rios.

"Yeah, but it's not going to matter right now."

The deputy from the pursuit helicopter was walking around with a laptop with a 3G connection. He moved towards one of the bins and pointed it out. Two deputies ran over and turned it over spilling a pile of mail on to the highway.

The deputies quickly sorted the mail into a pile of letters and a pile of packages. A bomb tech walked over with a handheld scanner and waved it over the packages. He pulled three from the pile and set them on the highway.

The deputies cleared away the other mail while the bins were loaded back into the truck.

A bomb sniffing dog was brought over to inspect the packages. He sniffed at them then looked up bored. The dog was walked back to his car.

The county Chief of Detectives walked over and looked at the packages. He picked up one and walked it back to where Brooks and several other higher-ups had parked their cars. He set it on the hood of an SUV.

Simmons and Rios walked over to get a look as a technician with rubber gloves slit open the small box. He reached inside and pulled out Mitchell's iPhone. The lock screen had a screen grab of a page from the note pad app as its background image.

The technician held out the iPhone for everyone to see what the note said.

'When I think you're serious about helping me I'll send up three flares so you can find me. Until then, no surrender. Mitch.'

37

After helicopter footage of sheriff's deputies searching through mail on the highway aired on FOX, CNN and MSBNC, another shoe dropped. Someone had leaked footage of the mall incident and the Super Center robbery to the major networks. Although the footage was being held for release by the city police department, it had passed around so many different agencies, there was nowhere to point a finger.

To the general public and news pundits, Mitchell's claims that something odd was happening to him gained much more credibility when they could see for themselves how strangely people behaved in the footage.

The 'contagious hysteria' meme was quickly dropped. Talk shows began using terms like 'rage virus' and 'zombie gas'. Mitchell had gone from being called a public menace to a one man WMD.

Baylor got the news in the middle of a conference with Homeland Security's South Florida Emergency Response Co-ordinator. He went through the roof. He left the room to make a phone call.

"I thought I asked you to keep the footage from being released!" he shouted at the man on the other end of the phone.

"We tried. But there were too many copies out there. It was going to happen sooner or later," said the man.

"Damn it. I wanted this contained before this got out."

"Wanted what contained, Baylor? Is this one of your projects?" asked the man.

"No. Of course not." Baylor hesitated. "From what we've seen in our lab we have reason to believe that this may be the work of a foreign power."

"When did you learn this?"

"Twenty minutes ago. I was just sent the results from our blood work on the mall victims. We found evidence of an aerosol in the lungs that was used as a dispersant," Baylor lied through his teeth.

"How do you want to proceed?"

Baylor ran his fingers through his hair. He needed a way to call the shots on the matter behind the scenes. If it was still handled by local authorities he wouldn't have as much influence. If it went to a federal level he had the connections to make sure that he and his group wouldn't be in the line of fire. "We need to elevate this to a Federal matter."

"On what basis?" asked the man.

"On the belief that this man has in his possession a chemical agent that induces panic. Most likely supplied by a foreign power or terrorist group."

Baylor had thought about saying that he actually believe that Roberts was infected with a form of weaponized Mongolian Flu, but that was too close to what the actual truth was. If he could get Roberts into custody, the right custody, he wouldn't have to worry about suspicion falling onto project Great Wall.

"You think this man is a terrorist?"

Baylor paused. Saying 'yes' brought in a whole new
set of problems. The FBI and CIA would start digging
around for any kind of connection between Roberts and
foreign groups. A connection Baylor knew didn't exist. If
Roberts had been Muslim and traveled overseas in the
last ten years, any kind of connection could be made.
Unfortunately, he was a white man with no strong
religious beliefs. If any of the Aryan supremacist groups
could put together something more sophisticated than a
fertilizer bomb, he might be able to make a compelling
case for Mitchell being part of one of them. but sadly no,
he thought.

"Do you think this man is a terrorist?" asked the voice
again.

"No, I don't think he's willingly part of any terror
groups." Baylor thought briefly about saying Mitchell
was acting alone, but knew that wouldn't wash. A
weaponized version of Mongolian Flu wasn't a kitchen
table project. "I think he may unwittingly or under the
threat of coercion is carrying a dispersant on his person."

Baylor thought of the footage he'd seen. In the mall he
had on a backpack. In the Super Center he was wearing a
large coat. The idea that Mitchell had a device on him
that sprayed a chemical agent was starting to gain traction
in his mind.

"Do we need to apply containment to the all of the
locations where the dispersant was used?" asked the
voice.

Containment meant sealing the mall, the Super Center
and everywhere else Mitchell had been. It also meant
other agencies looking for evidence of the dispersant. A

dispersant that Baylor only half believed could actually exist.

Saying 'no' would attract suspicion that he knew more than he let on. He decided to hedge his bet.

"Although we think the agent would most likely break down in direct contact with oxygen and UV light in the open air, we think it's prudent to seal the affected areas," said Baylor. This was going to cause a bigger lock down than the anthrax scares from a decade back.

"Alright," said the voice. "I'll go across the hall and inform the Vice President."

The line went dead. Baylor stepped out of the empty office where he had been talking on his cell phone and looked down the hallway of the Homeland Security building as people went about their work. He'd just manufactured an entire account about a WMD. Charitably he could say that he misinterpreted the information he had. But there were no domestic or foreign intelligence agencies he could point out and say that they'd reached the same conclusion as he had.

There were no dissident scientists claiming it existed. He didn't even have a madman dictator to single out. When the search for a physical WMD came up short, everyone would look to him for an explanation.

It would be much better if they found something. He walked back into the empty office and made another call.

The line made a click as it was routed through a secure connection.

"Hello," a precise and almost eloquent voice answered.

"Mr. Lewis, I have another favor to ask," said Baylor.

"Is this a personal favor?" asked the voice using 'personal' as a code word for something else.

"No. I need to get a gift for someone. I'll have a friend supply the bow."

An hour after Baylor got off the phone the South Florida Director of Homeland Security and the FBI's District Supervisor called a press conference.

They announced that Mitchell Roberts was now believed to be in contact with a dangerous chemical agent and that he shouldn't be approached by local authorities without proper protective gear. They explained that the Park Square Mall was going to remain closed until further notice and that the Super Center was going to be placed under containment while the FBI conducted their investigation.

Despite the fact that they carefully avoided using the term WMD or terrorist, the press had no such restraint. The largest manhunt in the nation's history began with Mitchell Roberts at the center of it.

38

After driving all night Mitchell arrived at the small island in the Intracoastal before dawn. He'd pulled the boat as far ashore as he could and covered it with palm fronds and branches. From just a few feet away the boat blended into the thick brush.

The island was a one acre dense tangle of mangrove trees, palm trees and various shrubs. To move more than a few feet required climbing over and stepping through a labyrinth of vegetation. Inside there he felt safe. He would be able to hear anyone coming and have time to move away from them as the island slowed them down.

His camp was a green tarp he'd stolen from the Super Center laid across the ground. That morning he'd used a life preserver from the boat as a pillow, wrapped part of the tarp over himself like a blanket and slept.

The island was filled with a hundred different sounds from small insects to larger things rooting around. Despite the surroundings, the exhaustion and stress washed over him and he slept for six hours.

He awoke to the sound of something moving through the brush near his encampment. His body jerked upright while his hand grabbed the hilt of the baseball bat he'd slept next to all night.

The masked face of a raccoon looked back at Mitchell trying to figure out what he was doing on his private domain.

"Sorry pal," said Mitchell. "You're going to have a guest for a little while."

The raccoon seemed placated enough with the answer to wander off. Mitchell pulled an energy bar from from the duffle bag and had a quick breakfast then turned on his radio to listen to the news.

His original plan was to keep going up the Intracoastal during the day when all the other boat traffic was on the water and make camp at night. He'd figured that hiding in plain sight was better then getting caught by Marine Patrol alone at night.

After driving the boat that night he'd seen that there was more traffic than he'd expected late at night and early into the morning as different boats headed out to go fishing or came back from late night expeditions. Traveling by night seemed like a better option. He could run without his running lights and stick close to shore by the small islands that dotted the waterway and be invisible to anybody looking out across the water.

He was certain that Marine Patrol had night vision and could spot a small boat trying to go by unnoticed. But seeing him meant looking for him in the first place. As far as he knew, nobody had made the connection between him and a missing boat.

Until the event with the Postal Service truck made news, the big talk was still on the events of the mall, the tractor-trailer truck crash and his YouTube video. Everyone seemed very confused by what was going on.

Mitchell didn't fit into anyone's profile of a mass murderer or master criminal. The YouTube video increased demand from the media that authorities release the surveillance videos. People were having a hard time trying to understand what it was that Mitchell was supposed to have done.

His heart skipped a beat when he heard a reporter interrupt a discussion with a legal expert to say that they'd gotten word that authorities had pinned Mitchell down and were about to make an arrest. When Mitchell heard a helicopter fly over ahead he dropped the radio and scrambled through the brush to look out on to the waterway.

All he could see were a couple of leisure craft. The helicopter blew right by the island and kept heading north. A half hour later the news reported that police had stopped a tractor trailer truck on the highway and were searching it. Mitchell hadn't realized how closely the path of the mailed iPhone would match his. He'd addressed it to the FBI headquarters in Quantico, Virginia, for lack of a better idea.

Mailing it seemed like a better way to put some distance between himself and the phone. The onscreen note about using three flares to signal them was an afterthought when he realized that without the phone he'd have no way to tell police he was ready to surrender.

Mitchell knew that it was only a matter of time before they caught up with him. The best he could hope for was to make sure that when they did, they understood that something was wrong with him and took the right measures to make sure nothing bad happened to him.

The police told news agencies that the phone had a note on it but left out the part about three flares to avoid having pranksters send them on false leads. Interesting and frustrating to Mitchell was that they were calling his request for medical containment a 'demand' like he was a terrorist asking that they let his friends in prison go free.

From what he could make of the coverage of the mail truck incident, it didn't sound like the arresting police were using protective gear of any kind. He was certain that if he had been driving the truck or hiding in the back he'd be dead by now.

News reports were still calling it 'contagious hysteria' until the surveillance video footage was scrutinized. A retired Army chemical and biological weapons expert speaking on Fox News pointed out the reactions of people who didn't have Mitchell in the line of sight. The idea that there was something actually causing people to behave this way besides Mitchell's actions was gaining traction.

When the FBI and DHS held their press conference Mitchell felt good to hear them finally say they thought there might be some kind of chemical agent involved. The idea that he had something on him was ridiculous. Although in a fit of paranoia he searched through the duffle bag and his backpack again for anything strange, he of course came up short. Mitchell was certain that when he surrendered the authorities would see that something was wrong with him and then they'd understand. He was one of the few people, if any, that was relieved to find out that he'd gone from a local fugitive to the target of a Federal manhunt.

To Mitchell that meant agencies like the FBI and Center for Disease Control taking what happened more seriously than a local police department that wanted to charge him for shouting 'fire' in a crowded movie theater.

Mitchell began planning how he would surrender. He wanted to wait another day to make sure that the authorities had the right precautions on place. In Mitchell's mind that meant men wearing hazardous material suits and some kind of hermetically sealed chamber in the back of a truck where they could take him to a special hospital and find out what was wrong.

He was ready to be treated like a patient and not a criminal. As soon as he knew they were going to do that he'd walk right into their hands. Mitchell was confident everyone would understand his actions once they could see for themselves what was going on.

39

Instead of moving on, Mitchell decided to stay put on the island until he had reason to believe he could surrender without harm. He listened to news reports through out the day waiting for information indicating it would be safe to turn himself in.

Listening to Rookman's show that night gave him second thoughts.

Rookman's familiar theme music began and his gravelly voice started talking. "Well folks, what an interesting turn of events out there. Public Enemy Number One, our own little Mad Mitch is now accused of being a one man weapon of mass destruction.'

'Our own expert on these kinds of things, Dr. Lovestrange, not his real name, is with us on the line from his secret location. Doctor, what do you make of all this?"

Lovestrange spoke in his usual calm voice, "Well Rookman, I have to say one thing. Don't believe it. There's something else going on here. As you know, there's the story they know and the story they want you to know."

Rookman replied, "How do you mean? What they've said sounds pretty scary. They've tented up a shopping mall like an exterminator tent and they're wrapping the

Super Center in plastic. If they're not trying to cause a panic, they've failed."

"Then explain the logic to me here." said Doctor Lovestrange. The government is saying that Mitchell has come in contact with some kind of chemical agent that is making people go crazy. Okay. Here are two problems with what they're saying. First, how come Mitchell hasn't gone crazy? Everything I've seen indicates a very sane, rational man trying to run from people pursuing him. Second, what's the logic in creating a WMD that makes people want to kill the person using it? That gives suicide bomber a whole new definition."

"Playing devil's advocate," said Rookman. "What if Mitchell has been given some kind of antidote to this, and the fact that people were attacking him wasn't the intended effect?"

"Possible," said Lovestrange. "It sounds like a very bad plan. It also brings up another set of questions. Who made this? Everything we worry about terrorists getting a hold of is smaller versions of stuff we have like nukes and anthrax. An agent like this is technically way beyond their capabilities and probably most governments. It's also I might add illegal under International laws and treaties."

"So who made this?" asked Rookman.

"Certainly not Mitchell acting alone. Three countries have the expertise and weapons program to make something like this, Russia, China and the United States. Is Russia or China going to hand over one of their most state of the art chemical weapons to some radio host to spray in a shopping mall? Why?"

"Maybe it was a test run," said Rookman.

"You don't test run chemical warfare agents you want to keep a secret inside a foreign country."

"How do you test them?" asked Rookman already knowing the answer.

"You do it on your own people," said Lovestrange.

"Wait up a minute Doc, you don't mean to say our own United States government would use its own citizens to test something like this?" Rookman exaggerated his disbelief knowing full well how Lovestrange would respond.

"The CIA exposed subway passengers to an aerosol based LSD in the 1950s. In the 60's and 70's we conducted tests to see how quickly bacteria could spread in urban environments. This is nothing new."

"That was then Doc. We exposed all of that and put a stop to it."

"Did we Rookman? We did those things when we were acting of fear from the cold war. After 9/11 we learned a new kind of fear. A whole generation of brilliant minds started imagining all of the scary things that bad people could do to using genetic engineering, computer viruses, nanotechnology and a thousand other technologies.'

'Once you start thinking about that stuff you can't stop wondering what the other guy has got. Your biggest fear is getting hit by something you don't understand. And there's only one way to try to understand these kinds of things. The first atomic bomb didn't blow up in Hiroshima, Japan. It was detonated in the middle of New Mexico in the United States. That next day a radioactive cloud covered half the state and the public was none the wiser until we dropped the bomb on Japan."

"Are you saying this was an intentional test of a weapon by our own government?" asked Rookman.

"Not a weapon in the traditional sense. This isn't some kind of device used to spray a crowd with crazy gas. The government said 'chemical' agent. Which implies a device to distribute it. There is no device. Because this isn't a chemical. It's a life form. We're looking at a genetically engineered bacteria or a virus that's causing this. Mitchell is just patient zero."

"But why didn't effect him?" asked Rookman.

"I don't know. In some diseases you have carriers. Maybe he's just a carrier for it. Somewhere he got accidentally exposed to it. Maybe he was intentionally exposed and the people behind this wanted to see what would happen if they sent him into a crowded population." Lovestrange paused. "What better way to get rid of a dictator then to have the whole world watch as his people tear him apart on live television."

Rookman let out a whistle. "That's some serious stuff Doctor. So what advice do you have for our boy out there?"

"Keep you head down and make sure when you're caught its by the right people."

"And who might that be?" asked Rookman

"Not the ones who did this. If they get a hold of Mitchell we're only going to hear one side of the story because Mitchell is either going to vanish down some dark hole or be killed in a fake escape attempt."

"Mitch, if you're out there, trust no one. Only come in when you think it's safe. If you think they're not being straight with you, run brother. Run."

40

Up until Rookman's show the thought had never entered Mitchell's mind that he was a pawn in some kind of plot. The paranoid yet sane sounding Doctor Lovestrange had him even more worried.

What if he was infected with some kind of secret government experimental virus, he wondered. The scenario Lovestrange laid out about using it to kill a dictator made a lot of sense to him. Was he really just some kind of guinea pig?

Mitchell thought about when he had been sick for the past two weeks. Was that an incubation period? Did someone sneak something into the food in his apartment? His mind kept racing with questions.

The idea of surrendering no longer sounded as appealing to him. Could he trust the people he surrendered to if they were the same people who did this to him? *Who could he trust?*

His best chance was to make himself look as innocent as possible. He needed to do whatever he could to make sure that in the public's eye he was a victim and not someone who was part of a terrorist plot.

Mitchell decided that when he surrendered he needed to have an escape route. His surrender point would also be the most public place he would be. He needed to make sure that the things they were going to accuse him of wouldn't hold up in the public's eyes.

He made his way through the tangled brush in the darkness and out to his boat. He pulled off the palm leaves he'd covered it with and pushed the boat back into the water.

Mitch pulled the starter cord and drove the boat five miles back to a spot he'd seen earlier that morning.

It was a medium-sized marina catering mostly to luxury yachts. Several of them had 'for sale' signs on them. A sign of the Florida economy.

One of the things he'd learned when he worked in a marina was that when an owner tried to put a boat up for sale after the first month they let go of any crew they had to save costs. Large vessels weren't as much of a target for theft because it took to long to get them out to sea.

There was one noteworthy exception. Mitchell had heard of a man and a wife who managed to get a boat all the way to the Bahamas by taking the time to change the name of the boat on the stern and the registration to a similar boat. When Marine Patrol and the Coast Guard saw a vessel that matched the description of the stolen one, they'd run the name and registration and come back with a boat that wasn't reported missing.

The biggest problem was fuel. Any boat he found wasn't likely to have enough on board to get very far. That wasn't going to be a problem for Mitchell. He didn't need to go too far with the boat.

Mitch drove his little boat into the harbor and started looking at the different boats. He drove by one 200 foot yacht that still had its lights on. It was obviously occupied, and not the ideal boat for Mitchell, but it gave him an idea.

He pulled out the iPod he'd stolen and turned it on. Sure enough, the yacht had an an open WiFi connection. Mitch pulled up a web page showing a list of all the yachts and powerboats in the area that were up for sale along with all of their features.

Originally he thought about just stealing a luxury yacht and waiting for SWAT to storm the boat if the surrender didn't go right. Then he had another idea. Why not just get a large power boat instead? He'd never be able to outrun the full force of the federal government, but he could at least buy some time.

Mitch began looking up listings for fast boats. The kind Scarface would want to use. One in particular caught his eye. It was a model that wasn't too obscure and would be easy to mark up as another vessel if he could get the tools to do it. What really stood out was a piece of equipment that it came with. *Mitch had to have it.*

Mitch put the iPod away and patrolled the marina until he found the vessel. The vessel had "Highlander" written across the stern. It was a 40 foot Donzi.

He climbed over the transom and lifted the covering that was buttoned over the cockpit area. He slid underneath. There was a row of seats in back and two chairs in front. The boat was intended for two things; scuba diving and going really fast. It was the kind of boat you'd take for an overnight diving trip to the Bahamas or the Keys to bring back lobster or a hundred kilos of cocaine.

The control console was covered with a metal sheet that was locked into place with a thick lock. The entrance to the main cabin had a similar lock. Mitchell could see there was no way he was going to be able to use his tire iron to pry the locks off. He was also certain he wasn't going to find a spare key hidden on the deck.

If he could get past the lock on the cabin he was sure he'd be able to get inside and get the lock for the console and the key for the ignition. He looked at the lock on the cabin again. Bolt cutters wouldn't do it. He'd need a power tool.

Mitchell peeked out under the covering and looked at the dock in front of the boat. He could see a power outlet. He needed a metal grinder. He took out the iPod and opened up the WiFi panel. He was still getting signal from the large yacht. Mitch pulled up a list of nearby Super Centers and made a mental shopping list.

41

His last raid had been an act of improvisation. He'd been able to outrun the old greeter to get to where he needed and get some of the things he wanted. Items like the paintball gun and a few other things were useless to him in the store that prior night while still in their packages.

Mitchell had come to realize that when people raged out and went homicidal, they lost whatever kind of control that made them rational and capable of planning. He hadn't seen anyone throw punches or try any kind of stylized fighting technique. This gave him some kind of advantage. He could predict how they'd come at him--at least he thought he could.

While he now had more insight and preparation to help him, he was going to need a little more than a paintball gun and pepper spray. This store had a police car parked on the curb out front--a precaution that was undoubtedly influenced by the previous night's raid in the store 40 miles to the south.

Mitchell looked at the car from a row of hedges that faced the store. He contemplated walking the three blocks back to where he'd parked his john boat in a canal and making other plans. The cop car meant at least one armed police officer, maybe more.

"Fuck me." said Mitchell.

He couldn't get the idea out of his head that bad things only happened to him when he was ashore.

The previous night he'd been lucky with the deputy who got caught off guard. This time there was someone waiting for him.

There were a few cars in the parking lot. Nothing screamed unmarked police car. Mitchell pulled the scanner from his pocket and turned it to the frequency he found on RadioReference.com. He listened for a half hour while he watched the parking lot. He heard various dispatches to different areas of the city but nothing that sounded like it was near him.

If there was some kind of covert surveillance going on it was likely they were using scrambled frequencies. The scanner could only tell him what was going out on public frequencies. If the cop parked in front of the store called for more units he could hear that. The scanner could also tell him where the dispatcher was trying to coordinate police cars to find him if a call went in.

Mitch decided the car was there as a deterrent and not as part of a stake-out. There were just too many Super Centers in South Florida for that to be practical. Other than the cop inside the car, it wasn't likely there was a police presence. Of course, one cop was enough to deal with.

His safest bet was to take the police officer out of the picture. If he walked near the car he ran the risk of the officer raging out and trying to kill him or possibly shooting him. If he was spotted from too far away, the officer was likely to call it in. Since Mitchell was the target of the largest manhunt in the nation's history, it was easy to assume that there were a lot more police out that night than usual. He could expect backup to arrive on the scene very quickly.

He needed a distraction that would let him get into the store unnoticed. The problem then was getting past the inevitable greeters, which if the store had any sense, weren't going to be as feeble as they were the night before.

The best approach would be to walk to the main entrance as casually as he could and enter in plain sight of the police officer. From there he'd have to take care of the greeter and run into the store to get what he needed and then exit through the back.

Without any fellow shoppers trying to kill him he could probably be in and out in under two minutes. With any luck he could be almost back to the boat before the police knew he was there. Counting on luck wasn't something he planned on doing. He'd need to figure out some way to create some.

Mitchell rehearsed where he needed to go and walked across the parking lot to the entrance. He used an earbud to listen to the scanner in his back pocket under his jacket. The paintball gun was tucked into his waistband along with a can of pepper spray. He was in full-on Mitch mode.

He reached the last row of cars before crossing the road in front of the store. Through the glass doors he could see a man about his height with a stocky build acting as the greeter. Mitch began to bring his hand towards the can of mace. As the doors whisked open he shot a glance into the police car. It was empty. That wasn't good.

The doors opened and the greeter looked at him. Mitch gave him a nod. The greeter was halfway into returning the nod when his face changed. Mitch pulled the pepper spray out with his right hand and shot him in the face with a blast. "Sorry bud."

The greeter screamed then wiped instinctively at his eyes. His arms lashed out trying to find him. Mitch ducked under his grasp and ran past him into the store.

A young man in his teens with a shaved head and a pierced lip looked out from the checkout counter and came towards him. Mitch switched the pepper spray into his left hand and pulled out the paintball gun. He fired two balls into the young man's face covering his eyes with paint.

The cashier, a thin woman with a long ponytail, jumped up on the counter and snarled. Mitch shot her once in the face before she leaped at him. The paintball didn't faze her. He shot her in the eyes with the pepper spray and continued running in to the store. She fell on her side knocking over a candy rack and screamed.

Where was the police officer? This had Mitchell worried. If the cop saw him from far enough away and told him to freeze, he could drop him with one bullet if Mitchell tried to run. While the rage made people more deadly with their own bodies at short range, they seemed to lose all mechanical aptitude for things like door handles and guns.

Mitch ran towards the hardware department. As he ran past rows of shelves he shot a quick glance for other shoppers and to look for the cop. Not that he wanted to run into him, he just needed to know where he was.

Mitch reached the hardware section and grabbed a bucket to throw stuff into. The paint he needed was behind glass. Mitch placed the pepper spray and paintball gun into the bucket and picked up a ladder. He smashed the front of the case sending sharp glass shards every where. He grabbed a few different colors including the one he needed. He ran down another aisle and found an angle grinder. Mitchell impulsively reached for the cheapest one before Mitch reminded himself that price really wasn't an option at that point in time.

He ran to another aisle and grabbed an extension cord. He poked his head into the main aisle and saw the greeter, the pierced teenager and the cashier running in his direction. It was clear that they couldn't see where they were going but something else, most likely Mitchell's scent, was driving them forward.

Mitch ran back the opposite way and took the aisle farthest from them. He was about to go into the boating section to grab letters for the power boat he was going to steal, then froze. He cursed himself for being stupid. If he grabbed boat letters they'd know that night what he was up to. There would be police swarming every marina as soon as they saw the surveillance video and looked at what he stole.

He needed to think of something else to use that wouldn't be obvious. He ran back down the aisle he just came from and ran face first into the stocky greeter. The man's thick fingers grabbed him by the neck. Mitch kicked him in the balls as hard as he could. The greeter didn't flinch.

The teenager with the piercing lunged at Mitchell grabbing him around the waist. The three of them fell to the ground. Mitch managed to knee the teenager in the chin and kicked him in the chest sending him backwards.

The greeter was still choking Mitchell and bringing his teeth in to bite him. Mitch's hands grabbed at the shelves trying to find something to use as a weapon. He felt a heavy box and grabbed it. He slammed it into the side of the greeter's face as hard as he could. The greeter didn't relent. Mitch hit him again just above his eye splitting it open. Blood poured down his face but he didn't stop.

Mitch brought his knees up to his chest and kicked out at the man. He kept his legs pressed against the other man and kept shoving. He finally slipped out of his grasp.

Mitch scrambled backwards on the floor on his backside and looked for something else to use as a weapon. The teenager crawled towards Mitchell's foot. Mitch kicked him in the face.

The greeter jumped at Mitchell again. This time Mitch pulled himself to the side by grabbing the edge of a shelf. The man hit the tile next to him. Mitch used his free hand on the shelf to pull himself up. As he leaned on it, the shelf came loose and fell on top of the greeter sending a pile of toolboxes on him.

That wasn't going to stop him. Mitch looked at the box in his hand, it was for a kitchen fire extinguisher. Mitch pulled it out of the box and yanked the safety free. He sprayed the other men directly in their faces covering them in a cloud of white powder.

Mitch found his bucket of stolen merchandise and ran to another section. He found some rolls of black electrical tape and shoved them into his bucket. He stepped out into the aisle and saw the ponytailed cashier approaching. Mitch pulled out the paintball gun and shot her twice in the face and ran back to the automotive section. Five more people were coming from the other side of the store. They were 30 yards away and gaining.

Mitch looked around for another weapon. There was a stack of motor oil to his left. He set down his bucket and pulled the fish knife from his waistband. He started stabbing holes in cans and throwing them between himself and the people running at him. A heavy man wearing a football jersey ran over one of the cans and his heel slipped on the oil. He lost his balance and pulled down an display of 2-liter soda bottles with him. A tall stock clerk jumped over the oil spill and came charging at Mitchell.

Mitch grabbed a can from the display and just hurled it at his head. The can hit the man in the cheek, but he kept running. Mitch threw another can at his head and missed. Desperate, Mitch slid the whole display of motor oil on to the ground covering the closing gap between them. The man's foot slipped on one of the cans and his face slammed into the pile with so much force a can popped open spewing oil like blood splatter.

Mitch could see other people getting closer. He wouldn't be able to fight them all off. He ran towards a pair of double doors in the back of the store.

He entered a long storeroom. He felt a shudder as he remembered what happened the day before in the department store. Mitch wanted to block the doors but didn't see anything to use so he ran down the aisle pulling large boxes onto the floor behind him.

Halfway to the exit he could hear the double doors open behind him. His pursuers struggled through the boxes. To Mitch's right he saw a fire axe and a fire hose. He reached for the axe then noticed an electrical power box. Mitch set down his bucket and used two hands to slam the axe into the cable above the power box.

The lights went off. He could hear footsteps and snarling getting closer. *Fuck.* Mitchell realized that they didn't need sound to find him. They could still follow his scent. He was blind. They weren't.

Mitchell held the axe ready to slam it into anything that came close.

Damn it! He knew hitting someone with the blade would kill them. Self defense or not, that would be murder. Mitchell turned the axe around so the blade was under his hand. He'd use it like a club, but not a bladed weapon. Concussions were fair game.

Mitchell heard a box crunch near him. He swung into the dark and felt the handle connect. Something fell backwards. He heard something to his right. He swung again. He heard a crack and felt a spray of blood hit his face and open mouth. He spat it out.

Something grabbed his ankle. Mitchell brought his foot up and slammed down on a hand. He could feel the bones crunch under his heel. He felt around and grabbed the bucket.

Mitchell slid around the back wall periodically jabbing the axe handle into the darkness. He felt it connect again.

Something clicked behind him. He stopped for a moment then realized it was the back exit. Mitchell bolted through it and almost dropped the axe. There was a police car in back of the store.

Mitchell froze until he heard footsteps behind him. He shoved the door closed. Fists slammed against it from the other side. Mitch picked up the axe and slammed it into the middle of the door just below waist height. He ignored the cop car as he tried to shut the door.

The axe lodged in a wedge shaped gash. Mitch pushed down on the end of the handle until it hit the ground. Hands behind the door found the release and pushed the door open. The axe slid backwards a few inches then came to a stop when it hit the metal railing that lined the walkway behind the door.

Mitch looked over at the second cop car. It had to have been empty. Nobody was trying to kill him. He hopped over the railing and landed on the hood. He had the impulse to slash the tires but decided it wasn't worth losing time.

Mitchell took his bucket and ran back towards his boat. He could still hear the dispatchers and police officers on the scanner talking, but nothing about the store. He considered that a good thing. But he was nervous that he hadn't seen the two cops anywhere inside the store.

Mitchell ran two more blocks and found his boat where he left it. He threw his stolen booty into it and kicked off from the canal. He gave the engine a start and headed back to the marina.

On the way back he realized that in fact he had seen the cops. He understood why his nut kick hadn't had any effect. The stocky greeter was one of the cops. When Mitch kicked him in the testicles he probably kicked him where he had his gun hidden. The other cop was probably disguised as one of the stock clerks. Most likely the Hispanic one that kept coming.

He felt good about narrowly averting a close call with the cops and also for not doing permanent damage to the man's balls. No matter how sore Mitchell's throat felt, he knew he couldn't blame the man for trying to kill him. What did make Mitchell upset was the fact that if the cops were waiting for him to show up, how come none of them had any kind of protective gear like a gas mask on them?

For sure if they did, Mitchell would be in custody or dead right now. But if they still weren't taking him seriously, he was even more worried about surrendering.

For all the effort he just went through and the bruises on his neck and rest of his body, Mitchell was glad he was going to take some extra steps to protect himself when he surrendered. The crazy James Bond shit Mitch had planned probably wouldn't work and would only get him killed, but at least he wouldn't go down easily if all hell broke loose.

42

Mitchell brought his johnboat in back of the Highlander and tied it to the dive platform. He looked around the marina. The lights had gone off in the super-yacht he'd seen earlier. Other than the lights from fixtures on the docks, the only other light came from a small building at the front of the marina. In an upscale marina like this one, he could be certain there was a guard sitting inside in front of a bank of screens that showed different camera angles from around the harbor. It was also a certainty that he would make periodic rounds.

Mitchell debated whether or not to change the boat lettering while he was in the marina. The last thing he wanted to do was try to cut off the lock on the main cabin. The sound might not carry all the way to the guard, but he might hear it when he walked his rounds. Thinking of the truck stop the night before, Mitchell had the added risk of there being people asleep on any of the boats around the marina. When he worked at a marina he met several colorful characters that lived on their boats and yachts year-round.

The lettering could wait until he was safely away from there. He used the WiFi network to look at a Google map of the area to figure out where he wanted to take the boat. Thirty minutes north of him the Intracoastal ran into a bay with a bunch of small islands like the one he had been on. He could take the boat up there and park it behind one of the islands that night and change the name and registration numbers.

Before he took the boat out of the marina, assuming he could get to the key, he needed to look for a GPS antenna. On a boat that cost over $300,000 it was a given the owner would install a security system that would tell him if it had been moved more than fifteen feet from where it was berthed.

On most boats it would be mounted to the canopy. The Highlander didn't have one. It was just an open cockpit. Mitchell climbed under the covering and searched around under the inside of the sides of the boats. He couldn't find anything that felt like a unit, but he found two cables that ran from the cabin to the back of the boat under one of the locked covers.

One of them was probably the antenna for the alarm system. The other was probably an electric cable control for the back hatches. He pulled on them both. One of them let out several feet of slack. That was most likely the GPS cable. Installers tended to roll the slack up into coils and zip-tie them inside of a well in case the owner wants to move the unit. Mitchell cut the cable and looked at the cross section. It looked like what he thought it should. Before leaving the harbor he'd do another pass through the interior and take a look at the electrical system.

With the alarm system out of the way, Mitchell was ready to cut the lock. He gathered all the gear from the john boat and put it under the canopy. He set the flashlight he was using on the floor and put a metal grinding disk in the angle grinder. To keep the lock from flopping around, he taped it to the hatch.

He plugged the extension cord into the grinder then poked his head out from the covering to see if anyone was near. The dock was empty on either side. He couldn't do anything about the security cameras so he just went for it. Mitchell leaned out over the edge and plugged the cord into the outlet on the pylon nearest to the cockpit.

He ducked back down and pulled the covering back in place. With any luck nobody would notice the sound. With slightly less luck, they wouldn't know where the sound came from. Worse-case scenario: he could hop into his john boat and go find another island.

He'd seen an angle grinder used to cut a lock, but had never tried it himself. Mitchell gripped the grinder and held it over the lock. He was about to find out real quick if observing was the same as doing.

He turned the grinder on and touched the spinning disk to the lock. The cockpit was filled with an earsplitting sound while his legs were showered with sparks. Mitchell squinted as they bounced into his face. He cursed himself for not getting eye protection or ear muffs.

After a few seconds of abuse the lock gave up and fell open. The small space under the cover was filled with the smell of burnt metal. Mitchell's ears were ringing but he could still hear the sounds of dispatchers in his ear bud as they responded to the latest crisis he caused at the Super Center.

Mitchell grabbed the lock then jerked his hand away from the heat. Dumb move, he told himself. He used the edge of the jacket he had taken off to pull the lock away. Mitchell opened the hatch on the cabin and shined his flashlight inside.

On his left he could see a panel of green lights that showed the systems that had power. He flashed the light around and saw a sink, the head, and the 'U'-shaped couch at the front that also served as a bed.

Remembering back to the marina he worked at, he pulled up the carpet beneath the hatch. There was a small door that opened to the bottom of the hull. Mitchell reached down there and felt a box the size of a thick wallet. He yanked it free. It came out attached to two cables. He was looking for the key but found the GPS alarm system. He unplugged it and tossed it aside.

Mitchell reached his arm back down again and found a plastic bag wedged between some cables. He pulled it out. Through the plastic he could see several keys. One for the hatches, one for the ignition and another one that unlocked the lockers that held the dive gear and the reason he wanted to steal this boat in particular.

Mitchell made sure the john boat was firmly fastened to the stern then made his preparations to leave. He leaned out and undid the line at the stern. To avoid being seen on the dock, he climbed into the cabin and up a hatch and unfastened the line attached to the bow.

He looked out over the marina. It was still quiet. He paid careful attention to the scanner. On that frequency, Mitchell would have heard a police car dispatched to the marina. It would also let him now if they had alerted the marine patrol.

Mitchell gave the dock a push and sent the bow of the boat in a gentle arc away from the dock. He climbed back into the cockpit and peeled away the front of the covering. He slid the key into the ignition and gave it a turn. The power boat started with a powerful roar.

He looked around the marina but nothing stirred. With his right hand on the throttle and his left on the wheel he reversed the boat and slowly pulled it backwards out of the harbor. When he was clear of the last boat he nudged the throttle forward and slipped the shifter into forward. The vessel moved away from the docks and Mitchell and his latest prize faded into the night in search of a quiet place where he could finish his home improvement project on the boat.

Fifty miles away from Mitchell, the man called Mr. Lewis had his own shop project. He set a briefcase on the hotel room table next to a bag of things he'd purchased at a drug store. The Discovery Channel played in the background.

The briefcase had been with him his whole trip from Virginia on board a private aircraft. Any prying eyes that had a look inside it would have had a lot of questions. But Mr. Lewis wasn't in the business of answering questions. At least not truthfully. His job was to stop people from asking them, or at the very least make them ask the wrong ones.

Mitchell opened up his case and pulled out a few parts and some tools. He took apart a hand-held cutting torch and used the pieces to make something new. He took a can of spray-on sun-tan lotion and drained it into a wastebasket, then used a Dremel tool to saw it neatly in half.

He took a half hour break to watch a documentary on snow leopards, then returned to his work.

He used some epoxy on a few parts then used a drill to make several punctures into the top half of the sun-tan spray canister. Two hours later it was finished. It was obviously a rushed job by his standards. It was put together with the minimal amount of craft needed to make it looked plausible. The device was just a prop for a larger piece of theatre.

With the addition of Mr. Baylor's 'bow' it would look like a plausible device. The CO_2 cylinder attached to the valve from the hand torch led to a small valve that extended outside the thin aluminum cylinder. The valve opened up to a small chamber lined with very thin gauze. Two screws would hold in place a glass cylinder like the kind used to store a blood sample. A third screw, this one a thumbscrew, would break the glass cylinder when it was twisted. The open valve would blow a blast of compressed gas into the chamber and blow whatever was in the glass cylinder into the open air, quickly filling every corner of whatever room it was in.

Prop or not, it was still a lethal device when the 'bow' was added to it. Mr. Lewis wanted to make sure that he was well clear of it after planted it.

He placed his tools back into his case and put his left-over materials into the plastic shopping bag to be disposed of away from the hotel.

He sat down on the bed and sorted through various ID badges and chose the one he wanted to use when he got the call to proceed. The advantage of working for the people that he did was that most of them weren't forgeries.

43

When Baylor arrived at the Super Center, fire engines blocked the streets while hazardous materials teams under the direction of the DHS were in the process of sealing off the entire building. Baylor watched the scene from next to his car as large pieces of plastic were wrapped around the entrances, exits and air handlers.

The misfortunate people who were inside at the time were being held in sealed trailers parked near the garden center while men and women in blue and yellow hazmat suits with different agency names written on them went about the process of containment.

Since Baylor was on the scene in an advisory capacity his access would be determined by the DHS director. Fortunately for him, the director knew of his political connections. Getting access wasn't going to be a problem.

The real challenge was going to be trying to contain the story. He needed to make sure that attention wasn't directed to where he didn't want it. His work for the country was too important for that.

A rental car sedan like his pulled up next to him. A man got out dressed in slacks and a blue polo shirt. Slightly receding hair, middle-aged, he looked like any of the dozen other government functionaries running around the scene. At his waist was a ID badge that said he was with FEMA.

Baylor nodded to Mr. Lewis and went to his trunk. He took out a locked box from a suitcase and opened it. Inside were three small glass cylinders. He carefully removed one and placed it into the folds of a towel he'd put in the trunk for that purpose.

Mr. Lewis took the wrapped object and sat inside his car and finished the assembly of the package. Baylor shielded him from view and watched as he worked. The spray canister was a stroke of genius.

Mr. Lewis finished sealing the glass vial inside then wrapped the canister in the towel. He finally turned to Baylor and spoke.

"You have a preference?" Baylor looked at the Super Center. It would be tempting to have Mr. Lewis plant the canister inside, but too many people had already been on the scene. He also didn't know what kind of coverage the surveillance cameras had. He trusted Mr. Lewis's sleight of hand, but wanted to avoid anything that could even bring up the idea that it was planted.

It was one thing to have the press start spreading conspiracy theories, it was something else to have different federal agencies suspicious. From experience he had no doubt believing that they would accept the narrative he created, no matter how many gaps and leaps of logic, if all the puzzle pieces looked like they were part of the same picture.

"I'm going to tell DHS and the FBI to go out of their way to tell Roberts that they're ready to go along with him. That should bring him in faster. When he surrenders

I want you to put that somewhere on his person or his belongings." He looked at the ID Mr. Lewis was wearing.

"When he surrenders I'll tell them to keep a 500 foot perimeter and to only approach him using hazmat suits. Once you're in a suit you should be able to move about the perimeter freely. Try to put it in a bag or a pocket if possible."

"I can put a strap around it so it'll look like he wore it under his clothes slung from his shoulder," said Mr. Lewis.

Baylor nodded. Mr. Lewis was a practical man. "Very good." Baylor pointed to the towel with the cylinder inside. "Is that a functional device?"

"Functional enough. Do you want me to use it?"

Baylor shook his head. "Good lord no. What's inside of there isn't quite the same as what I think is wrong with Roberts." Baylor paused. "It's not as discriminating."

Baylor wasn't sure what the canister would do if unleashed in a crowded area. The most likely scenario was the Mongolian prison experiment, but this time on hundreds of police and rescue personnel. He decided to stay well clear of the location for the surrender.

Of course, if the material in the glass vial was released, it would solve the problem--at least partially--of the lack of evidence of aerosols at the other locations. If the object found in Robert's possession was shown to cause the rage on a large group of people, it would make a much stronger connection between him and the device.

"I might have you solve two problems at once. If it's possible to spray it on Roberts and then get him in proximity to someone without a suit, I want you to take the initiative. If you can end-of-life him on the scene we can clean things up more easily.'

'Also, as a backup, keep a set of respiratory gear with you at all times in case we do need to activate it." Baylor reminded himself to ask for a hazmat suit to keep in the back of his car if need be.

"Anything else?" asked Mr. Lewis.

"One more thing after this. I'll send you the information. I'm going to need you to take the other two cylinders to Los Angeles. I have an Estonian post-doc working at UCLA in a lab theoretically capable of this. I think he would make a good point of origin.'

'We've already got evidence of him soliciting the Chinese for certain things from the lab. I just don't know yet if we want to go with a Chinese connection or a Middle-Eastern one.

After Mr. Lewis left, Baylor walked over to a group of vans and trucks parked in the middle of the parking lot. The regional FBI director was talking into his cell phone while trying to get information and give orders to a dozen people. He put his hand over the mouthpiece of the phone and looked at Baylor.

"I think you need to tell the press that you're willing to meet Roberts' request." For Baylor's plan to work, he needed to convince them that they were putting on a show for a man that wanted to believe he was contaminated, while making sure that they took the precautions they needed to avoid actually getting exposed to Mitchell.

"I'm with you," said the director. He tilted his head towards the Super Center. "One more day of this and people aren't going to want to leave their homes."

"How's the search going?" asked Baylor.

"We still haven't found any cars with the license plates he stole last night. We're trying to figure out why he's still in South Florida if he has a car. We think he may have an accomplice that's driving him around."

Baylor knew that was an almost impossibility but nodded his head. There was still a possible third person in the Oklahoma City bombing. The FBI was never fully clear on who was responsible for the Anthrax scare. The Olympic Park Bomber, Eric Rudolph, also had supporters who were never charged. There was a precedent there. The more they bought into the idea that he was involved in a conspiracy, the less he would look like a victim.

Baylor told the director he would be available if he was needed then walked back to his car to call Steinmetz back at the lab.

"Ari, I need you to come down here."

"What's going on? Is it ..." asked the concerned scientist.

"We don't know yet. But I want you to be on the scene so we can take possession of the body."

"Body? What body?"

Baylor backtracked. "Sorry. It's chaotic here. I mean when Roberts comes into custody I want us to run some tests on him."

Baylor hung up the phone. It was stressful keeping track of who needed to know what. But that was the burden he had chosen.

44

After he heard the latest press conference announce that they took Mitchell's claims seriously, Mitch had spent the night going over every police stand-off he could remember. The first goal was to not get shot by some police sniper ordered to take him out if he looked like he was going to do something threatening to anybody else. Given that Mitchell's own body could be considered a threat, this was going to be a little problematic. He had to make sure that proper distance was going to be kept from him.

To do that he needed some kind of threat he could use that wouldn't pose a risk to anybody else. When the location came to him, he thought of a way to make only himself vulnerable to the threat. Hopefully that would keep trigger happy police from off-ing him.

Another contributing factor for the location was proximity to television news cameras. Mitchell didn't want to get caught in some remote place like the little island he hid out on the day before. Rookman had made him paranoid enough to think that there might be some greater conspiracy going on. He stood no chance against anything like that. All he could do was look as much like a victim of circumstance as possible.

The next morning, Mitchell docked his john boat on a sea wall below the South River drawbridge. He waited until the morning rush hour was over then climbed the stairwell that lead up to the pedestrian walkway. Mitch took four road flares from his bag, lit them then used them to block traffic coming from one side of the bridge.

He walked to the other side and did the same. Before the last road flare was lit, Mitch could hear sirens. He walked towards the middle of the bridge and shot three flares into the air before pulling one more thing out of his bag then tossed the bag over the side. Mitch looked up at the bridge-tender's control room and waved his hands at the man to stay away.

When the bridge tender saw the crazy man in his underwear walk across the bridge and start throwing flares onto the road he immediately called the police before he realized he was looking at Mitchell Roberts. He pressed the button that lowered the barriers that told traffic not to cross then locked the door to his control room. He'd wait for the police to tell him what to do next.

Mitch hopped up on the railing and waited. It was embarrassing being in his underwear, but it seemed like the only way to convince people that he didn't have a weapon. He knew it made him look like a loon, but he could explain afterwards why he did it. It made sense to him at least. He tried to put the idea out of his mind that governments had a habit of humiliating dictators and terrorists with leaked photos of them in a state of undress.

The other precaution made him look unstable, but it was the only way he could think of to make everyone stay clear. If he could have climbed to the top of a building and have a practical escape route, he might have done that. But he didn't. He had to improvise.

A sales manager for Channel 8 heard the sirens and looked out his 18th floor window that overlooked the South Bay bridge. "Holy cow," he exclaimed. He shouted to the rest of the office to come look. "Hey guys check this out!"

Half a dozen people rushed over. A minute later the newsroom upstairs was notified. A camera was aimed out the window down at the bridge. Mitchell was live on the air five minutes after the first police car arrived. The feed went national three minutes later when people realized the man on the bridge in his underwear with the orange electrical cord tied around his neck like a noose was Mitchell Roberts.

Mitch had no intention of snapping his neck with the noose he'd tied to the bridge. It was a desperate measure, but he needed a way to make himself look as vulnerable as possible. If the police stepped past his perimeter he would threaten to jump.

He knew that in situations like that, where the only person at risk was the suspect, police had a lot more patience. The only life they had to protect was his. Or at least he hoped.

He left three conditions for turning himself in on his iPhone notepad. The first was that the arresting team wore the proper hazmat gear so they didn't kill him in the act of apprehension. The second was that they show him that they had a means of transportation for him that would keep him isolated from everyone else. The third was that no one single agency would have access to him. He wanted to make sure that there would be some kind of oversight. If he was the victim of a conspiracy, he didn't want to fall into the hands of the people who were responsible for it.

The first police officer to arrive on the scene had received the briefing to stay well clear of Roberts under the suspicion that he might have a chemical weapon on him.

He parked his car across the entrance to the south side of the bridge while another police officer did the same on the north side. Their instructions were to contain him until federal officials arrived and under no circumstances to engage him directly.

As an added precaution, the officer stretched a line of crime scene tape across his side of the barrier as if it would form some magical barrier between everyone on the outside and whatever was wrong with Mitchell Roberts.

Mitch held up his hands when the first two police cars arrived to tell them to stay back. He didn't even have to show them the noose around his neck to threaten them. He leaned back on the railing and waited for the people in funny looking blue space suits to arrive.

He cast a glance up at the Channel 8 building and could see crowds gathered around the windows. He spotted a camera aimed at him and gave it a wave and a nod. If he acknowledged them, he at least felt it would look like he was partially in control of the situation.

For the millions of people watching at home it was a different sight then the usual police stand off. Mitch wasn't waving his hands around in the air. He didn't have any weapon other than the noose around his neck. Standing in his underwear, his lean physique made him look more like a college swimmer waiting for his swim match.

While news commentators waited for a response from the federal officials who were arriving on the scene, the biggest topic of conversation was the state of Mitchell's body. One of the Channel 8 cameras zoomed in and revealed the various scratches, bite marks and bruises all over his body.

One female CNN correspondent trying to buy time while they waited for more information put it succinctly. "This man doesn't look like a terrorist. He looks like a rape victim."

The confused and afraid public didn't know what to believe. Mitch's YouTube video had played over and over again the previous day while amateur and professional sleuths looked at his online footprint for any kind of insight into Mitchell. His playlists were scrutinized and his broadcast archives were listened to for anything that would give them a reason to think his behavior was somehow premeditated or the final chapter of a bizarre life.

The search came up with a relatively normal man a few years out of college trying to make his way in broadcasting. His friends described him as an affable guy with the same interests as everyone else. He had no political agenda and not a single person could recount a violent thing he'd said or done prior to two days ago.

The sincerity of Mitch's YouTube video had won a lot of people to his side. The experts on talk shows who explained the sheer difficulty of trying to make the chemical weapon that he was rumored to be in possession of made the WMD story line difficult for people to swallow.

Talk of a rage virus or 'reverse rabies' seemed equally difficult to accept, but people found themselves divided into two groups. There was the WMD camp and the patient zero camp. The lack of any apparent agenda on Mitchell's part made many of the WMD group suspect that maybe he was an unwitting pawn.

30 minutes after Mitch had arrived at the bridge the first person in a hazmat suit approached the outer barrier. Other people in suits were moving the barrier even further back and clearing all the roads another block back. Mitchell thought this was a hopeful sign.

The man in the spacesuit waved at Mitch and motioned that he wanted to walk towards him. Mitchell nodded and felt a wave of relief that this nightmare was about to be over.

45

Special Agent Joseph Merritt, the FBI's designated negotiator, walked towards the man in his underwear with the orange electrical cord around his neck standing in the middle of the bridge. DHS and his district supervisor had given him specific instructions on what to tell Roberts. He was to not contradict Roberts's claim that he was somehow infected and he could promise him anything within reason if it could get him clear of the bridge and the noose.

At the outer edge of the perimeter, an FBI SWAT team watched as the negotiator approached Mitchell Roberts. They had been informed by DHS that it was likely a chemical agent that Mitchell had been using. When it was obvious that he wasn't concealing anything on his body that fit the profile, their commander gave the order for them to use gas masks instead of the more cumbersome tactical nuclear/biological/chemical suits they had in their truck.

Mitch held up his hand for the agent to stop when he was 15 feet away. Mitch could make out the man's face through the glass on the helmet. He had a broad grin and thinning red hair.

"Hello, Mitchell," said the agent. He used the informality as a way to put Mitchell at ease. "I'm not used to talking to people with a spacesuit on. I feel like I should be asking you to take me to your leader."

Mitch stared at the man for a moment. He was about to ask if the corny jokes were a tactic to wear him down but thought better of it. "I'm not used to negotiating in my underwear." Mitch paused. "Begging, yes."

Agent Merritt smiled. Through his earpiece he could hear one of the people listening in on the microphone let out a muffled laugh.

"My name is Special Agent Joseph Merritt. You can call me Joe. My job is to negotiate with you and listen to your demands. I'm empowered to make anything happen that we think is reasonable."

"Wait a second," interrupted Mitch. "Demands? Demands are what bank robbers and terrorists have. I don't want anything. I just want to know that if I surrender I won't be torn to pieces. And that I'll be safe from whoever is responsible for this."

"Who do you think did this to you, Mitchell? I'd like to help."

The question was posed with the calm sincerity of a parent talking to a child about monsters.

It took every bit of Mitchell's will power not to react sarcastically or get angry. Acting defensively in either way would make him look paranoid and unbalanced. "Look, Joe, I don't know what's happening to me. I hear all the crazy things that people say on the radio. I see first hand what happens when people come near me." Mitch looked down at his body. "Look at me, man! This is real. Those bite marks and scratches happened. I want an explanation for all of this." Mitch looked at the crowd of law enforcement officials on either side. "We need answers for all of the people who got hurt."

"Let me help you get some answers. What do you need?"

"I need to know that anyone who comes near me is going to be wearing proper protective equipment."

"Protective of what?" asked Merritt.

Mitchell blinked. The question came out sounding like a probe. "Protective of me. My scent. Maybe I've got some kind of rage virus like they said."

"Who said?"

"Talk show hosts. People on the radio filling air time. I don't know who, man. It's just one of those things that come up when people are looking for an explanation."

"What else do you need?" asked Merritt.

"I need to know that you have a safe way to transport me from here."

"A vehicle to keep you from getting attacked?"

"Yes," said Mitchell.

Merritt held up a finger as he was getting instructions through his ear piece. He looked at Mitch and nodded. "That's not going to be a problem."

"Okay ..."

"We're going to transport you in an armored truck. That way nobody can get at you and hurt you. Does that sound good?"

Mitch shook his head. "No, it does not. Ask the people on the other end of your radio how an armored truck is supposed to keep people from smelling me or getting wind of whatever makes them attack."

Merritt held up his finger again as he got more instructions. "They're designed to withstand tear gas attacks and are sealed tight."

Mitchell felt the hair raise on the back of his neck. He realized that it wasn't just the negotiator acting in a patronizing way, the people he was dealing with really didn't think there was anything wrong with him. They had bought into some other theory about a weapon. Mitchell had to call the bluff. He leaned back on the railing and looked over the edge of the bridge for a moment.

"Joe. Special Agent Merritt," said Mitch. "I'm sure the people you're talking to will promise me the world if you think it will get me away from the edge of the bridge and this stupid thing off my neck while a thousand cameras are on us. The one thing I am asking for right now is the truth. An armored truck is designed to keep things on the outside from getting in like people and tear gas. Air may be filtered on its way in, but not on its way out.'

'Either the people you are talking to know that and are just trying to bullshit me because they're under some false pretense that I'm up to something or they're incompetent and can't be trusted with my life." Mitch waved his arm at the buildings and pointed at the Channel 8 camera. "Or the lives of everyone else around me. A truck that's not airtight is a menace to everyone we drive past."

"Mitchell, we're being totally straight with you," Merritt said in his most sincere voice.

"If you want to believe I'm acting under some kind of delusion or have some kind of sinister plan, for the sake of everyone, have the courtesy to treat my delusion with some kind of consistency."

Agent Merritt listened for instructions. He nodded. "Alright, Mitchell, here's the deal. You've got a lot of people scared right now. Traffic is shut down on highways, people are afraid to go into public spaces, there's a lot of families upset with you.

"I've been doing this for twenty years and I've met a lot of different personality types. I had you figured out the moment I saw you standing here with the silly cord around your neck. If you were serious, you'd have a gun to your head or you'd be up some place high. You're just a guy that wants attention and to pretend he's a victim in all this. Obviously it's not on you. We'll find it though."

"What?!" asked Mitchell.

Merritt reached down and turned off a knob at his waist. The suit began to deflate as the pressurized air coming from his backpack came to a stop. He reached to undo the seal under his helmet.

"Please stop!" shouted Mitchell.

"You can stop this any time, Mitchell. Tell us where we can find the other canisters."

Mitchell heard a hiss as the latch opened. He looked at the rows of people on either side of the bridge. "For god's sake! Somebody stop him!" he shouted. He looked up at the Channel 8 building, his eyes filled with desperation.

Merritt tossed the helmet aside and held open his arms. "Don't feel like jumping, do you, Mitch?" Merritt took in a large nose full of air.

Mitchell backed towards the railing. He could feel the metal against his back.

"I'm not going to miss that..." Merritt's voice turned to a snarl as he bared his teeth and ran towards Mitchell with his fingers curled into claws.

Vulnerable, naked, with nothing to use to defend himself, Mitchell held his hands in front of his face and knelt down. As Merritt closed in on him, Mitch grabbed him by the legs and picked him up in the air. Mitch threw his body to the left as hard as he could.

Merritt fell on his side. The air tank on his back slowed him down as he tried to get up. He rolled over on his stomach and came at Mitchell in a four legged crawl. Mitch's foot hit the helmet on the ground. He picked it up and swung it at Merritt's head so hard the glass cracked. Blood drops splattered from his broken nose.

The SWAT team got orders on their ear pieces to take Mitchell down. They swarmed past the barrier with their guns drawn. The .3 micron filters on their gas masks provided no stopgap for the air around Mitchell. Once they passed the barrier Mitch had set up their posture began to change.

Millions of people watched on television as cops with gas masks turned from highly disciplined law enforcement officers into a pack of rabid dogs. Several of them dropped their guns as they clawed out at the air when they ran towards Mitch. Two of them reflexively pulled their triggers, sending a wild barrage of gunfire that ricocheted off the bridge and hit nearby buildings and the vehicles on the other side of the bridge.

The Channel 8 camera zoomed into the terror in Mitch's eyes as they came at him ready to rip out his throat and tear him to pieces in a violent slaughter. The world watched as Mad Mitch pulled the noose tight over his neck and jumped over the edge of the bridge.

46

Driven by the rage, the SWAT team members leaped over the edge after him in their full armored gear. Not to save him, but to kill him. The cord around Mitchell's neck snapped and he fell into the water. Black armored SWAT team members rained down around him as they hit the water.

Another wave of law enforcement officers swarmed onto to bridge. 20 more people were overcome with the rage and leaped into the water. Bystanders were paralyzed with panic as they realized that whatever reflex it was that made people go mad overpowered every other instinct. Men thrashed in the water and began to drown as they bared their teeth and clawed out furiously trying to kill something they couldn't see.

As the presence of Mitchell subsided, rescuers were eventually able reach the thrashing men and pull them to shore. EMTs and police officers worked quickly to resuscitate those that had a drowned.

News anchors tried to make sense of what happened for their viewers while they watched it unfold. Expert pundits began to doubt what they had been told. What should have been a simple surrender was botched in the worst way possible.

The FBI District Director barked some orders to his subordinates then turned to his DHS counterpart. "What the hell is going on?"

The other man shrugged.

The FBI district director answered his ringing Blackberry. "Yes sir. I understand sir."

The Deputy Director of the FBI was on the other end of the line and was furious with what he'd seen on the news.

"We were acting under information that this was caused by a weapon of some kind. No sir, I believe that information is incorrect." He looked over at the DHS director. "I think we proceed under the assumption that this is a public health crisis and not primarily a criminal investigation. Yes sir." He hung up and started giving orders.

The DHS director's phone was ringing too. He looked at the FBI district director.

"We're asking the Center for Disease Control to step in and provide assistance. We're going to the patient zero hypothesis."

From his vantage point the FBI district director had clearly seen his negotiator break down and attack Mitchell. An attack that he was sure had gone out live to millions of viewers. The response of his SWAT team confirmed, in his mind, that absent any kind of dispersant on the bridge or some other weapon, the most likely hypothesis was the one that Mitchell had been telling everyone all along.

Where the fuck was that weasel Baylor, he asked?

Baylor watched the disaster on his hotel room television. The moment he saw that Mitchell had stripped down to his underwear, he knew the current plan wasn't going to work. If the canister wasn't found on his person, then the allegations of it being planted were going to be too loud. He had half a mind to text Mr. Lewis and ask him to go in after the drowning men and throw the canister in the water to be discovered. The problem at that point would be that what they found in the canister wouldn't be found in the men's lungs.

The FBI was going to want to do their own tests on the blood and tissue and match it to the material in the canister. It would be apparent to them that whatever caused the reaction wasn't the same as what was in the spray can. He needed to figure out a strategy for the patient zero hypothesis that could minimize blow-back and protect Great Wall.

He called Mr. Lewis to give him instructions on how to proceed.

After rescuers had pulled all of the law enforcement personnel from the water, the search continued for Mitchell Roberts. Rescue divers searched the bottom of the waterway in a spiral pattern moving outwards around the bay and Intracoastal. The outgoing tide gave them a half mile radius to search, and that was growing by a mile every hour.

City and county police were sent to watch along the waterfront to see if he climbed ashore anywhere. Marine Patrol and Coast Guard boats were brought in to canvas the area while helicopters from four different agencies swept the area around the bridge and surrounding city looking for any sign of Mitchell.

47

Naked and exhausted, Mad Mitch climbed onto the dive platform of the newly christened "Monkey's Paw". Two miles away he could hear the helicopters as they buzzed around the South Bay bridge and the manhunt continued. He had very little time until the search extended outwards and law enforcement started stopping vessels in the water near him.

The necessity of an escape plan came to Mitch after he listened to the paranoid Dr. Lovestrange on Rookman's show. Up until the FBI negotiator had tried to patronizingly convince him that an armored car was going to serve as an airtight transport, he was fully committed to the idea that they believed him, or at the very least, were willing to give him the benefit of the doubt.

The attack on the bridge proved otherwise. Mitchell had been lied to. He still wasn't sure if it was out of incompetence or the machinations of someone trying to cover up something. The effect was the same. Mitchell couldn't trust anyone.

The idea for the escape came to him when he was looking for a boat to steal. Originally he thought of taking a bigger yacht in the event he got stuck in a prolonged stand off. What attracted him to the Donzi was the piece of equipment that had just saved his life.

The SBS 730 was an underwater propulsion device used by very rich scuba divers, the military and drug smugglers. Shaped like a cross between a torpedo and a jet ski, it could go up to 8 miles an hour underwater and had over a twenty mile range. What made the SBS 730 unique was that it had its own sonar system, making it possible to navigate in the limited visibility of the waterway and Intracoastal. The unit cost half as much as the boat Mitch had stolen to get it.

Before Mitch tied the john boat to the shore by the bridge, he found the exact middle and dropped the SBS 730 overboard tied to a weighted-down duffle bag filled with dive gear.

When he had no other option except to jump, he made sure to land on top of his underwater stash. He hit the water after a few milliseconds of panicked free fall when he wasn't sure if the extension cord was going to break like it was supposed to.

Once he hit the water he swam straight down ten feet to the muck covered floor below. It took him a frantic minute before his hands found the propulsion unit and his duffle bag with the compressed air tank.

He hadn't gone scuba diving in years, but his instincts kicked in and he remembered how to clear the mask and strap the tank on underwater. He ignored the sound of bodies hitting the surface overhead and focused on getting away as fast as he could.

Somewhere in the 2 miles between the South Bay bridge and the power boat he lost his underwear in the turbulence as the propulsion unit carried him through the water. Adding just one more indignity to his plan.

To get back to the boat while underwater he relied on the sonar and compass as he looked for the mooring lines of boats he remembered passing on the way in. Finally he reached the Monkey's Paw and surfaced near the dive platform. Before he struggled to pull the SBS 730 on board, he ran to a dive locker and found a diving suit to wear.

Looking down at the skin tight suit, he wished he could have worn that instead of his underwear when he tried to surrender on national television.

Although he had narrowly escaped that time, Mitchell was sure they'd cast a tighter net the next time around. He had to make sure that when he surrendered, it was to the right people. He started up the boat and had to decide which way to take it.

He had three options. Going further up the Intracoastal and away from South Florida meant traveling through less populated areas. The advantage was that it was away from where he'd been. The disadvantage was that there were less side canals and avenues to escape.

He could take an exit that led straight out to sea and follow the shore line north or south. But that would put him well within the Coast Guard's cross-hairs and only give him the beach as an escape.

His other option was to head back south. There were numerous canals and natural harbors where he could blend in and make it ashore if he decided to abandon the boat.

It felt like backtracking. *But backtracking from what?* He'd never had a final destination. Heading to a more populated area might give him more options for surrendering. He felt safer knowing that millions of people would be watching from news helicopters.

He also had to deal with a limited amount of fuel. If he ran out he'd rather take his chances stealing another boat than getting stranded nowhere near another escape route. There was also the idea that they wouldn't expect him to go south since his travels had all been to the north.

Mitchell pulled up anchor and pointed the boat towards the south. He sat back in the cockpit chair and tried to look like just another boater out for an afternoon trip.

Fifteen miles away Mr. Lewis was planning his own afternoon trip. He'd received new instructions from Baylor. It took him a half hour to arrange it. Fortunately, he had a number of associates in the South Florida area that could help facilitate what he needed.

When he pulled into the hanger near the small private airport near the Everglades, his associate, Mr. Travis was finishing marking up the tail letters of the helicopter. He pointed out a long case to Mr. Lewis.

He walked over to a table covered in tools and opened the case. Inside was a sniper's rifle with a high magnification scope.

"It's going to be a bitch to shoot that from the air if he's on the water," said Mr. Travis.

"The current plan is to have you drop me near an overpass so I can shoot from the ground as he passes by. If that doesn't work, we have other options."

Mr. Travis stepped back to look at the new lettering on the tail. "If they run it they'll know it's bogus."

"I'm not worried about that right now. Every bird in South Florida is going to be out looking for him. I just want plausible denial about where the chopper came from," replied Mr. Lewis.

"Good thing. I like my job here."

"Never get too attached," said Mr. Lewis as he looked through the rifle scope and aimed it at fuel truck across the tarmac and dry fired.

Mr. Lewis was already suspicious that Mitchell had been using the waterways to get around. When Mitchell vanished after the dive off the bridge he informed Baylor of that. Baylor was about to tell the FBI that was where they should be directing their search efforts when he realized he had an opportunity.

When it was clear that Mitchell's body wasn't going to be found, Baylor had called Mr. Lewis with the new plan. If Mitchell was shot out of sight, it would point to an accomplice that wanted to keep him silent.

Baylor didn't care if Mitchell talked. He didn't have anything to say. The real advantage to his death was that it would appear that he knew something worth getting killed for. If one of Baylor's associates could get access to Mitchell's body before any of the other agencies, he could misdirect them as need be.

48

Mitchell passed the inlet that led towards the part of downtown where he'd made his escape. Police and news helicopters flew around looking for a naked Mitchell hiding out somewhere around town.

The underwater propulsion device had made his escape a practical impossibility to anyone watching. A strong scuba diver would be able to swim one mile an hour at most in no current. He'd covered the distance in 20 minutes, giving him an hour head start from the most optimistic position of where he could be. That was of course assuming people were thinking logically. Mitchell had little reason to think that was the case.

Mitchell kept the boat going south on the Intracoastal and focused on what he need to do next. He set the scanner on the dashboard and turned the volume all the way up so he could hear it over the engine noise.

As a precaution, he laid out his dive gear in the rear seats so he could get to it quickly if he needed to and checked the charge on the underwater propulsion device. It still had a half charge left. That was more than enough to take him to shore or pretty far down a side canal.

Knowing he had some kind of backup escape cleared his head and made it easier to think. The problem he had earlier was that nobody took him seriously. He hoped the unfortunate incident at the bridge was enough of a wake up call.

To find out what the reaction was, Mitchell turned on the boat's stereo and tuned it to a news channel. He still kept one ear on the scanner, periodically tuning in to make sure he wasn't about to be surrounded.

Mitchell hadn't realized the unintended consequence stripping down to his underwear had on people's perceptions. The bite marks and scratches hurt like hell when he thought about them, but he'd been too focused on moving forward to stop and get a look at himself.

When the public saw them they became more sympathetic. It gave them an image of Mitchell as a wounded man trying to avoid getting hurt. When the FBI negotiator attacked him, even people defending how law enforcement agencies were handling the case found it hard to defend what took place.

A popular discussion on several of the news stations was what should Mitchell do next. According to the reports, his @MadMitchFM Twitter handle was flooded with people decrying what happened and offering advice. One suggestion repeated by a reporter made a lot of sense: "**@MadMitchFM Get a fucking lawyer on these assholes**."

He needed a third party to negotiate for his surrender. Someone who could verify that the authorities were living up to their word. He needed the advice of someone who could help him, not just find out what was wrong with him, but make sure he didn't spend the rest of his life in prison.

Mitchell realized that if he had surrendered that morning and hadn't been attacked and the magical armored truck didn't put him in a riot in the middle of downtown, he probably would have walked right into their hands without any legal protection. While he bargained for his life, they would have conned him into agreeing to spend the rest of it in prison.

For sure he'd done some very criminal things, but nothing he should go to jail for, at least in his mind. As far as he was concerned, guilty feelings or not, he was only trying to survive. Mitchell began to get angry at the thought that he might actually have to go to prison for what happened. His hand pushed the throttle forward as he fumed.

When he realized he was making a wake big enough to get stopped by the marine patrol, he slowed down. The last thing he needed was to start a boat chase over a 'no wake zone' ticket.

When he got the chance to make a phone call, he'd try to contact a lawyer. The bigger loudmouth the better. He wanted some kind of OJ Simpson-level dream team.

If he got surrounded or stopped before then, that would be his one request. He wanted someone else to deal with the unctuous negotiators. He began to form a legal strategy in his mind. Of course he was sure the lawyers would have better ideas. It just made him feel better to have a plan.

If Mitchell was killed before he got to a lawyer there was going to be no brilliant defense, no pardon and no cure.

49

A half hour later, Mitchell was lost in thought thinking of his legal defense when the police scanner inexplicably flew off the console. At first he thought it was from the wave he just drove through. When he leaned over to pick it up he saw the bullet hole. An instant later he felt something graze his right shoulder.

"Fuck!" he screamed as he ducked down behind the console. He put his hand on his shoulder and felt where the bullet had almost gone through his arm. It burned like hell but there was no blood.

The second bullet sounded like it was coming from one of the islands to his left up ahead. He'd reached a part of the Intracoastal where it was mostly mangroves on either side. A perfect place for an ambush.

He desperately wanted to pop his head up and look, but he knew that's what the sniper was waiting for.

Mitch reached a hand up and slowed down the boat so he wouldn't overtake the sniper's position and leave himself vulnerable in the open cockpit. He had to go past that point sooner or later. Otherwise the shooter could just work his way through the brush to a better position.

Why was he being shot at? Didn't the FBI warn you before they did that kind of stuff? It didn't make any sense to him.

Mitch looked around the boat for anything he could use to protect himself. He could hide in the cabin, but that would mean leaving the boat adrift. Sooner or later he would hit the shoreline and the shooter could hop aboard and finish him.

Somewhere in the distance heard the sound of a helicopter. He had the urge to wave them down, but knew that outcome probably wasn't going to be a good one either. He looked at the console above his head. He could try to navigate the boat without looking. If he looked at the tree line in back of him he could gauge where the middle of the waterway was. That would still leave him open when he passed by the sniper's position.

Mitch decided to hell with it. He'd aim the boat down the middle as best as he could, throw the throttle forward and go duck down into the cabin. It was a cowardly way to confront the crisis. But he didn't have any other options.

Mitchell opened up the cabin door and got an inspiration when he saw the mirror over the small sink. He climbed inside and ripped it off the wall. He climbed onto the bed that was directly under the bow hatch and carefully lifted open using the edge of the mirror. He looked at the trees where he thought the shot came from. He saw something move then the mirror shattered, followed by the sound of a loud bang. The hatch slammed shut as broken pieces of mirrored plastic fell on him.

"Asshole!" shouted Mitch.

The boat was still drifting forward. He needed to do something fast. Mitch searched the cabin for anything. He found an emergency transponder in a drawer and threw it aside. He opened another drawer and dumped it out onto the bed. There were two flare guns like the ones he'd boosted from the Super Center the night before.

Mitch grabbed them both and climbed back out to the cockpit. He pulled the safety off on one and gripped it in his right hand. He only had a vague idea where the shooter was so the most he could hope for was a distraction.

He pulled the cabin door wide open so it would act as a shield. Mad Mitch quickly reached his hand up and fired. The flare shot across the bow trailed by a plume of smoke.

Mitch pushed the throttle half way forward then ducked into the cabin. He could see part of the shoreline as the boat moved by where the sniper was hidden.

From inside the cabin he shot the other flare in the general direction of the shooter. He climbed out of the smoke-filled cabin and ducked under the console to try to steer the boat away from the sides of the waterway.

The boat became more difficult to control the faster it went. Mitch decided to push the throttle all the way forward and get back behind the wheel. He made an effort to keep the boat moving erratically until he was out of range.

Mitch rounded a bend and put the small peninsula between himself and the shooter. He had no idea if there were other snipers lying in wait for him. He decided at this point it was better to keep the boat going full throttle.

He had no idea who was shooting at him, but he'd prefer a chase from marine patrol than getting shot at by hidden snipers.

He was half-tempted to get on an open channel and ask why people were shooting at him. He decided to wait until he knew his position was completely compromised. For all he knew, it was the government trying to take him out. The sooner he got to a more populated area, the safer he would feel. Safe as long as people kept their distance.

Mitch had the throttle fully open and was flying down the waterway. The boat would hit small waves and glide through the air. He passed several fishing boats, sending them into the trees. People shouted curses back at him.

In ten minutes he would pass from the undeveloped section of the waterway into more residential areas. If he slowed down there he might be able to make it by at a more reasonable speed. His hope now was to be able to slip up close to a marina or a housing complex and steal some WiFi to make a Skype call on the iPod he'd stolen.

Mitchell heard the sound of a boat getting closer behind him. He turned around and froze for a moment when he realized it wasn't a boat. It was a black helicopter flying just a few feet above the water gaining on his stern.

Fucking black helicopters?

A man leaned out the side with a large rifle. Mitch ducked down and jerked the wheel to the left sending the boat in a tight circle bringing it to the opposite side of the helicopter as the shooter.

The helicopter made a tight turn too. Mitch tried to bring the boat underneath the helicopter to stay out of the shooters range. The pilot pulled the helicopter off to the side in a movement Mitch couldn't replicate with the boat and brought the shooter in direct line of site with Mitchell.

Mitch turned the wheel to the right bringing the left side several feet higher as the boat turned into another circle. He was running out of options. The helicopter could outmaneuver him and go twice as fast.

He looked ahead and saw a narrow channel between an island and the ocean side of the Intracoastal. Mitch aimed the boat for there while swerving back and forth. The top of the seat next to him erupted in padding as another shot rang out.

The boat slid under a small canopy of trees. Mitch pulled the throttle back. He could see the helicopter fly overhead and come to a hover.

Mitchell could jump from the boat and try to make it through the thick vegetation and find a place to hide. But for how long? He had little doubt a sniper would be able to find him there.

He needed some way of minimizing the helicopter's advantage. Mitch opened up the lockers in the stern to look for something he could use. All he had were wet suits and dive tanks.

He opened up another locker and saw the dive belts. He could try throwing them at the windshield. Maybe if he cracked it.

Mad Mitch had a better idea. He ran to the console and pushed the throttle forward a hair sending the boat out from under the canopy.

Mr. Lewis and Mr. Travis watched as the boat drifted from under the cover of the trees. The cockpit was empty. That meant either Mitchell had jumped off onto the island or was trying to wait things out inside the cabin.

Mr. Travis looked at Mr. Lewis for instructions. Mr. Lewis set the rifle between the seats. He pulled on an oxygen mask and slung the tank over his shoulder. He gave the valve a turn then pulled a 9mm pistol from a holster at his side.

"Bring it down," he said through the the mask.

Mr. Travis brought the helicopter a few feet above the stern and matched speed with the boat as it glided along. Mr. Lewis hopped down from the passenger side door and landed in a crouch on the back of the boat.

He kept his body away from the line of sight of the cabin. One of Mitchell's flares had already come close to burning the hair off the left side of his head. He wouldn't let him try that again. He hopped from the top of the stern engines into the main cockpit. His finger prepared to squeeze as he shot anything that moved inside the cabin.

He took a step closer and was beginning to make out the interior when everything went dark for a moment.

Hands grabbed him and shoved him into the water before he could understand what had just happened. He looked up from the water as Mad Mitch hurled a dive tank from the locker at his head.

It hit the gun and knocked it from his grasp. He turned to dive for it when Mitchell hurled another dive belt at his head. It hit so hard he felt the urge to vomit.

Mr. Travis had watched as Mitchell emerged from the locker in the stern and swung the weight belt at Mr.

Lewis' head. To the man's credit it seemed to only phase him and not knock him out. Mitchell used the distraction to throw him overboard.

While Mad Mitch looked for more heavy objects to throw at Mr. Lewis as he tread water. Mr. Travis pulled his sidearm from his ankle holster.

Mad Mitch turned around as Mr. Travis was sliding a window open on the pilot side door. Mad Mitch looked down at his feet and opened another hatch. He reached in and pulled out a metal anchor.

Mad Mitch began swinging it by the anchor line in huge circles. When it was at the top of its arc aimed at the rotor, he let go. Mr. Travis shouted then pulled back on the stick to avoid losing the helicopter. He heard the sound of metal hitting the hull.

From the stern of the boat Mitchell looked up in shock. He thought he'd only hoped to hit the anchor against the window and crack the glass. When the pilot pulled back he'd tilted it so the skid acted as a catch for the anchor.

The anchor went through the gap between the skid and the hull and fell to the water. Mitchell watched as the rope at his feet unspooled.

The pilot pulled the helicopter into a hover when he thought he was at a safe distance from the anchor oblivious to fact that he had just been hooked.

Mr. Travis spotted Mr. Lewis floating in the water. He was waving furiously at him pointing at the helicopter. Mr. Travis brought the helicopter down to pick him up.

Mad Mitch didn't want to lose his chance and have the man in the water ruin his catch. He ran to the console and slammed the throttle forward. The boat raced away from the helicopter.

Mr. Travis watched it try to get away out of the corner of his eye. He'd have plenty of time to catch up with him when he picked up Mr. Lewis. He turned to look at the water below then noticed the line running from the boat under his chopper. He felt something yank on the skids.

"Oh fuck!" he said, as he realized the anchor had just grabbed his chopper like a grappling hook. He jerked the stick forward to avoid being pulled from the sky.

Mad Mitch had the throttle wide open and was starting to catch air as he hit the crests of waves. The helicopter had to either match speed or run the risk of Mitchell pulling it into the water. It could come down on top of him for all he cared at that point.

After two days of constant abuse it felt good to be able to strike out in anger and not feel bad about it. He kept the boat headed south. He could see the north end of the next city coming into view.

There was no way he was not going to attract attention with a helicopter tied to his stern. The advantage of that happening was that it would lead to a lot of questions that would be embarrassing for whomever was out to kill him. He was sure the guy that had jumped onto his boat and the pilot weren't just a couple of assholes with a helicopter and rifle.

Mr. Travis was in an awkward situation. He tried to get over the boat then gain altitude to try to snap the anchor cable. Physics wasn't on his side. The helicopter had a lifting capacity of 900 pounds. The anchor rope had a tensile strength of 4,000 pounds.

Gaining altitude only raised the back end of the power boat a few inches and increased his chances of crashing into the water. He opened up the sliding window on his door and aimed his pistol out the window.

Mad Mitch looked at the suicidal man then turned the boat sharply to the right. The pilot had seconds to match course or get pulled down. Mr. Travis opted to match course. He also realized that shooting Mitchell wouldn't help him get his helicopter loose from the boat. If anything it might make matters worse if the boat ran aground.

He decided to try to wrap the rope around the boat. With any luck it would get cut by the propellers. He brought the helicopter in a tight arc bringing it alongside Mitchell in the driver's seat. Mad Mitch looked over and flipped him off. The pilot pushed the throttle forward and brought the helicopter just inches off the water.

Mad Mitch looked back and saw the slack the helicopter pilot was building up. Mitchell had been water skiing enough times to know what the pilot was doing. Mad Mitch ran back and grabbed the end of the line near where it was tied off. He pulled the slack rope into the boat cockpit until it ran taught from the skid to Mad Mitch's hand.

Mr. Travis brought the helicopter across the bow while hovering less than a foot over the water. He looked back to see if the rope went under the bow. Instead he saw Mad Mitch holding on to the slack and flipping him off again. He was grinning at him.

God damn punk! Furious, he pulled up on the stick yanking the rope from Mad Mitch's hands. Both he and

Mad Mitch were so engaged in their back and forth that they failed to notice the marine patrol boat heading towards them or the Channel 11 news helicopter that was following.

Dozens of people had called in 911 about the helicopter and the power boat that were fighting on the Intracoastal.

The Channel 11 helicopter was heading south to get footage of the Park Square Mall when they saw the battle taking place. Emergency news coverage about Mitchell was interrupted by a special news bulletin about the helicopter and the speedboat.

It took ten minutes before news anchors watching the feed realized that the man driving the boat was the same person the FBI was dredging the bottom of the South Bay bridge for.

Police helicopters from two different jurisdictions and an FBI chopper were now in pursuit of Mad Mitch and his catch. A county sheriff's boat had also started on an intercept course. Coast Guard cutters were moving into positions along all the ocean access points.

Mr. Travis looked down at Mad Mitch and the growing armada surrounding them both. He knew that the tail numbers were already being run and coming up as bogus. Voices in his headset demanded that he identify himself.

Part of him just wanted to ram the chopper right into the boat and kill them both. He was sure Mr. Lewis would be happy with that outcome. Unfortunately for Mr. Lewis and his employers, Mr. Travis didn't have a death wish.

He would wait for the right moment and jump into the water. With the right commotion he might be able to slip away.

Mad Mitch looked at all the heat on him and decided there was no point in not making plans for when they finally forced him to stop. Mitchell took the handset for the VHF radio and shouted over the sound of the helicopter overhead.

50

Baylor was watching the unfolding drama of the helicopter hooked to Mitchell's boat with a sense of dread. Reporters were trying to track down the helicopter's owners. A quick search on the FAA website revealed that numbers on the tail were fake.

His phone rang with an unfamiliar number. "Hello?"

"It's Lewis. We have a problem."

"Please tell me you have nothing to do with that helicopter. Where are you?" said Baylor.

"I got picked up out of the water by a fisherman. I'm going to fix the problem. I need to know if the package is expendable?"

Baylor looked at the news chopper footage of the helicopter hovering over the boat as it raced down the Intracoastal. If the pilot made it away somehow, it wasn't likely he would get very far. Although Baylor's hire wouldn't point directly back to him, the man was going to be in a position where he was likely to tell them everything he knew. Which included Mr. Lewis and the package that was left on the helicopter.

"The package is expendable. After that, we need to salt the earth. I mean, you need to."

"I understand," said Mr. Lewis.

Mr. Travis was thinking about getting on his VHF radio and asking marine patrol why they hadn't stopped Mitchell's boat and cut him free. Maybe if he acted petulant enough, he could get away and find a place to bail out near a crowded area.

He could hear his phone ring through the connection to his headset. He answered.

"Mr. Travis, this is Mr. Lewis. It seems we have a problem."

"God damn we have a problem! I was just supposed to be a taxi." He looked out the window as almost the entire South Florida nautical and aviation law enforcement fleet gathered around his helicopter and the boat below.

"I left something on board in my bag that can probably help you. It's an incendiary device. I'll tell you how to activate it. When you drop it onto Robert's boat it should cause a large enough fire to burn the rope. Once you do that and bail out in a safe place, I'll call you to help you relocate."

Mitchell was in the middle of explaining the new conditions for his surrender when the sound of the helicopter behind him changed pitch. He looked over his shoulder and saw the helicopter heading straight at him. The spinning blades were at eye level and starting to pass over the back of the stern.

Mitch jerked the wheel to the right and threw himself to the floor. He felt a jet of air push down on him as the rotors came inches away from the top of the deck. The helicopter skids scraped the left side of the boat before the helicopter nosedived into the water. Mitchell cowered as far down as he could when the tail rotor passed overhead and ripped apart the seat he'd been sitting on just moments before.

Mitch stood up to look at the wreckage then heard a huge crack and was thrown forward with a jerk. He ducked back down then realized that was the sound of the anchor rope tearing the anchor cleat from the stern.

He looked at the wreckage behind him. He could see a rage-filled face with blood shot eyes pounding his fists and face against the glass cockpit bubble. *How could the man even smell him?* Mitchell was confused. He had no idea how it was possible the man in the chopper could have got his scent through all the downdraft.

Off to his right a marine patrol boat was pulling alongside him. A man on a bullhorn shouted at him to shut down his engine. Mitch picked the radio microphone he'd dropped when he heard the helicopter coming at him.

"I've already told you to keep your distance! No boats! No more god damn helicopters!"

A voice came over the emergency channel. "Mr. Roberts, if you stop your boat we can negotiate."

Mitch looked at the two marine patrol boats on either side of him trying to keep him boxed in.

"I don't see any kind of protective gear on anyone around me. Didn't you guys learn anything today?"

"We'll pull the boats back if you slow down," said the voice.

"Every time I slow down people try to kill me. I've told you what I need, for your sake and mine."

"We're considering it."

Mitchell knew it was a waiting game. Sooner or later they'd try to use a high-powered rifle to take out the engine or just wait for him to run out of gas.

After that, he'd be metaphorically, and possibly, literally, dead in the water.

He needed something to bargain with. He could threaten to kill himself, but he wasn't sure if they'd take him seriously having realized he'd had an escape plan the last time he said he would do that. Mitchell thought about that for a moment. He was still an unpredictable element to them. There was something to creating a bluff that they'd be afraid to call him on.

He also knew that he had the public watching what was happening. Mitch looked down and saw one of the spent flare guns. He picked it up and slid it into the zipper of his diving suit.

"Let me ask you a question. Do you believe me now that there is something medically going on with me that's making people attack me?" he asked into the microphone.

"We don't know what to believe. If you stop your vessel we can talk about it."

"That's not a helpful answer. I've already told you what I need in order for me to stop this boat." Mitchell looked up to his left and saw the orange and white colors of a Coast Guard helicopter. He remembered how they'd stop go fast boats like his.

"If anybody else shoots at me today..."

The voice interrupted. "Nobody has shot at you today."

"Did I imagine gun fire on the bridge? Is this bullet hole in my suit a hallucination?"

"The bridge was unfortunate."

Mitchell was shocked at how hard it was to get through to these people. "Yes. It was unfortunate. Unfortunate because it was your fault."

"We're going to handle things differently. Please power down your vessel."

"Here's what I'm going to do. If you do the simple thing I asked for, which quite honestly is not asking for much and is just as much for your safety as mine, then you will have my surrender when I think it's safe." Mitch held up the flare gun. "If you guys insist on handling this wrong and doing something like trying to shoot my engine or me on live television, I'm going to straddle the gas tank on this boat and shoot a flare into the leak the helicopter made."

"Mr. Roberts," the voice interrupted.

"I'm not finished! Here's the best part. That explosion is going to send me into a billion tiny little parts all over the Intracoastal. Maybe nothing will happen, maybe everyone around for a hundred miles will get to breath in a little Mad Mitch.'

'Maybe I'm not the suicidal type like the last guy said, but I know I'd rather go out by my hand than yours. I've told you what I want."

There was a long pause. Finally the voice came back on, "Alright Mr. Roberts. Just let us have your assurance that you won't try to hurt anyone."

"I'm not the one who needs to make that promise. But I will. I've acted as open and ethically as I could. I beg of you to do the same."

"Agreed."

The Naked Man in the Forest was in a different place. He didn't know where to look for the face of the Earth mother. The trees and the plants were different. This wasn't his familiar spot. Of course it was all part of the Earth mother. He just needed to be able to see that.

He dropped a half tab of the blotter and waited.

He jerked his head to the side when something scurried through the brush. He hoped it was Earth mother. Instead it was just an armadillo. Just an armadillo? He felt shame for denigrating one of her creatures. It was a thing of light. Not a thing of dark like him.

The Naked Man in the Forest scratched a huge welt into his leg for thinking that he was special. He looked down at the red mass of his testicles and penis. Hadn't he learned his lesson already from the poison ivy? This time it was going to be worse. He'd failed the Earth mother. For the first time, he feared her eggs may be in danger.

He had come far away from them and wasn't able to protect them. All because of that damn man. That horrible man shrouded in darkness. Because of him he was sure the Earth mother was going to make him pay.

Wind blew through the clearing and the Naked Man felt a cold breeze on his back. She was here. But she wasn't showing herself. This was bad.

"Earth mother," he pleaded. "I'll do anything you ask. Anything."

I know my child.

Her voice was sweet. He began to turn his head to look behind him where the voice came from.

Do not turn around!

The words came out like thunder claps. The Naked Man in the Forest froze.

The eggs. Protect my eggs.

Her voice was sweet again.

"Why can't I see you right now Earth mother?" He began to wail.

I don't want you to see how angry I am right now. I don't want you to see my face and forget that I ever loved you.

Loved?

"What can I do Earth mother?"

Are my eggs ready?

"Yes Earth mother. They've been ready."

Then go to them. Stop this man if you can. But go to my eggs. I may have you bring them to him.

"Bring them to this man? I don't understand?"

The entire forest shook with her fury. Tree limbs snapped and a cold wind stirred up a tornado of dead leaves.

DON'T QUESTION WHAT I ASK OF YOU!

The Naked Man in the Forest buried his face in his hands.

When you came to me you were lost. You were confused about the things you did. You didn't understand what was light and what was dark. Who showed you?

"You did Earth mother," he whimpered.

Who told you what to say? Who told you what to do? Who told you about my eggs?

"You, Earth mother. Everything I owe to you."

Then if I tell you to bring my eggs to this man, then that is what you will do.

"Yes Earth mother. Yes."

He felt her presence leave the clearing. He sat alone, naked. 'Loved', she had said. She said she *had* loved him as in the past tense. All because of this horrible man.

He put on the Otherself's clothes. He would do what she asked. He'd try to bring the eggs to this man. But she hadn't said anything about trying to stop him before then.

She would love him again. She would love him when she saw that the eggs were his responsibility. That he, The Naked Man in the Forest, not the horrible man or his Otherself was the one to see to it they were hatched.

He heard a twig snap behind him as he put one leg into the Otherself's pants. He turned his head and saw an athletic man with cut off shorts and a tank top whistling at him. The Naked Man in the Forest froze. He'd never been seen changing back into the Otherself.

"You don't waste time. I like that."

The Naked Man in the Forest tried to focus on the man's face but the acid was making his goatee stretch and distort into a beard. He just smiled back.

The man walked towards him. "So what's your thing?"

The Naked Man in the Forest looked around the clearing. "Over here." He pointed to a log. "Sit here and watch."

The man sat down on the log and looked up at him. "Alright. Now what?"

"Close your eyes."

The man looked up at him skeptically.

"Just close your eyes. Let me get something out of my wallet."

The man closed his eyes. The Naked Man in forest leaned down to his pants and grabbed a large rock.

"This better not get..."

The man's words were cut off when he was struck in the temple. He struggled to get up but The Naked Man from the Forest hit him again and again until his skull cracked open and blood poured on to the ground.

For a moment the man's face changed into the face of the hunted man on the television but The Naked Man From the Forest knew that was just wishful thinking.

51

Mitchell slowed the engine down and looked at the pier. Once they'd come to terms for his surrender his escorts gave him a wide berth. The fact that none of the men on either the Coast Guard or Marine patrol vessels had proper gear also made a difference. The people Mitchell was negotiating with didn't want a replay of what happened that morning.

The pier ran 1,000 feet out into the ocean. Mitchell could see that it had been cleared of fishermen and sightseers. The beach on either side had also been evacuated in a mile radius. He looked to his left at the various Coast Guard and other patrol vessels. They were moving into position to keep other boats away and to form a blockade if Mitchell decided to run again.

He could count at least three different television news helicopters in the sky along with various law enforcement ones. Since that morning, having things be public wasn't as reassuring to him. They had no problem acting stupid with the world watching. From the news reports, it was clear they were catching hell for what happened.

One hundred feet away from the floating dock at the bottom of the pier, Mitchell stopped the boat then went into the cabin. He dug through some drawers and found a roll of high-test fishing line.

He took the other flare gun from the floor of the cockpit and tied the fishing line around the trigger. He flipped open the gas cap and pointed the flare gun down into the tank. He then gently pushed the throttle forward and brought the boat up alongside the dock.

Still holding the spool of fishing line, he tied the boat off. He knew it wasn't going to work because he'd already shot the flares from both guns at the sniper in the trees. He'd found extra flares, but decided to only reload the one he had on him.

The fishing line was his own bit of theatre. Maybe they could tell the trigger probably wouldn't work. But as long as there was the possibility it would, it gave Mitchell's threat some additional weight.

Mitchell unspooled the fishing line and walked up the stairs that lead to the pier above. As per his request, there was a table and a chair at the end of the pier within sight off the boat. On it were two cell phones, a walkie-talkie, a bottle of water and a bag of take-out from Outback Steakhouse.

Mitchell hadn't eaten all day and didn't want to enter into negotiations on an empty stomach. He walked over and sat down.

A voice came over the radio, "Are you happy?"

Mitchell looked inside the take-out bag, "You forgot the steak sauce."

"It's inside the container."

Mitchell opened the Styrofoam container. "Oh. Thank you."

"Are you ready to talk now?"

Mitchell pulled the food out and unwrapped the knife and fork. "I need to make a phone call first."

He looked down at the food. He'd heard stories about the police drugging food they sent to hostage-takers. "If I feel the least bit woozy after eating this, I'm going to pull the cord. Is it safe to eat?"

"Yes, Mr. Roberts. No games on our part."

Mitchell picked up the phone and dialed. Rookman's familiar voice answered. "Mad Mitch! I'm watching you eat right now on television. Couldn't you have gone a little more upscale?"

"I'm sticking to what I know," said Mitchell as he ate a mouthful of baked potato. "Do you have a name for me?"

"Yep. I got the biggest cock puncher of them all for you. He's the guy you go to whenever somebody needs to stick a thumb in the government's eye."

Mitchell remembered the name from a few different high profile cases. "Thanks. So what do you think my chances are?"

"You know how in movies it's your most trusted friend telling you its safe to come in? I'm telling you it's safe to come in. So where are you?"

Fuck. Mad Mitch dropped a piece of steak back in the container. Rookman telling him things were safe was his way of telling him things were absolutely not safe. In every thriller, if a friend tells you its safe and then asks where you are, it means people are coming to get you.

Mad Mitch stood up. He looked around. There was nobody anywhere near him. Of course he knew that didn't mean there weren't NAVY Seals using gear like he had, waiting to disable his booby trap and shoot him.

Mad Mitch picked up the radio. "Is there anyone within 500 feet of me on land or in the water?"

There was silence. "Everyone is a safe distance away from you."

"That's not answering the question!" Mad Mitch looked over at the boat. How would they try to disable his threat? He looked at the water around the boat. There was less than a foot of visibility. "If I see so much as one drop of fuel come from the side or some hole one of your divers made in the bottom of the hull to empty the fuel tank, the deal is off." Mad Mitch thought for a moment. "I'll tell you nothing."

"Tell us nothing about what?"

Mad Mitch took the cell phone and the radio off the table and walked back down the stairs to the floating dock. He put the cell phone in his suit and pulled the other flare gun out and aimed it at the boat. He couldn't see any fuel leaking into the water, but that didn't mean they weren't about to try.

Mad Mitch stepped into the cockpit. He looked at his console and turned on the depth finder. The screen showed him a sonar image of the ocean floor below.

"I see two very large fish under my boat." Mad Mitch flipped a button that made a sound whenever something came within a few feet of the hull. It pinged. He held the radio to the speaker. "I shouldn't be hearing that sound."

The voice on the radio spoke up. "It's a fishing pier. There are going to be fish there."

Mad Mitch was looking at two very big fish on the screen. "Then tell Aquaman that he needs to call his friends back." Mad Mitch looked over at a gaff stick under the sidewall of the boat. He picked it up and held it aloft for the helicopters to see.

Mitchell spoke into the radio, "Are we being sincere with each other?"

"Yes Mr. Roberts. We're very sincere."

"Then if I stick this gaffing stick under here and try to stab the 'fish' under my boat you won't be bothered by that?"

There was a pause. The images on the screen drifted away. The sound of the depth finder dropped. "We may have had some people who were trying to secure the area who drifted away from their position."

Mitchell did a face palm. He let out a sigh then spoke into the radio. "Listen man. I know what happened today was a cluster fuck of epic proportions and you guys are profoundly embarrassed by what happened. I'm sure some genius there is telling you that you can make up for it by doing some commando style shit to get the upper hand on me.'

'I got news for you. You probably can outsmart me and wear me down and have your guys take me down in some kind of face saving way that makes it look like you guys are in control and some third-rate DJ nobody listens to is no match for you. But that won't erase the fact that you guys didn't listen to me earlier and people got hurt. It also doesn't mean you suddenly have a grip on the situation. There's something seriously fucked up going on. The sooner we can come to simple terms, the sooner you can march me down that pier and we can all figure out the bigger problem.'

'You've got a lot of people watching us on television right now and listening in on our discussion. You've told me twice that you were up to no tricks. There's no hostage here. You're not ethically obliged to lie to me to save them. I want to help.'

'If you send some NAVY Seals to shoot me or tranq me while my back is turned, all you've done is shot the guy who knocked on your door to tell you your house is on fire. I didn't start it.'

'And the more crazy-clever bullshit you try to pull on me the more people are going to be convinced that the reason you're trying so hard to not let me surrender the way I'm asking is because you're the ones who started the fire. Are you the one who started the fire?"

"No Mr. Roberts. We are not."

"Do you have any idea who that helicopter belonged to and why they were trying to shoot me and decapitate me?"

"No Mr. Roberts. We do not."

"Then please keep your word to me. Let me finish my phone calls and take care of what I need to on my end to make sure everything can go smoothly." Mitchell stepped out of the boat and walked up to table and sat down. He pulled out the cellphone.

"You got all that?"

"Yes sir," replied Rookman. "I'd get a hold of that lawyer soon."

"I agree." Mitchell hung up with Rookman and got the number of the lawyer from a Google search on the phone. While he assumed the Feds could listen to the phone call, he was even more paranoid about them pretending to be the lawyer.

A receptionist answered.

"I'd like to speak with Trevor Smith," said Mitchell.

"Who shall I tell him is speaking?" she asked.

"My name is Mitchell Roberts."

"Hello Mr. Roberts. We've been waiting for your call. I'll put you right through."

Finally some courtesy thought Mitchell.

"Mr. Roberts, I'm so glad you called." The booming voice had a calming effect on Mitchell. "It looks like you've had a bad couple of days."

"Not as bad as the people who got hurt, sir."

"That's true. I just want you to know that I'm on your side. Everyone is on your side. Especially after the way the Keystone cops handled it today." He paused, "Yes, I'm talking to you buffoons listening in. I'd remind you that I've got attorney client privilege if that would make a difference. Either way, they can hear what I'm going to tell you anyways. I don't want you to step a foot off that pier until they give you full immunity for everything that's happened."

"That sounds great. Can you get them to agree to that?"

"My office has already been talking to the attorney general. We pointed out that if they wanted to charge you for acting in self-defense then they would be obligated to charge half the agents on the bridge for attempted murder," he said.

"Yeah, but they couldn't help it. There's some kind of rage virus thing," said Mitchell.

"That's exactly the point. Either they acknowledge that there's something real that's out of your control and agree to not charge you for trying to save your own skin, or they say its hogwash and have to try two dozen FBI agents for attempted murder."

Smith went over a few more legal points with Mitchell then got off the phone to speak to the head of the CDC, the governor's office and the US District Attorney. He laid out his legal arguments and made the case that for everyone involved it was best to have Mitchell as a willing patient. He pointed out that he could get an injunction against them using any blood or tissue samples without his consent. And without those, they put their investigation into jeopardy.

After they agreed in theory he called Mitchell back to tell him that the immunity offer was only relating to the events of the past three days. He explained that they wanted to keep legal options available in the event Mitchell was found to be part of some larger plot.

"Is three days going to be enough?" asked Smith.

Mitchell stopped to do the math. "My first encounter was a girl four days ago. She just ran and screamed at me. I just ran away."

"I'll include that," said Smith. "Is there anything else?"

Mitchell realized that Smith, ever the lawyer, was giving him the opportunity to ask for help if he was actually tied into some kind of terrorist plot. "No, that's fine. If they can give me this and make sure I'm going to be safe, they'll have my full cooperation."

Smith called back to say that paperwork was being drafted on the immunity. "The next issue is your care. I've asked that you be admitted to a private hospital of your choice, but they're insisting you be taken to the CDC. I don't think we can get them to budge much on that."

Mitchell thought about that. "Wait, what if they can't cure me? Then what happens?"

"I'm going to have a trustee appointed to make sure that they provide the best care possible for you. They won't be allowed to just lock you away in some dark room."

Mitchell hadn't contemplated the idea that he had something that might not go away. What if people tried to kill him for the rest of his life? The only safe place would be locked away like a virulent disease.

He still didn't have any answers about who was trying to shoot him. Terrorists trying to cover their tracks? A renegade part of the government?

After another hour Smith called him, "You'll be allowed unrestricted use of communications. I've got three Noble laureates who have agreed to act as trustees. Amnesty International and the Red Cross have offered to oversee your treatment."

Mitchell's appreciation for the well-connected lawyer grew every time he called.

Behind him the sun was beginning to lower in the horizon. He'd finished the last of his steak an hour ago. The final step was for a courier in a spacesuit to bring him the papers to sign.

A voice came over his radio. "For us to allow the courier to come out to you we need you to disable your explosive device attached to the gas tank."

Mitchell still had Smith on the phone. He told him to proceed. Mitchell climbed down to the boat to pull the flare gun out of the gas tank. A sudden wave of paranoia overcame him. He pulled out the phone to call Rookman.

"Rookman, I've been in the middle of negotiating and haven't listened to anything on the news in the last few hours. What have they said?" Mitchell was afraid that it was too good to be true; the pardons and Smith's smooth tactics were all an act and that he was just talking to an impersonator.

"They've been saying that Smith was making a deal for you," said Rookman.

"Should I go along with it?"

"Listen kid, I don't think they're going to try anything more today. But I wouldn't put it past them to try to find a new way to screw you later on. When, not if, they do, scream. Make a big noise."

"Thank you," said Mitchell.

Mitchell unplugged the empty flare gun from the gas tank and threw it onto the floor of the cockpit. He climbed back up the stairs and sat down.

The voice on the radio spoke, "Please sign the documents as soon as you can so we can get you proper care."

A few minutes later a man in a blue hazmat suit walked down the pier. He set down a sheaf of papers and a pen on the table. Mitchell looked through the documents. There were two copies of the pardon, two more saying that the government was responsible for any liability claims made against Mitchell and another document underneath them with an 'X' next to where he was supposed to sign. He read the first few paragraphs then picked up the cellphone. He gave the courier a look and the man stepped out of range.

"Mr. Smith, why is there a document here about an agreement to limited liability?"

"That's to make sure the government is responsible for any liability claims against you," replied Smith.

"Yeah but there's two here. One is different then the other."

"What? Read it to me," said Smith. Smith listened then blurted out, "Those assholes. They want you to give up your right to sue them."

"To sue them?"

"Of course. We're going to file papers on your behalf tomorrow," replied Smith.

"This isn't about money."

"It's about leverage Mitchell."

"What do I do?" asked Mitchell.

"Tear it up."

Mad Mitch tore the document up then signed the others. The courier looked down at the torn up document and gave Mitchell a wink. He turned and walked back down the pier.

Ten minutes later the voice came on the radio. "We're bringing a container down the pier for you to get into. It's airtight with its own oxygen supply. From there we're going to bring you to a temporary staging area to look at your wounds. Then we're going to transport you via plane to the CDC in Atlanta. Are you ready?"

Mitchell called Smith to get a reassurance that it was safe to proceed. Smith told him to cooperate and that he would meet him at the staging area--behind glass of course.

Mitchell told the voice on the radio that he was ready. At the far end of the pier he saw four men in yellow hazmat suits push a larger stretcher out onto the pier. When it got closer Mitchell got a good look at it.

It was small plastic bed that looked like a sled with a plastic covering over the top. To Mitchell it looked like a glass coffin.

The men lifted the clear top off the stretcher. One of them spoke, "Mr. Mitchell, if you would please have a seat here, we can make sure you're securely fastened inside.

Mitchell eyed the container warily. In his mind he'd been hoping for something a little bigger, like an airtight limousine. Already mildly claustrophobic, the added paranoia wasn't helping him any.

The lead medical technician spoke to him. "After we take you to the staging area we can give you a sedative for the trip."

Mitchell just shrugged and got on the stretcher. Nobody protested when he put the phone in his pocket. Another technician fastened an air mask over his mouth. After he put his legs up they covered him with a blanket. The lid came down and he could hear the sound of it sealing. The lead medic gave Mitchell a thumbs up. Mitchell nodded weakly.

He'd gone from a man on the run to letting them put him into a box smaller than the coffin he felt bound for. The medics began pushing the clear coffin down the pier and towards a large van designed for transporting hazardous materials. Mitchell tried to calm himself by accepting the fact that everything was out of his hands now. No more running. No more seeing people get hurt.

In the back of his mind were a hundred different paranoid thoughts. *He should have asked for Secret Service protection.* He should have demanded a 24 hour live internet feed showing the world his treatment. *Damn,* he could have been streaming the whole thing. Overhead he could see news helicopters still flying around. What happened when he was put inside the van or locked away for treatment? Why didn't he just aim the boat for the ocean and keep going? He'd have to have felt safer than he did at that point.

They finally reached the van. The medics slid the casket into the sealed-off back area headfirst. The wheels were locked into grooves on the floor. The first medic, the one who gave him the thumbs up stepped inside.

Another medic began to step into the back, but was waved off by him. That was odd, thought Mitchell. You'd think they'd have that kind of thing sorted out. The doors were shut. Mitchell looked around the interior of the van and then at the one man inside of it with him. He was trapped.

52

Restricted by the glass casing, Mitchell tried to turn his head to look at the man in the hazmat suit sitting just past his shoulders. It was hard enough to make out a face through the glass shield of the helmet without Mitchell's own scared face reflecting back at him from inside the plastic dome that trapped him.

Mitchell could feel the van begin to move. He thought about shouting for help, but knew no one would hear his muffled voice through the respirator and the van's thick walls. The man in the hazmat suit slid across the metal bench so Mitchell could more clearly see him. The man looked out the small window at the rear of the van then back towards him. He placed a gloved hand on Mitchell's casket.

"Mitchell," said the man's voice from behind the ventilator in his mask. "I guess the only way to explain things is to just come right out and tell you." The man paused. "When they get you to the facility, they're going to find out that there's nothing wrong with you."

Nothing wrong with me? Was this guy crazy, thought Mitchell.

The man continued. "And then its going to be even worse for you. People will begin asking questions. Questions that others don't want answered. And that's why they want to kill you."

Mitchell's eyes bulged behind his own oxygen mask. Was this man an assassin? He ran his fingers along the edge of the container trying to find some way to crack the seal and get out.

The man looked down at Mitchell struggling. He reached into a pouch and pulled something out and set it on top of the plastic casket. Mitchell's eyes tried to focus on the object just inches above his head. It was a screwdriver.

"You'd need something like this to get yourself out. But I don't suppose you have one on you. No matter." The man leaned back and looked at a watch strapped to the outside of his suit. "We have a little time."

Mitchell looked down at his feet. He braced his hands against the side of the container and began to kick. Maybe it wouldn't set him free, at best it would attract the driver's attention.

The man in the suit put another hand on the casket and shook his head as he looked down at Mitchell. "Mitchell, I'm not here to hurt you. I'm here to help you."

Mitchell stopped kicking and looked up at the man. "Who are you?"

"I'm part of this Mitchell, but I never wanted to be a part of this." He tapped the casket. "I'm a doctor. I'm part of a group that spends its time worrying about worst case scenarios and trying to prevent them."

"Like this?" asked Mitchell.

The man shook his head. "Much, much worse Mitchell. This was a side effect. A mistake that happens when people act without thinking. When they do things out of fear. We're at war Mitchell."

Mitchell tried to look into the man's eyes to read if he was being sincere or just trying to calm him down so he didn't alert the driver. "At war with who?"

"The future, Mitchell. It has many faces, many threats. We take tiny pieces of information and, from those tiny pieces, we try to extract a bigger picture. Sometimes that picture is more horrible than you can imagine. When that happens you have to act. You're here because certain people decided to act in a certain way. I told them they were too motivated by fear. But it didn't matter. What they saw was too terrifying to act any other way."

Mitchell was silent as he tried to make sense of what the man was saying.

"A few months ago we found something. A virus, basically a modified version of a pneumonia-causing virus, the kind of virus everybody has in their body but that their immune system keeps in check. But this virus had something special in it, a set of instructions that would flip a switch in your body that's been dormant for a hundred million years.

"Ever wonder how animals can tell family members apart? It's in the pheromones. Chemical fingerprints. Everybody has them. They're what makes us want to fuck. They're what makes women jealous when they smell another female on their mate. They're what make men want to kill each other in bars filled with available women.

"This virus had been engineered to make people want to kill each other when they smelled other human pheromones. Any kind. It turned on the fight or flight response in our brains and turned us into reptiles trying to rip the throat out of any other animal with that same chemical fingerprint.

"The virus is highly contagious and we knew it could spread quickly if it got loose. In a few weeks every man and woman on this planet would be trying to murder each other with their hands and teeth."

"Who would make something like that?" asked Mitchell.

"The Russians, the Chinese, us, maybe the Indians. It could be something an ally made and it got loose. The problem was that we knew it was out there. Somebody had it. And we had to do something about it. That's when some clever people came up with an idea for how to inoculate us against it. We'd heard that Chinese party officials were getting vaccinated for some mysterious reason and we had to act.

"The problem is that the virus works even in its weakened form. So we needed to create something that acted just like it and prevent it from infecting in the first place, and if it did, override the chemical triggers it sent to the brain. That's when we had the idea, my idea, to change the pheromone trigger from a general one, to a specific one. Instead of targeting any human, only one unique pheromone could set it off."

The man gestured towards Mitchell. "And that my friend is where you came in. It was a simple mistake. A mislabeled vial here, a truncated database, I don't know the specifics, but I can draw you a picture.

"You donated blood three years ago on your college campus. A sample of it ended up in a lab looking for pheromone triggers in blood. Yours wasn't special, no offense, it was just a control sample. From your blood we sequenced the part of your DNA that coded for one of your unique pheromones. Some we all share, others are one-in-a-sextillion combinations that will never occur in a billion years of human history. Instead of creating a random one to plug into our counter-virus, we fucked up. We used yours.

"A few weeks ago we got the go-ahead to covertly inoculate the population. We began spreading the virus in subways, restaurants, everywhere. It's symptoms were so mild we were able to run under the cover of a convenient flu outbreak. I suspect the only person who got noticeably sick was you. Your body didn't know what to make of it. That's why you were sick at home. That might be why you've lasted this long.

"And so there's the problem. If other people get a look at you they're going to realize that you're perfectly healthy. We're the ones who have been infected. We've covered our tracks so far by modifying gene libraries of pneumonia viruses and made sure that epidemiology reports are filtered through friendly hands. But it's a small group of people trying to maintain a large conspiracy. That can't last for very long if you're alive.

"That's why they're going to come for you. They don't see themselves as murderers. So they won't come at you with guns and knives. They're doctors. They'll kill you via committee. A group of people will prescribe a treatment for a condition that doesn't exist and just to be cautious they'll treat you for other conditions as well until you're dead. They'll cure you to death so that people who know better can keep the real secret hidden.

Once you're dead your body will be sealed up and buried away in some basement where they keep vials of smallpox and polio. A tentative explanation will be given, some kind of hormonal trigger you give off and that will become the accepted wisdom because there will be no more Mitchell Roberts around to test and poke. The end."

The man began to unlatch the buckles holding the top of the casket in place. "Of course then the people who did this will get overconfident and the next time they might get even more sloppy. Or even worse, someone might decide we need to be proactive and create a virus that only gets the 'bad' guys and go ahead and release it. Or maybe the 'bad' people. It's not like a nuclear missile where you need a thousand people to build, maintain and launch these things. All it takes is one asshole with a test tube."

Mitchell watched as the man finished unlatching the casket. He picked up the screwdriver and lifted the container open like a clam shell. Mitchell eyed the screwdriver. The man turned it over and handed it to Mitchell handle first.

"Too bad they didn't search you for this when you got inside," said the man.

He reached to the floor and pulled out a small bag. He produced a syringe. Mitchell recoiled.

"Don't worry, it's for me. Not you. We need to switch places, you in my suit, me in the casket, but in order to do that I'm going to have to be unconscious, unless you want to fight me off. I'd rather we didn't do it that way."

"What do I do then?" Mitchell asked.

"When we come to a stop they'll unload me thinking I'm you. That's when you need to get out and make it to my car. The keys are in the bag. From there you need to get away as fast as possible. In my car you'll find my laptop. There's a file called 'Great Wall'. It's what you want."

Mitchell tried to put all of it together. "Is that a cure?"

The man laughed. "No. The only cure right now is transparency. You'll need to share that file. It's got everything in there about what happened. The problem is you can't just email it to people or upload it to Google.'

"Ever since Wikileaks, we've taken some extreme measures to filter and protect sensitive information. Filters on email servers. Worms on storage servers that cause disk failures when certain phrases show up. There's even rooms full of people that do nothing now but create credible looking forgeries of government documents to confuse and waste the time of people trying to find the truth."

"So what do I do?" asked Mitchell.

"Keep doing what you've been doing. Run. Stay alive and when you find a way, tell people everything. Broadcast it. The only safe place for you is in plain sight."

The man opened the wrist of his suit and injected himself. "Place my body inside and cover my head with the pillow. Then move. You'll have maybe two hours before they realize I drove my own car and my lab assistant is using the rental with the tracking. Then find some other way to keep going."

The man's eyes began to get droopy. Mitchell tried to think of anything else to ask him. A million questions came to mind.

"What's you password?" asked Mitchell.

"Password ... almost ... for ... got ..." The man's body began to go slack. Mitchell had to grab his shoulders to keep him from falling over. "password ... is ... Lovestrange."

53

The van came to a stop. Mitchell was convinced the moment they opened the doors they'd see he'd made the switch and the gig would be up. He did his best to look down at the plastic casket at the face of Dr. Lovestrange, or whatever his name was, covered with the pillow and a towel, and act as casual as could be. Four more men in spacesuits were at the back of the van waiting to unload the casket.

Mitchell helped them move it out while avoiding eye contact. He kept his eyes down on his 'patient' while trying to scope out where he was. Four sets of work lights illuminated the area where they were unloading the van. Directly ahead was a large plastic door, the kind of thing you saw in movies before you saw the bodies of crashed aliens behind it.

In and around the work lights were several other people in spacesuits watching the proceedings. The whole area looked like some kind of improvised processing facility.

What looked like a hundred police cars with their lights still flashing surrounded the area beyond the lights in a perimeter. The police were staying inside of their cars to avoid 'contamination' or whatever they were calling it.

At first he panicked at the thought of moving through them, then he realized all the attention was on the casket. Mitchell allowed the men pushing it to move away from him as they headed towards the big plastic door. Once they got close to it, Mitchell stepped to the side and walked between two of the huge work lights into the shadows where other people in spacesuits were watching from behind a barrier.

Acting like he had business elsewhere, he walked right past the line of police vehicles and nobody looked twice.

Past them he could see a parking lot filled with cars, various government vehicles and trucks. That's when he realized that the processing facility was actually the Park Square Mall. Mitchell knew criminals often returned to the scene of the crime. For him it wasn't a choice.

He moved out into the parking lot and towards a cluster of cars. Nobody stopped him, so he kept moving. Off to one side there was a small encampment of trailers with people in and out of suits walking around. Somewhere he was sure there was probably a decontamination booth and lockers for the suits, but since nobody stopped him, he kept walking towards the cars. There was no time to waist acting guilty.

Mitchell fumbled the key from a pouch and clicked the unlock button. A dark blue Ford Explorer's lights blinked a dozen cars away.

He wasn't sure how suspicious he'd look getting into the car with the suit on, but he was even more afraid of what would happen if he was approached with it off. Mitchell also didn't know if it would be possible to drive with the bulky oxygen canister strapped to his back.

Mitchell waited until the last second as he got to the car and quickly stripped the suit off and tossed it into the passenger side on top of the laptop bag. He'd put it back in its duffel bag later. For the time being he just needed to get out of there.

Mitchell started the SUV up and headed towards the exit. All of the entrances to the mall had police cars at them making sure that no unauthorized people entered. He hoped that they assumed anybody inside there had business in there and could leave without having to show any identification.

Even so, Mitchell's face was the most recognizable one in South Florida. He looked around the interior and found a pair of reading glasses in the center console. Mitchell put them on as he headed towards the exit where a cop with a flashlight was standing.

Act casual, thought Mitchell. He reached down and picked up a cell phone Lovestrange had left behind. He put it to his ear and had a pretend conversation when the cop looked over at him. Mitchell nodded. The cop pointed towards the main highway and waived Mitchell on.

Mitchell pulled out of the mall for the second time in three days in a car that wasn't his own with no idea where to go next.

Baylor couldn't make up his mind if he wanted to follow the motorcade surrounding the ambulance or keep a careful distance away. He'd gotten Steinmetz onto the processing team. But all he could hope for from him was information. He wasn't a team player. Steinmetz had trouble with the difficult choices. Baylor couldn't count on him do the really hard stuff. For that he needed Mr. Lewis. By this time he should be finishing up cleaning the mess he and Mr. Travis had made.

A little arson and an incriminating letter about trying to stop 'The Islamic Traitor Roberts' and they had a credible Jack Ruby in Travis. Helicopter pilots were kind of nutty to begin with. Baylor could make sure that a record of Post Traumatic Stress was available on the man and he'd just be an odd footnote in the Mitchell Roberts story.

The next step was making sure that story ended in the next day. The longer the CDC and others had a live specimen, even worse, a lawyered-up specimen, the more problems for Great Wall.

Baylor decided his next step would have to take place somewhere after Mitchell left the South Florida area. The CDC was pushing to have him brought to Atlanta. That would be too problematic for Baylor. If he could get the Pentagon involved, he could have Mitchell sent to an Army base where they dealt with bio-terrorism. There he could count on less civilians and more people tied into his own network.

He pulled out his phone and called his contact in the West Wing. He would follow the motorcade back to the mall at a more leisurely pace while he strategized on how to get who he needed on the committee that would actually be overseeing Mitchell's care.

54

The idea for everything had come to Mitchell when he realized he'd have to ditch the car sooner rather than later. He was 20 minutes north of the mall when he saw police cars behind him begin to line up on the exits on the highway. He took the nearest exit before a Highway Patrol car came to a stop in the middle of the off ramp.

Steinmetz, aka Dr. Lovestrange--Mitchell had found the name on a letter in the console--had meant well. But even he had no idea how intense this manhunt was going to get once they realized Mitchell had slipped away.

The escape made Mitchell appear far more resourceful than he was and also more sinister. The negotiation and the surrender seemed like some kind of mastermind plot. Now the authorities weren't treating him like a hospital patient on the run, his actions had implicated him in something much more global.

He had to tell the world about Great Wall, or else his actions would never make any sense. There was no way he would survive for very long at the center of such a massive hunt. He was in a race to get the word out before they caught him.

Everything came into focus for Mitchell when he realized he had one and only one goal; get the word out before they got him. To do that he needed a way to spread the message. He entertained the idea of breaking into a copy shop and holding them hostage while they printed out the contents of the computer files. But he knew that would take too long. He'd find himself surrounded before the first printout was finished collating.

Steinmetz's computer was going to have to be his printing press, if not online, then by making copies onto USB sticks and CD-ROMS. That meant one more stop before he dropped off the car and took an alternate means of transportation.

Mitchell pulled the SUV into a Walgreen's several miles from where he exited. He had a bold idea, but given the state of panic everyone was in, it could work.

He donned the spacesuit and walked in through the front door. The small Indian woman behind the counter gave Mitchell a curious look.

Mitchell turned to her. "He's been spotted in this area. Do you have a back room where you can hide?"

The woman nodded.

"Go there, but don't touch anything electrical, like a phone." It sounded stupid as he said it, but the woman was too scared to point that out. She ran off towards the back of the store.

Mitchell grabbed a shopping basket and walked over to the side of the store where they had USB memory sticks and blank CD-ROMS. He began piling them into the basket. Once it was full he headed back out the front of the store and got into the car with the spacesuit still on.

He got the helmet off, but had to drive with the seat pushed back at its farthest setting to accommodate the backpack.

His silly trick wasn't going to last for very long and he needed to get to where he could ditch the car as soon as possible.

Back when Mitchell was hiding out on the island he'd played around with the scanner listening to different frequencies. On one cluster of bands he found different voices talking about dispatching police cars, ambulances and other emergency vehicles. That was the one he paid the most attention to. While scanning around he found another band he couldn't understand at first. It took him ten minutes to realize that the talk of 'knuckles', 'drawbars' and 'gas cans' was railroad chatter. He was listening to rail yard workers somewhere not too far off getting trains prepped.

He remembered them talking about 'the ten fifteen North Atlantic'. At 10:40 he could hear the sound of a train passing somewhere not too far away from where he was hiding across the Intracoastal.

Mitchell pulled into the parking lot of a Best Buy not too far away from where he'd thought he remembered seeing the rail yard the calls had come from. He parked in the far side by a beat-up Ford Focus and stripped off the spacesuit. He shoved it into the duffel bag. His fingers touched the screwdriver Steinmetz had given him, which he realized he was supposed to have left behind, and had an idea. He took the license plate from the Ford Focus and shoved it into his bag. It worked before. Maybe it would work again.

Mitchell then climbed through the hedges and ran towards the railroad tracks that snaked around the back of

the Best Buy and towards the rail yard. Ahead he could
see the tail end of the 'ten fifteen'. By his watch it was
already 10:17 PM. He'd heard trains rarely left on time,
so he hoped he'd just had a bit of good fortune.

Mitchell ran along the side of the train that was in
shadows. He was looking for an open rail car. He didn't
know how common they actually were, but Rookman had
guests come on who talked about using them to travel
around like 21st-century hobos. Up ahead he could hear
the train blow a whistle and start up. There was the sound
of metal hitting metal as the 'knuckles' that connected the
cars began to pull against each other from the front to the
back of the train. The train would build up speed and
begin to overtake him if he didn't find a spot.

Car after car was either a tanker or a locked up freight
car. Mitchell was beginning to lose hope. If all else failed
he could just cling to a ladder and get off at some point
further on up the rail, but that meant being out in the open
and risk getting caught.

The train was beginning to match pace with Mitchell's
jogging. He had to run faster in order to get to the cars
that were further ahead. He rounded another bend and
could see the front of the train a thousand feet away.
Closer to him he saw several car carriers loaded with
brand new Toyota Land Cruisers headed from the port of
Miami to somewhere north. They had walls along the
sides but the backs were open.

Mitchell ran up to the closest carrier and threw the
duffel bag with the spacesuit and laptop onto the platform
at the end of the car. He grabbed the metal frame around
the back and pulled his chest onto the back of the car. He

didn't appreciate how high off the ground the back end was until he felt his feet dangle and drag in the gravel as he struggled to pull himself aboard.

He finally managed to get a knee, then both legs onto the carrier as the train picked up speed. Mitchell picked up his bag and climbed over the space between the hood of the last car and the top of the carrier. He didn't want to break the window of the outermost car.

Mitchell pulled out his screwdriver and got ready to slam it into the back window of a brand new silver Land Cruiser when he got the impulse to actually check if it was locked. He reached down and squeezed the latch for the rear hatch. It popped open. Of course. Mitchell threw his duffel bag into the back.

He looked at the sticker on the windshield of the rearmost Land Cruiser and tried to decipher the symbols. Origin was listed as MIA. Destination was listed as ATL. Atlanta. He tried to remember what was going on in Atlanta at that time. He knew the CDC had headquarters there. But there was something else. *Of course*, thought Mitchell. His endgame was in sight. First he needed to make several hundred copies of the files while the train drove through the night. Then he could plan out how he was going to cause a commotion.

55

Mitchell was sound asleep in the passenger seat of the Land Cruiser when a commotion not of his design shook him awake. He felt his body lurch forward then opened his eyes to see sunlight momentarily flicker from outside the carrier then suddenly get blacked out. Something pressed up against his face and he could smell a sharp pungent smell like battery acid. All around he heard the sound of twisting metal and explosions as the entire world seemed to be shaken apart.

He felt a moment of weightlessness then was thrown to the right as the world shifted around him. His brain tried to make sense of what was happening. Parts of a half-remembered dream still threaded through his consciousness. *The smell. The pressure on his face and the explosion he just felt to his side. Airbags.*

He was in a car. The car was in a train. The train had crashed. Mitchell could feel the rumble of metal sliding across gravel and hear the impact as cars hit each other. The train was still crashing.

The air bags began to deflate. The windshield was cracked from when the impact sent the cars in the carrier into the air, bouncing into the ceiling. His car and the carrier were now on their side. For a fleeting moment he thought he was back in the tractor-trailer truck he'd stolen what seemed like ages ago.

Mitchell could hear the sound of the railroad cars in back of him shutter and fly off the tracks as the impact that hit him rolled from the front of the train to the back like a giant wave. Twenty million pounds of steel cried out as the train was brought to a stop.

Mitchell regained his senses. He did a quick pat down to see if anything was broken. He was already bruised and banged up from the past several days; all he cared about was if any bones were sticking out of places where they shouldn't. Everything seemed to be where it was supposed to have been. It was dumb luck that he'd found the safest place on the train; inside a car with front and side airbags. If he'd found the open rail car like he'd been hoping for, he was certain his body would have been bounced around like a jelly donut inside a blender.

On top of everything else, thought Mitchell, now he was trapped in a train accident. He unfastened his seat belt and shifted his back to the side door so he could kick out the windshield. *Accident?* He cursed himself. There were no accidents of late. This was deliberate.

He thought for a moment. If it had been the cops and the feds, they would have just stopped the train. This was someone else. This was the work of the people who'd sent the helicopter after his boat. Somehow they'd tracked him. Mitchell had shut off the phone he'd taken from the pier and made sure that Steinmetz's laptop's wireless connection was turned off. *Damn it.* It was a government computer and undoubtedly had some kind of computer tracking system in it. The fact that the people who tracked him had used train derailment as a means to stop him, meant that Steinmetz's bosses hadn't told the feds where he was at.

Mitchell needed to get away before the scene was flooded with emergency personnel. He grabbed the duffel bag and climbed through the front windshield. There was a crevice of space between the top of the SUV and the carrier ceiling. Mitchell squeezed his body into it and moved towards the bright light streaming from the back of the car hauler.

It probably would have been easier if he'd just crawled through the back window, but he didn't feel like going back into the SUV. The airbag smell and broken glass would only depress him even further. If he stopped to think of himself as an accident victim waiting for help, that would just make him vulnerable.

Mitchell pushed himself through the tiny space then froze. Outside he could hear the sound of feet on gravel. Someone was walking towards the car carrier.

56

Tracking Mitchell Roberts had been easy. As soon as Baylor called Mr. Lewis to tell him that Dr. Steinmetz had been overpowered and injected with his own sedative, the first thing he did was put a trace on Steinmetz's cell phone and laptop. He ignored Baylor's suggestion that he focus on the rental car. Baylor was cunning in his own right, but he didn't get people like he did. The whole story sounded fishy to Mr. Lewis, but he kept his opinion to himself. His target was Roberts.

Once he tracked him within 10 meters of a railroad line, it wasn't hard to put two and two together. A charter jet flight courtesy of Baylor, and he was able to beat the train north of the Florida border on the Georgia side by a few hours.

The real problem was getting to Roberts before the real feds did. Mr. Lewis couldn't afford to wait for the train to pull into a yard or have the kid jump train before then. He needed to stop him in his tracks in the literal sense of the term.

Mr. Lewis had spent the two hour travel time trying to figure out how one goes about stopping several million tons of steel while making it look like an accident, or at the very least a crude form of sabotage.

He had enough plastic explosive in his travel bag to do the trick, but that would leave too many questions. He needed what his trainers back at The Woods had called an 'organic' solution. Mr. Lewis looked up every rail disaster he could to see what would be the most practical for him to pull off. For the small part of him that felt anything like excitement or enthusiasm, this kind of improvisation was his favorite part of his job. It was one thing to arrange for a Turkish scientist to have his tires get blown out on the Autobahn or to create a propane explosion in a medical facility at Oxford that would only take out one troublesome biologist. It was another to do something so spectacular that it would dominate the national news for days. It wasn't the kind of thing he'd put on his resume, but it certainly would give him a source of pride.

If it killed that asshole Mitchell Roberts in the process, that was an even bigger plus in his book. Mr. Lewis still chafed from letting the kid get the drop on him and making him and Travis out to be buffoons when he hooked the helicopter. Telling himself it was a one-in-a-million shot didn't solve the problem.

What was most frustrating with Roberts was that he wasn't any kind of professional. It's one thing to get thwarted by someone who has been trained to avoid assassination and kidnapping attempts. It was another to be chastened by a kid who hadn't even served in the military let alone had any kind of special training. Roberts had only one skill, and that was running away from danger like a scared rabbit. Most people were easy to catch because they had a moment of panic before they decided to take flight. That was when you went in for the kill. Roberts was like a twitchy rodent that didn't stop to think. He just kept moving and tried to figure out where he was going afterwards.

It was an admirable instinct. It was the kind of thing men trained for years to learn how to do. The trick was learning how not to think. Thinking took time. Thinking got you killed. Roberts had made it this far because he just didn't stop.

Mr. Lewis's sole mission in life at that point was to make sure that he did get stopped. His 'organic' solution was a tractor trailer truck loaded with a 50 ton steel cross beam destined for a highway overpass. He'd found the solution at a truck stop a mile outside of Waycross, Georgia - ten miles from the narrow trestle where he was going to put it to use.

He'd stopped the driver in the parking lot and showed him one of his more official looking badges. He punched the ruddy faced man in the nose when he got with in striking distance, stunning him. He then slipped him into a sleeper hold and snapped the man's neck as he pulled him into the cab.

The entire altercation took only four seconds, not that anyone was counting.

Mr. Lewis pushed the body into the passenger seat and took off back down the highway to the trestle. It took him eight minutes to get to the service road that lead up onto to the tracks and to the trestle. The chain barrier snapped like twine when he drove the tractor trailer truck though it.

He pulled the tractor trailer and its cargo half way on to the trestle at an angle. That way the train would hit it like a bullet through a blocked muzzle and be directed sideways. It would be hard to bring that much energy to a total stop even if he had a hundred trailers loaded with 50 ton beams. All he needed to do was to send it a few feet off to the side then inertia and gravity would take care of the rest.

After the organic solution was in place he checked his watch. He had eight minutes before the train was going to be coming through and meeting its immovable object. That gave Mr. Lewis plenty of time to get clear and to find his means of escape. He walked back the side road to State Road 84 and flagged down a car.

Rhonda Terrell was on her way to drop off a meal for her invalid mother before she went to work. She brought her Chevy Malibu to a stop when she saw a man in khaki slacks and a polo shirt wave her down. He had some kind of badge on his waist, so she figured he was probably a police officer of some type.

He walked up to her window and gave her a broad smile. She never noticed him pull the gun from his back and shoot two bullets through her forehead. The Tupperware container was sprayed with blood.

Mr. Lewis reached inside and popped the trunk lever. He looked both ways to make sure there were no oncoming cars then unbuckled the woman and pulled her into the trunk. He turned the ignition off, but left the keys in the car. He was fairly certain it wasn't going to get stolen in the next four minutes. He opened the Tupperware container and took out a piece of fried chicken then walked back to the side of the road where he had the best vantage point of the trestle.

He wanted to get close, but not too close. Off in the distance he could hear the train whistle as it went through the town of Waycross. He imagined that most of locals had learned to tune the sound of trains out entirely. It was just more background noise like a honking horn, although that was a rarity in this polite part of the South.

Two school buses passed by. Mr. Lewis watched as tiny faces looked out through the windows back towards him. He was almost sad they were going to miss the show. He could feel the rumble of the train as it got closer. His balls began to tingle as he looked through the trees at the steel beam and trailer wedged into the trestle. He finished the chicken and threw the bone to the ground.

As the train reached the point of no return he could hear the rolling sound of thunder through the trees. The horn blew as the engineer finally saw that the trestle was blocked. Then the sound of air breaks frantically being pushed into action raced through the air.

Mr. Lewis watched as the train engine slammed into the obstructed trestle. The trailer and beam bent inwards as the engine hit them with full force. The front of the train derailed and ran square into the trestle beams knocking the entire structure off its foundation and into the shallow stream below. The engine nose-dived into the ground and sent a bullwhip of energy backwards, lifting cars off their tracks and into the air. They buckled then fell on to their sides, skidding down the embankment and into the trees.

He watched with satisfaction as over a mile of steel and iron threw itself into the air and then against the ground like a giant serpent. He could hear the sound of groaning metal and small explosions as tankers ripped open, spilling their contents.

He ran forward, like a concerned bystander, to inspect the carnage and look for any survivors he needed to kill.

57

Mitchell slowly pulled his body back into the shadows of the crevice formed by the roof of the Land Cruiser and the ceiling of the carrier. It was such a tight space he had to control his breathing to avoid getting stuck. The duffle bag with the spacesuit hung in the air squeezed between the two walls.

The footsteps slowed down. Mitchell had a pretty good idea who they belonged to. He knew the shooter from the helicopter wasn't going to give up that easily. It just wasn't in the cards for Mitchell that the man would have just drowned when he threw the air tank at him.

Mitchell tried to think of what he had for a weapon. The screwdriver was in the duffle bag along with the laptop and the thumb drives he'd copied the Great Wall folder onto. He reached a hand towards the zipper of the bag and carefully began to open the bag. He kept his eyes forward towards the bright patch of light at the rear of the carrier.

The footsteps moved closer. A voice called out. "Hello? Is anyone in there?"

The calm and friendly nature of the voice chilled Mitchell. *This wasn't a man.* This was a sociopath who acted like men to trap and kill them.

Mad Mitch wanted to call back out to the voice, *come murder me in here, dumb fuck*! But he kept quiet. His hand probed around the plastic contours of the suit trying to find the screwdriver. Footsteps moved towards the back of the carrier.

Mitchell could see a shadow come into view. In just a few moments the shooter was going to poke his head in the back and look to see if there was anybody in there. How far would he go in? Mitchell lifted his chin so he could turn his head and look to the front of the trailer. There were four more Land Cruisers on their sides.

He could try to move all the way to the back, but then what? The further in he went the more trapped he would be. Mitchell tried to imagine what the shooter was going to see when he came around the corner. If the shooter looked at the back of the car to see if the hatch had been opened Mitchell might have a moment before the shooter noticed him in the tight space.

Mad Mitch's fingers felt the edge of the laptop. He still couldn't find the damn screwdriver. *Fuck it.* He slid the laptop out of the bag. At the very least he could use it as a shield.

The duffle bag lost some of its tension and fell to the aluminum siding that was the floor and made a metal clang. *Fuck.*

"Hey! Need me to go get help?" The shooter was giving Mitchell a plausible reason to speak up.

Yeah, go get help so you won't get infected by my reverse rabies, that's not really reverse rabies. Mad Mitch kept his mouth shut. If he spoke, even if it was an attempt to misdirect the man by telling him he was stuck in the car, he knew he'd lose the advantage.

The shadow grew as it came around the corner. Mad Mitch raised his left hand in an arc and passed the laptop over his head and into the grip of his right hand. The shadow paused. Mad Mitch could hear the man take in a breath of air through his nostrils.

Mad Mitch didn't even wait to see the man come into view around the corner. He knew a human predator like this was controlled by their killing instinct and would not hesitate. He slammed the laptop downwards as the shooter leaped into the crevice.

The thin metal edge of the computer slammed into the shooter's forehead and formed a crimson streak across his face. Mad Mitch stepped backwards. The shooter pushed his body into the crevice. His clawed hands shot at Mitchell's face trying to pull away flesh and skin. Mad Mitch slammed the laptop upwards at the man's chin. His head jerked back then snapped forwards as his teeth bared at Mitchell. He let out a growl sending a shower of blood and spittle at Mitchell's face.

Mad Mitch took another step back. The man forced himself further into the crevice. A hand grabbed Mitchell's shoulder. He could feel nails digging into his skin and trying to pull apart the sinew of his shoulders. Mad Mitch pulled backwards and tripped over the bag as he fell onto the metal siding.

The shooter pushed himself into the space where Mitchell had just been. His left hand clawed out into the space beyond the hood. He struggled to pull himself through, but the space was too narrow for his large frame.

Mad Mitch looked at the laptop on the ground. He got to his feet, picked it up and slammed it into the man's face with both hands while trying to avoid the reach of the hand. The shooter's nose shattered and sent a cascade of red fluid all over the laptop and Mad Mitch's hands.

The man's eyes bulged and looked at Mitchell without blinking. The hand tried to twist around the corner to reach out at Mitchell, but he was too far out of reach. The shooter tried to push his body into the narrow space. Mad Mitch could hear the sound of the Land Cruiser's metal roof pop inwards as he shoved his shoulders past the center.

Fuck.

Mad Mitch slammed the laptop into the man's face again. He heard a crack as the laptop finally began to crumple. He grabbed it by the sides, held it over his head and brought the corner into the shooter's left eye socket. Mad Mitch felt it crack through the case of the laptop. Blood sported out from the eye and it bulged even further outwards hanging loose.

The shooter kept snarling and trying to grab Mitchell with his left hand. Mad Mitch swung the laptop into the man's wrist. He could hear something crack as he dented the laptop even further on the man's thick wrist bones.

Lubricated by his own blood and sweat, the shooter began to slip past the roof of the Land Cruiser and the carrier ceiling. Mitchell looked to the front windshield of the Land Cruiser. This one wasn't cracked like the one he'd been inside. Mad Mitch kicked his right heel into the windshield hoping to break it. His foot was just deflected. Mad Mitch slammed the laptop into it. The computer broke into two pieces only leaving a small spider web of cracks.

Mad Mitch threw it to the ground. He picked up the duffle bag and crawled into the space where the wheels met the floor of the carrier. He ducked under the front wheels and shoved his body under the front forks. His spine could feel the axle pressing up against it. He kept moving.

The shooter finally burst through the crevice and into the space Mitchell had just left. He threw his body into the even tighter area Mitchell was in and grabbed wildly. His hands grabbed Mitchell's right thigh and began to dig their nails into the skin.

The shooter brought his mouth to tear into Mitchell's flesh. Mad Mitch reflexively jerked and sent his knee into the shooter's chin. He hear a loud crack as he dislocated his jaw. The hands didn't let go.

Mitchell fell backwards. He was half supported the pressure of his hips between the undercarriage and the side wall. His leg was still firmly grasped by the shooter who was pushing his body in further.

Mitchell heard the sound of metal clang. He looked to see if his screwdriver had fallen free. His left hand scraped the floor where he couldn't see. His fingertips grazed something metal. The shooter brought the top of his mouth onto Mitchell's leg to take a bite. His dislocated jaw couldn't close on the leg so he furiously slammed his upper teeth into Mitchell's shin.

It felt like an ice pick slamming into bone. Half upside down, stuck between the SUV and the carrier, Mitchell began to hyperventilate. He stretched his left hand back to try to grab the object. Mitchell let out a roar as he nearly tore his arm out of socket pulling on the car's frame.

His fingers grasped the object. It wasn't his screwdriver. He gripped the handle and brought the shooter's gun back over his head and pointed it towards the man's bloody mess of a face as he tried to fillet Mitchell's calf muscle.

Mad Mitch pulled the trigger and fired a round at almost point blank range. The back of the shooter's skull exploded, sending blood and brains into the back of the carrier. His body reflexively kept trying to bite into Mitchell's leg.

Mad Mitch fired two more rounds into the man's face before he could pull his leg free. His ears rang from the sound of the shots reverberating in the small space. Mitchell fell backwards and hit the ground. With his free hand he grabbed the duffle bag and went towards the light. He tried to ignore the searing pain in his leg as he stood up and limped from the back of the car carrier.

Outside he could hear sirens as rescue vehicles raced towards the mile long disaster of twisted metal. Mitchell could see two separate plumes of black smoke coming from tankers at the tail end.

He knew he only had minutes before rescuers found him and tried to finish what the shooter had started. Mitchell pulled a shirt from the bag to use as a bandage. He looked down at the spacesuit in his bag.

In all the commotion it was worth a try. It looked like a hazmat suit fire fighters used to put out chemical fires. If he could get it on quickly enough, he could pass himself off as one of them and get the hell away away

from the train and the dead body of the first man he ever
genuinely wanted to kill.

Mitchell found the car that Mr. Lewis was planning to
use for his escape. He was twenty miles away before he
noticed the blood stains on the passenger seat and
dashboard. He put two and two together and decided he
didn't want to look inside the trunk. It was a bad enough
feeling, knowing that the murder weapon was in his
duffle bag and he had gunpowder residue all over his
fingers.

It was just one more situation that kind of made him
look like a bad guy. He'd have to deal with this
complication in due time. For the present, his only
mission was to get the word out about Great Wall. Until
people understood what was going on, for most people at
least, he was just some shadowy figure in a strange plot.

His only tool was openness. His biggest problem was
that being out in the open usually meant people were
trying to kill him. The previous owner of the vehicle had
mercifully left him with nearly a full tank of gas. With
any luck, which was stretching things, he could make it to
his final destination in under five hours. From there he'd
let fate take its course. Mitchell was willing to put a big
bet on humanity, despite the horror of the last several
days, that when given the chance they'd make more sense
of the events of the past four days than the people trying
to control things from behind the scenes.

58

Mitchell took the exit off I-75 and drove towards the heart of Atlanta. The signs for Centennial Park reminded him of another innocent man who was wrongly implicated in the center of a terrorism plot. Richard Jewell, like Mitchell, unfortunately fit the profile some people were trying to box him into.

Mitchell took a right turn down Peachtree street and traveled the last few blocks towards his final destination. He pulled the phone from his pocket that he'd taken back at the pier. He didn't turn it on just yet. He had no idea how quickly they'd be able to track it. He needed to use it for just one thing.

Mitchell reached his final destination and parked the car in a no parking zone. He left the keys inside and took the duffel bag loaded with USB drives and the 150 CDs he managed to burn before he drained the computer's battery. Mitchell instinctively stayed to the less-populated side of the street and walked the last block.

He turned on the phone and opened up an Internet browser. He entered in his Twitter account information and began writing a tweet.

Over the last two days #MadMitch had been a nonstop trending topic. His @MadMitchFM Twitter account had over 700,000 followers. He had good reason to believe more than a few of them were in a three block radius.

Mitchell finished his tweet and clicked 'send'. Of course nothing happened at first. He just stood on the corner of Harris and Peachtree, just one more person in a spacesuit in the middle of Dragon*Con surrounded by 50,000 other freaks that had grown up isolated, wanting to connect and not knowing how.

He watched as elves, Klingons, zombies and hundreds of various super heroes walked around from hotel to hotel going to the different events scattered around Atlanta the one weekend out of the year the geeks took over.

Out of the corner of his eye he could see two girls with fairy wings running towards him. One of them was holding an iPhone and pointing at him. He watched the doors of the Hyatt Regency burst open as a crowd of men and women in Jedi costumes came running out of the hotel moving in his direction as well.

His tweet had been retweeted over and over again a thousand times in the span of just a few minutes. Some thought it was a joke. Maybe his Twitter account had been hacked. But anybody within walking distance had to come see for themselves.

at dragon*con.
Love me.
Hate me.
Come say hello.
Find the truth.
Don't worry. I have protection.

As dozens of bodies ran towards him, Mitchell held up his blue spacesuit covered arms. He closed his eyes and waited. If it was going to end, it was going to end right there. The USB drives, the CDs were at his feet. Some of them were bound to get out. And at that point, that's all he cared about anymore. He couldn't run anymore. If he just stopped, they won. If he ruined their secret, then Mitchell won. That's all that mattered. He could get torn into a thousand pieces for all he cared.

Mitchell heard footsteps getting closer. He kept his eyes shut tight. The spacesuit would only keep his scent in. It couldn't protect him from their anger. And that was fine. If they saw the devil, then they should pay him his due.

Mitchell shuddered as he felt the first body hit him. Only it wasn't a tackle. There was no growling or horrific screaming. He felt other hands reach out and touch him.

Mitchell opened his eyes and looked down at a petite teenage girl with thick glasses, stringy hair and fairy wings. She was hugging him. He looked around as dozens of hands reached out to him, not to rip him apart, but to connect with him. To tell him that he wasn't alone. To tell him they believed him.

Mitchell fell to his knees and opened the duffel bag. He began handing out the CDs and USB sticks. Some people pulled out laptops from backpacks and began to read what was inside. Others took them and ran back to hotel rooms and office centers to print out what was on there.

By the time the police showed, Mitchell had a ring of over 1,000 costumed misfits blocking the streets and sidewalks for two blocks in either direction. Many didn't know why they were there at first, but word quickly spread. They were there to protect Mad Mitch and get the word out.

Hundreds of blogs uploaded PDFs describing the illegal biological warfare that was taking place. Details of the unauthorized vaccination of the public with a faulty vaccine quickly spread. CNN, headquartered just a few blocks away, had anchors reading the contents of the documents on air as they tried to make sense of it all.

In the middle of it all sat Mitchell. He answered questions from the people all around him. Others walked by and gently patted him on the shoulder or gave him a hug. The girl fairy who had been the first to reach out to him helped organize people in a protective perimeter around him. Men and women in Stormtrooper uniforms from the 501st stood guard and helped keep the government officials far away by gathering crowds to block them.

Someone had the good sense to bring Mitchell extra oxygen tanks for his spacesuit so he didn't suffocate in the middle of the crowd.

By nightfall the whole world was trained on the events that were going on in downtown Atlanta. A group of CDC scientists who happened to be at the convention as cosplayers were able to make their way over to Mitchell's court and sit down and talk to him. They'd seen the Great Wall documents and were appalled. They talked to Mitchell about a strategy to get him to safety.

The Naked Man from the Forest walked through the crowd. He was wearing the Otherself's clothing. Of course, in that crowd, he might have blended in more easily if he had worn nothing at all like he did in the forest clearing.

In his backpack were the 12 eggs he'd been ordered to bring to the dark man in the middle of the crowd. He couldn't understand at first why the Earth mother had chosen this thorn of a man to have the eggs. Did she mean for him to break open the eggs in front of him? Was he just supposed to give them to him?

Breaking them all open at once didn't make any sense. Just one was enough to kill everyone he could see and bring pestilence to this continent. 12 was overkill. They were meant to be spread apart. Each one with its own plague.

Was the dark man chosen because he was a secret survivor? Was he chosen because his ordeal was just a trial? The Naked Man from the Forest paused when he thought that the dark man was chosen because he had bested him. Was that it? Had he failed so much in the eyes of the Earth mother she'd chosen his enemy as her new lover?

His stomach was in knots. He didn't want to give the eggs to the man. He wanted to prove himself. He wanted the Earth mother for himself.

He couldn't fight her. He had to try to follow her orders. He moved towards the dark man in the center. A hand reached out and stopped him.

"Who are you?" asked a man dressed in white plastic armor.

The Naked Man from the Forest hesitated. He couldn't say the name of the Otherself. He was a wanted man now. He tried to walk around the man. Three more people in armor gathered around him.

"What's in the bag?" asked one of them in a muffled voice.

A gloved hand reached towards the bag. Towards the eggs.

He swatted it away. "Gifts...gifts for Mitchell."

Two of the people wearing armor looked at each other. "Let's see the gifts."

The Naked Man from the Forest pulled away. He had been told to only give them to the man. He couldn't let them see the eggs.

More people gathered around. He gave them a nervous look. There was no way he was going to get to him. He tried. But he failed.

He pulled back from the people in the plastic armor. His eyes darted from left to right as people looked at his bag. He threaded through the crowd of costumed people and ran away. He'd tried. The Earth mother would have to know he was sincere.

This had been a test he decided. The Earth mother wanted to know if he was willing to follow her orders. He had. He was sure she would be proud.

At midnight the crowd was still growing. A CNN news crew had been allowed through and Mitchell told them everything even including the train wreck and the body he thought was in the trunk of the car. Another news team corroborated the story when they found a man had been pulled from the train wreckage with bogus Department of Transportation identification.

As dawn approached Mitchell had done what he had set out to do. The word was out. He'd told his side of the story and for the first time in what felt like an eternity, he was able to be in the middle of the crowd and not feel intense rage. In fact, he felt the opposite. Everywhere he looked he saw a sympathetic face.

A new deal was brokered and Mitchell left his spot where he'd been sitting for almost 24 hours and walked towards an ambulance waiting to take him into isolation over at the CDC a few miles away. People high-fived him and touched him on the shoulder as he made his way through the crowd that had answered his plea.

Mitchell got into the ambulance and sat next to two of the scientists he'd spoken to earlier. They'd changed out of their fantasy costumes and donned spacesuits like his. One of them mentioned a possible treatment they could give to Mitchell, which might change his body's pheromonal trigger. Another said they might be able to rapidly develop an anti-anti-Mitch-virus that would allow medical workers and other people to be around him without spacesuits and not try to rip his face off. Mitchell made a comment about being able to look forward to not having to post ads on Craigslist for women who were into gas-mask sex then fell asleep for the short ride to his new home.

59

The Vice President offered a letter of resignation the next day. On the orders of the President, the FBI raided the offices of Athena Biomedical. When a team in hazmat suits searched the labs they found the unconscious body of Nick Arturous near an open refrigerator. The back of his skull had been cracked with a fire extinguisher.

Miraculously, he survived. When he was finally coherent enough to talk, they asked him if he knew the whereabouts of Dr. Baylor and what was in the 12 vials that were missing from the refrigerator.

He requested a lawyer before he would say anything about the vials. All he would say was that it was Baylor who had hit him with the fire extinguisher when he came for the vials. That and that Baylor was inexplicably naked when he walked into the lab and his balls and dick were covered in red welts.

Steinmetz had gone missing as well.

Epilogue

The Naked Man in the Forest looked at the face of the Earth mother on the oak. He hadn't needed to touch a blotter for her to appear.

He placed the twelve vials proudly in front of her. She smiled down on him.

"What now Earth mother?"

Soon my son we will bring light to this world once and for all. We'll bring the 12 plagues to the four corners of the earth and end man's reign. Then it shall just be you and me in the garden. Helicopters flew by overhead looking for him. It would be in vain. He had the Earth mother to look out for him.

The dark man had been a setback. Like Great Wall, he had been a test. Because of it he knew that the contents of the eggs would reach far and wide when they were cracked open, each one would bring a different pestilence onto man.

He packed the vials back into the backpack and walked deeper into the forest. Earth mother told him that there were friends waiting, friends that would help him in their cause. Friends of the earth who knew that man's time must come to an end.

Author's note
As a social media experiment I thought it would be fun to make this book available in draft form to anyone who wanted to edit or make notes. Here are the Twitter handles of the people who helped out:

@JustinRYoung
@dandirks
@lachbur
@RKMagic
@rc6750
@themadgician
@giggleloop
@magicofdru
@sinimagic
@getkasha
@msnovtues
@neshCOMPLEX
@AdamD_Marcus
@dpowensj

And if you're curious about what Mitch is up to, you can follow him at @MadMitchFM

Sincerely,
Andrew Mayne
@AndrewMayne

About the Author

Andrew Mayne, star of A&E's Don't Trust Andrew Mayne, is a magician and novelist, ranked the fifth best-selling independent author of the year by Amazon UK. He started his first world tour as an illusionist when he was a teenager and went on to work behind the scenes for Penn & Teller, David Blaine and David Copperfield. He's also the host of the WeirdThings.com podcast. AndrewMayne.com

Also by Andrew Mayne

ANGEL
KILLER

A JESSICA BLACKWOOD NOVEL

ANDREW
MAYNE

NAME OF THE DEVIL

A JESSICA BLACKWOOD NOVEL

ANDREW

AUTHOR OF *ANGEL KILLER*

MAYNE

THE **CHRONOLOGICAL MAN**
{A Tale of Scientific Adventure by Andrew Mayne}
The Monster in the Mist

andrew mayne

HOLLYWOOD PHARAOHS

KNIGHT SCHOOL

ANDREW MAYNE

HOW TO WRITE A NOVELLA

IN 24 HOURS

AND OTHER QUESTIONABLE & POSSIBLY INSANE ADVICE ON CREATIVITY FOR WRITERS

ANDREW MAYNE

Made in the USA
Las Vegas, NV
09 January 2022

40958514R00216